DAGGER QUICK

Also by Brian Eames

THE DAGGER X

THE DAGGER
CHRONICLES

The
DAGGER
QUICK

∽ Brian Eames ∽

A PAULA WISEMAN BOOK

SIMON & SCHUSTER BOOKS FOR YOUNG READERS

NEW YORK   LONDON   TORONTO   SYDNEY   NEW DELHI

SIMON & SCHUSTER BOOKS FOR YOUNG READERS
An imprint of Simon & Schuster Children's Publishing Division
1230 Avenue of the Americas, New York, New York 10020
This book is a work of fiction. Any references to historical events, real people, or real places are used fictitiously. Other names, characters, places, and events are products of the author's imagination, and any resemblance to actual events or places or persons, living or dead, is entirely coincidental.
Text copyright © 2011 by Brian Eames
Cover illustration copyright © 2013 by Scott M. Fischer
Illustration of boy copyright © 2011 by Amy June Bates
Title page background and chapter head illustrations
copyright © 2011 by iStockphoto.com/Thinkstock
All rights reserved, including the right of reproduction
in whole or in part in any form.
SIMON & SCHUSTER BOOKS FOR YOUNG READERS
is a trademark of Simon & Schuster, Inc.
For information about special discounts for bulk purchases, please contact Simon & Schuster Special Sales at 1-866-506-1949 or business@simonandschuster.com.
The Simon & Schuster Speakers Bureau can bring authors to your live event. For more information or to book an event, contact the Simon & Schuster Speakers Bureau at 1-866-248-3049 or visit our website at www.simonspeakers.com.
Also available in a Simon & Schuster Books for Young Readers hardcover edition
Book design by Laurent Linn
Map illustration by Drew Willis
The text for this book is set in Minister Standard.
Manufactured in the United States of America
1013 OFF
First Simon & Schuster Books for Young Readers paperback edition November 2013
2 4 6 8 10 9 7 5 3 1
The Library of Congress has cataloged the hardcover edition as follows:
Eames, Brian.
The dagger Quick / Brian Eames. — 1st ed.
p. cm.
"A Paula Wiseman book."
Summary: Twelve-year-old Christopher "Kitto" Wheale, a clubfooted boy seemingly doomed to follow in the boring footsteps of his father as a cooper in seventeenth-century England, finds himself on a dangerous seafaring adventure with his newly discovered uncle, the infamous pirate William Quick.
ISBN 978-1-4424-2311-4 (hardcover : alk. paper)
[1. Pirates—Fiction. 2. Identity—Fiction. 3. People with disabilities—Fiction. 4. Sea stories.] I. Title.
PZ7.E119Dag 2011
[Fic]—dc22
2011004405
ISBN 978-1-4424-8368-2 (pbk)
ISBN 978-1-4424-2312-1 (eBook)

NORTH
AMERICA

Atlantic

Ocean

Location of Spice Island

Caribbean Sea

Jamaica

Panama

Site of the battle with
the PORT ROYAL

SOUTH
AMERICA

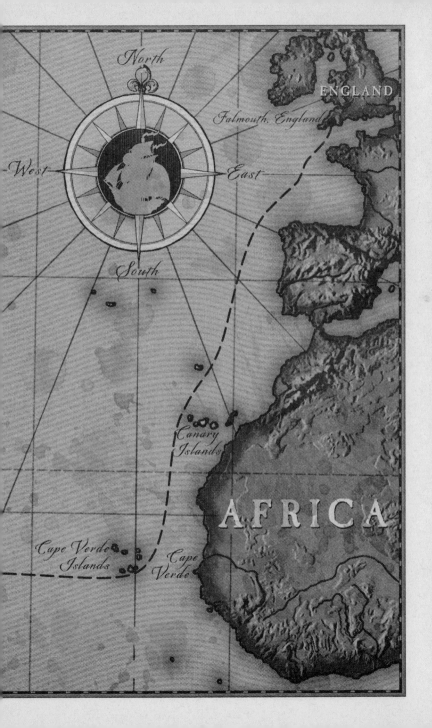

A tale of heroes, villains,
courage, cowardice,
torture, rescue,
love, loss,
loyalty, chicanery,
blood, gore,
sordid alleyways, rat-infested holds,
swordplay, marksmanship,
spice, sin,
greed, ambition,
and just plain good and evil.

CAST OF CHARACTERS

Christopher (Kitto)   son of Frederick and Mercy, clubfooted, age twelve years

Elias (Duck)   son of Frederick and Sarah, half brother to Kitto, age six years

William Quick   captain of the *Blessed William*, Frederick's brother, Kitto's uncle

Frederick   Kitto and Duck's father, maker of barrels (cooper)

Sarah (Mum)   Duck's mother, Kitto's stepmother

Mercy   Kitto's mother by birth, deceased

Henry Morgan   admiral of the Brethren of the Coast, buccaneer, lieutenant governor of Jamaica

Captain John Morris   privateer, longtime associate of Morgan

Spider   Morris's first mate

Van   member of the *Blessed William*'s crew, age thirteen years

Julius   Van's pet monkey

Isaac, Jenks, Peterson, Carroll, Swickers   crew members of the *Blessed William* who accompanied William Quick in Panama

Akin   formerly enslaved boy, age eleven years

CONTENTS

CHAPTER 1:

England, 1678

Simon Sneed flared thin lips, revealing a disgraceful mishmash of teeth.

"I was nice to you last time, wasn't I, cripple?" he said. "This time I'll not be so generous." Around Simon hovered a small tribe of dim-witted, large boys.

"You don't own the docks, Simon," came the answer. His name was Kitto Wheale—or so he thought—and unlike Simon, Kitto did not attract a circle of admirers. Kitto had been born with a clubfoot, a sure sign of God's disapproval.

"Not yet I don't own them," Simon said. There were six boys in all arrayed against Kitto. Simon and three others stood in front and blocked one end of the deserted alley; two boys behind Kitto blocked the other.

Six to one—poor odds. Next to Kitto stood his little brother, Elias, known to all as Duck. Duck glared the most menacing look a six-year-old could muster.

"Leave us be, Simon Sneed!" Duck said. "We wasn't bothering you."

Simon leaned to the boy beside him. "Nick that little

ankle biter." Two stout fellows stepped forward and took Duck by the arms.

"Let go of me! Let go or I'll show you what!"

"Shut it, Duck," Kitto told him. "You're just giving him what he wants." Kitto swept a hand across his dark curls. "Let him go, Simon. You've got me closed in, haven't you?"

"I'll do as I like." Simon looked down at the wet thing balanced in his gloved hand: a turd, freshly deposited in the alley only a few minutes before by a horse sweating beneath a load of coal.

"We get lots of visitors here in Falmouth this time of year. From all parts." With his empty hand Simon pointed at Kitto's clubfoot. "You come around here with that thing, and people get the wrong idea. You're a smudge on our good name, you are, and it's my job to see you cleaned out."

Duck stomped on the toe of one of the boys holding him. "Stop squeezing me!" The larger boy let out a howl. He and his mate hurled Duck to the ground, and the wounded one pinned him to the cobblestones with a knee to the back.

"If I was any bigger!"

Simon snickered. "He is a feisty one, that brother of yours," Simon said. "He doesn't get that from you, though, does he? But I guess he's got a different mum, eh?" It was true. The woman Kitto called "Mother" was so only by marriage, making Duck his half brother.

"Yes, he's got a feisty mum, doesn't he, that brother

of yours? That Sarah Wheale is a *feisty* one, ain't she, boys?" Simon's eyebrows jounced.

Kitto knew just then he would not try to run. There were some insults that should not be borne.

"Your lesson will be a little different this time, cripple." Simon gestured with the gloved hand. "You smear this horse apple all over your face so all Falmouth knows exactly what you are. Do that, and we let you go."

Kitto stared back. "Better to keep it yourself, Simon. Holding that makes you look less ugly."

Simon's sneer vanished. "Take it."

"I ain't touching that."

"One way or the other you are."

Kitto shrugged. "I rub it about and you let us go? Both of us? And no beating?" He eyed the glistening stool warily.

"I am a man of my word, ain't I, lads?" Simon turned to his cronies.

Kitto leaped forward, chopped one hand at the crook of Simon's elbow, and with the other he swept up, hitting the back of Simon's gloved hand. Simon's arm bent. He struck himself in the face, mashing manure across his nose and cheek.

There was an instant of shocked delay, and then mayhem erupted. Simon shrieked. The boy kneeling atop Duck stood, and in a trice the six boys threw Kitto to the cobblestones. They beat him and kicked him and stomped him.

"I'll kill you! You crazy cripple! I'll kill you!"

"Kitto! Kitto! Get up, Kitto!"

Kitto curled tight and buried his head in his arms. He squeezed his eyes shut.

The boys kicked and punched, spurred on by Simon's fury.

"Get him! Get him and don't let up!"

An adjacent door to the alleyway opened, alerted by Duck's pounding. A huge man stepped through it. His name was Pickett, and he was a blacksmith. He held a long bar of iron that glowed red at one end. Pickett took a few steps forward. The boys scattered like cockroaches before a lantern, Simon at their lead. Halfway down the alley, he turned.

"You'll get yours, Kitto Wheale! Just you wait and see!" he shouted, then ran on.

A woman emerged from the smithy behind Pickett. She stared first at the retreating boys, then at Kitto. The look of concern on her face melted into disdain.

"You know that lad was Simon Sneed, don't you? You know who his father is?" she demanded of her husband.

The blacksmith looked at Kitto with sad eyes. Kitto turned away, unable to bear his pity.

"Do you think we can afford to anger Preston Sneed? The most powerful man in this town?" She glared at Kitto. "For the likes of *you*!"

The man guided the woman by the elbow. The door closed behind them, leaving Kitto and Duck alone.

Kitto uncurled his body. He could feel the bruises forming on his back, on his head. He'd protected his face, at least. Maybe Father would not know he had been fighting.

"I got the blacksmith, Kitto! I did what I could to help!" Duck said cheerfully.

"Is it a help, Duck, when a six-year-old rescues his brother?" Kitto shoved at Duck, and the little boy fell away bewildered. His blue eyes filled.

"But what was I supposed to do, Kitto? What could I have done?" Tears rolled down his rosy cheeks.

Kitto knew Duck could never understand.

"Just leave me alone, Duck. Get on home and leave me be!" Kitto pushed through the pain to his feet, and as best he could he set off at a run. Down the alleyway toward the main lane he went, his head bobbing as he limped.

Kitto cut past a crowd of sailors and made his way to the seawall. He threw himself to the ground at the wall, disgusted and miserable. He hated Simon Sneed, who was cruel, and he hated Pickett and his wife, who saw only his bent foot. He hated his father, who would not listen, and his brother, whose body was whole. But mostly Kitto just hated himself and the twisted leg he hid beneath him.

He sat there a long time, staring and hating. After a while, the sea began to work its magic. He watched the ships swing on their anchors, and a few others round the head at Pendennis Castle. And while he sat, Kitto imagined he had found a spot where the world might leave him be for just a short while.

He was wrong.

CHAPTER 2:

The Captain

Captain John Morris smiled. It was not a smile of joy.

"Here. Have a look yourself. Must be him." Morris handed the spyglass to the other man in the rowboat. The second man peered through it across the harbor waters toward the spot where Kitto sat on the wall. The man holding the spyglass bore a black tattoo that entirely covered his left eye: an astonishingly realistic spider with articulated legs reaching out across his forehead, cheekbone, and the bridge of his nose. The tattoo was so striking that it had become the name by which he was known.

"The lad, Captain?" Spider said. "What of him?"

"Look at his foot, Spider. Look close."

"Aye, sir. I see now. All bent, ain't it so?"

John Morris dabbed at his nose—or rather, what remained of it—with a kerchief. The last inch of his smelling organ was missing; two dark and ragged black holes remained, leaking fluid. Besides the hacked off nose, he had two purple scars that curved up from each corner of his mouth, forming a sickly smile.

"Don't you remember, Spider? The clubfooted boy?"

Morris asked, in mock surprise at Spider's stupidity. Spider grunted but said nothing.

"That boy there. He explains why William Quick has come to England!"

"Just for a boy with a clubfoot?" Spider asked, looking again. His grimace revealed bloodred teeth, dyed from the leaves of the betel plant he chewed—a habit he'd picked up in the South Pacific.

"Not for the boy, you idiot, for his father! The cooper!" Morris snatched back the spyglass. "William Quick has come here to get new barrels made. *New barrels*. You *do* remember what that means, don't you?" Morris glared across the boat.

"It means the treasure's still there," Spider said, flashing his bloody teeth. Morris nodded slowly.

"It means that all proceeds according to plan," Morris whispered.

A long red tongue uncurled from Spider's mouth and swept across his thin lips, leaving a glistening trail.

"So what do I need to do to the boy?" he asked hungrily.

Morris stiffened in his seat, and he snatched back the telescope. He peered through it intently.

"What is it, Captain?" Spider said. Morris lowered his voice to a hiss.

"It's Quick! Right next to the boy, Spider!"

Sitting on the wall, Kitto kicked up his right foot and held it out in the sunlight. He had taken off his boots now, and his pale skin gleamed. The right leg started out promising and grew true through the knee, but at the shin it began its unnatural curl. At the ankle it became grotesque, wilting like an old lettuce.

"Disgusting! Hateful!" Kitto muttered. He knew the foot was what kept him in Falmouth, chained to the trade of making barrels like his father. A lame boy could turn into a beggar without a trade to practice, and Kitto's father made certain he would have the skills he needed. Kitto had proven to be an excellent apprentice, but he found the life of a cooper dreadfully dull.

Lost in dark thoughts, Kitto did not notice—as the two in the rowboat had—that a man had sidled up beside him.

The man wore a fine burgundy jacket, black trousers, and newly polished boots. A mustache adorned his upper lip, finely tapered at each end to a deliberate point.

His name was William Quick, and he was obviously a captain.

William drew on his pipe and blew a plume of smoke into the wind so that it was carried before Kitto. Kitto coughed and turned a mildly irritated look. It vanished instantly.

"I am sorry, sir! I did not know." Kitto jumped to his feet. He watched the captain's gaze travel his body, coming to stop on Kitto's deformed limb. The man grinned.

"Is there some help you need, sir?" Kitto said with a bite. "Directions to the nearest public house?" A captain is a powerful man. A boy should watch the way he speaks to one.

"Does my face look familiar to you, lad?"

Kitto puzzled. "Your face, sir? No, it does not. Should it, sir?"

The captain puffed more on the pipe and faced the sea.

"You're a bit old for idling the day away looking at ships, eh?" There was the faint smile again.

"So my father says, sir, I just . . ." Kitto turned away, flushing. "I like it here."

The captain blew another plume of smoke.

"'The sea chooses the lubber and his heart will have no other.' Ever heard that saying?" Kitto shook his head.

The captain pointed the end of his pipe down at Kitto. "The sea chooses the sailor, not the other way around, boy. Maybe it has chosen you."

Kitto blushed and looked down at the water. "My father says I shall outgrow it in time."

The man snorted in response. "Twelve years you have?" Kitto nodded. "I was just your age when I deserted such a man and put to sea for the first time almost directly where we stand."

"You, sir? And became a captain?"

The man shrugged. "I could say I earned it, but I know luck has played a leading role. Hard work, yes— lots of that—but plenty of luck."

Kitto dared a sidelong peek at the captain, and something caught his eye. There was a black mark, a tattoo, on the captain's hand. It did not look to be an image at all, simply a black square just more than an inch on a side on the back of the hand.

The captain moved the hand behind his back.

"Much time has passed since I was last here. Yet here I am in Falmouth again, tangled up in sordid business."

"And what sort of business is that, sir?" Kitto said.

The smirk sprouted again. "Well, lad—or young man, I ought to say—my affairs . . . they are my own."

"I did not mean to pry, Captain."

"Of course not. And were I inclined to share my plans with anyone in all of Cornwall, I would likely be safest in choosing you." Kitto beamed at the flattery. "But experience has taught me to keep a still tongue." The captain paused. "There is a way you might help me, though."

"It would be my honor, sir!" Kitto replied.

"Tell me your name."

"My name?" Kitto puzzled. "It's Christopher Wheale."

The captain grimaced. *"Wheale!* Wheale! That's the very surname of the stepfather tradesman I ran away from when I was your age. But that does help me, indeed."

"It does? I don't see how . . . ," Kitto began, but the captain turned and was walking away. After several steps, he spun around.

"There is one more thing, Kitto," he called back.

"Sir?"

"Don't tell your father about me. I do so like to be

surprising." The captain's smirk curled and his eyebrows arched. He whirled again and strode off down the wharf.

In the distance, Kitto heard the peal of the church bell. Still reeling from the strange encounter, he jammed on his boots and set out at an awkward jog home. As he passed the Custom House Quay, the thought struck him like a blow.

That captain called me "Kitto"! I never told him my nickname!

Kitto took one last look toward the sea, and so doing his gaze rested for a moment on an odd sight: a rowboat, two men filling it, one holding a telescope aimed toward shore. For a moment Kitto had the peculiar feeling that they were looking at the captain, who was striding along the wharf in the opposite direction. The wharf was busy, though. It could have been anyone they were looking at. Then the telescope turned on him. Kitto felt the skin prickle on the back of his neck.

Don't be ridiculous! Kitto told himself, and picked up his pace.

Morris snatched back the instrument. "He didn't see you, did he?" Spider shook his head, his hand staying suspended in the air a moment. It, too, bore a tattoo: small, about an inch square, of a skeleton hand. Morris trained the scope on the retreating figure.

"Well, now we know, don't we?" Morris said, lowering the telescope. "The Pirate Quick has come home."

CHAPTER 3:

No Place for Dreams

Father looked up to see Kitto stumble into the shop.

"Look what the cat dragged in," he said, "and late as well. Hand me that copper stripping," he said, pointing. Kitto fetched it and watched while Father wrapped the metal ribbon around the top third of a large oak barrel.

The two did not speak as Father tacked up the strip of copper about the newly warped boards, or staves. Kitto eyed Father's thick eyebrows for a clue to his mood.

Father swung his right leg on top of the barrel and let it rap soundly against the lid. It was not a leg, really, but a thick stump of dark wood.

"You see that, don't you?"

"Yes, sir."

"This stump tells you more about sea life than what you see at the wharf!" Father swung his leg back down. He knew where Kitto had been.

Kitto had been told that Father had lost his leg at sea, some sort of accident that led to a festering wound.

"Yes, sir."

Silence won out inside the shop, broken only by Father's grunts as he tightened the strip of copper with a hand crank.

Kitto mustered his courage.

"Francis told me that Mr. Pickett is letting his boy Edward—you remember Edward, he is the one who helped me deliver that load of wet barrels to the *Orion*—he's letting Edward head out on the *Drake's Pride* in two weeks. As a midshipman."

Father snorted. "Yes, I know. You told me they were looking for a ship." His head shot up. "Were you hoping I would do the same for you? Be such a fool with my own children?"

Kitto shrugged. "There's no shame in it."

"Your home is here, boy. It ain't such a bad life, is it?" Father asked.

Kitto did not answer.

"You are the son of a cooper and a cooper, too, will you be." Father spun the hand crank violently.

Kitto watched him work.

This is not the life for me. This is not the life for me. Those are not my barrels, this is not my home, this is not the life for me.

"Father," Kitto said softly, "what if I do not want to be a cooper? What if . . . what if 'the sea chooses the lubber'? . . ." he said, using the captain's words.

Father startled as if he had been stung. He slammed the hand crank against the barrel, knocking it over.

"Where in God's name did you hear that? 'Sea chooses the lubber'!" Father mocked. "I don't give a good bloody awful whit if it does—" Father could feel the heat rising in his face, his cheeks burning.

He knew his anger was not fair. The boy remembered nothing. Nothing of what had happened.

Father spun on his heel to pace, but the movement threw his balance. He reached for a post to steady himself.

"Kitto . . ."

There were things he wanted to say, tender things, yet the words caught in his throat. He was no good at it, this being a father.

Father began again. "Kitto, I don't tell you things. Things a father should. I leave it all to Sarah, but I know that is wrong." Father's voice trailed to a whisper. "You're so very important to me, son," he managed. Kitto held his breath.

"I know being a tradesman is not the life you would choose, but it will take care of you. You will *need* that. This world is no place for dreams, Kitto.

"It might not be right for me to hold you here, but I know no other way. If your mother were here . . . she would say just the right thing. You are more like her than me, I am afraid. But she is long departed. And . . ." His voice grew softer still. "I don't know that I could bear to lose you as well."

Kitto felt a warm sting in his eyes. He stood over the upturned barrel, blinking.

The far-off peal of a church bell made the silence between them loom.

Father stood, quietly considering whether to tell Kitto more. Could he tell Kitto what really happened to his mother?

"Kitto," Father began. "What did I tell you about this . . . my leg?" His back still to Kitto, Father thumped the wooden stump against the floor. "Infection, I told you, isn't that right? An accident?" Father spun around.

"Yes, sir. An accident."

"Well, that . . . That is a lie!"

At that moment an elongated shadow in the shape of a man spread across the dusty floor. It was a man who would change Kitto's life forever.

The captain filled the narrow doorway. He wore the same curious smile, only now there was a challenging air to it. A pistol belt draped over his shoulder. He took a few steps into the shop and struck an arrogant pose.

Father stood mute. Dumbfounded.

Kitto stepped forward. "Good day, sir. Is there some way in which we might be of service?" he said, hoping the captain would not reveal that he had been bold enough to chat with a captain.

The captain said nothing, but continued to stare at Father.

"Frederick!" he said finally. "I would say the cat has scampered off with your tongue. I suppose you have a right to be surprised to see your only kin. But *so* surprised?" One hand twirled the end of his mustache. "Your lack of faith disturbs me."

Kin? As far as Kitto knew, there survived no family on Father's side.

The captain's words seemed to release Father from his trance. "Seven years it's been, William. Seven."

The captain nodded. "Seven, and a half to boot, I believe. Yet here I am as I promised I would be. Lucky I am to have found you." The captain flashed his eyes at Kitto.

"You have raised this one well from the look of him, Frederick." The captain winked. "Trying to make a cooper of him, eh? But surely I do see a *quick* glint in his eye, don't you think, Mr. *Wheale?*" He nearly sneered the words.

"I'll admit I am surprised, William. It has been some years." Father's voice was grim and cold. "I thought you were dead. As for the 'faith' you mention, I hope you will not be disappointed to hear I have none. Not in you." Kitto turned in dismay toward Father but held his tongue.

"No, Frederick. I am not disappointed. Nor surprised. But given the nature of my arrival, I should think a scintilla of gratitude might be in order." Again the captain twirled the end of his mustache.

"Gratitude?" Father scoffed. "What is it, William? Have you more schemes with which to tempt me? Have I not grown poor enough scrabbling for your riches? Have I not lost enough?"

The captain's face clouded.

"Ironic it is, brother, that with such anger you greet me when I bring you so much and have endured so much to do it. It is not new interests that bring me here, but rather our former ones. The same ones you know so well."

Brother? Kitto gaped. *Father has a brother?*

"Did you think I had been off squandering your share all these years?" the captain demanded. He ran his eyes over the room. "I can assure you that you have enjoyed more creature comforts than have I."

"I have done passably well," Father said.

From outside came a familiar giggling. Duck darted around the corner of the door. A blur of scrabbling limbs, he nearly careened into the captain's legs. Duck grabbed a fistful of the captain's trousers as he dodged. Two steps more and he jumped for Father spread-eagled. Father snatched Duck from the air and lifted him to his hip.

"Did I scare you, Daddy? Say I did!"

Now the boy's mother rounded the doorway. Sarah Faith Wheale walked past the captain, giving him a polite nod.

"I *am* sorry, my dear, but it is like keeping hold of wet eel." Sarah pulled Duck from Father's arms.

The captain stared at her. Sarah was a beautiful woman. Her sandy blond hair peeked out from beneath her lace bonnet, and her brilliant blue eyes sparkled with wit.

"I do hope you will forgive the interruption of your business, Mr. . . ." Sarah waited for the captain to finish her sentence. William's mouth opened, closed again. Sarah's eyes caught the flash of brasswork on the pistols at the man's chest, and her smile melted.

"This shop is also my home, Captain. I can assure you, sir, that here you need not bear arms." Sarah, a Quaker, loathed guns.

"Can I touch it?" Duck asked, reaching out for a pistol. Sarah hooked a finger in his collar.

"Ah, William, madam, William," the captain stammered. He looked down at his pistols. "Please excuse my caution, madam. I did not mean to offend." A long moment of silence followed. Sarah looked to Father to put an end to the awkwardness, but he did not. Duck squinted up at the adults. He reached again for a pistol, but Sarah gave him a sharper yank.

The captain broke into a grin. "Frederick, you old devil! You have not wasted a moment of time," he said. He reached out to pinch Duck's cheek. Duck pulled away and glared.

"What is your name, lad?"

"Duck," he answered.

"'Tis not!" Sarah corrected. "When a captain asks, young man, you give him your Christian name."

"Elias Bartholomew Wheale, sir!" The boy saluted smartly. The captain returned the gesture.

"And what's yours?" Duck asked him.

"Duck!" all three of his family members protested.

"My name? You can call me 'uncle.'"

"Uncle?" Duck's face wrinkled. "That's an odd name you've got." Duck felt his collar tighten again. "I mean, that's an odd name you've got, *sir!*"

The captain winked and stood.

"Sarah, I am afraid we still have business to conduct, Mr. . . . the gentleman and I," Father said haltingly.

Without a word Sarah scooped Duck into her arms and disappeared behind a door that led to a flight of stairs.

Father spoke softly. "I have done well, brother. And I have a family, for which I care greatly. I know you have little understanding for such feelings. What happened seven years ago happened, William. The interests we shared in the past we no longer share now. The blood money is yours to keep."

Blood money? Kitto did not understand.

The captain stepped toward a stack of barrels and ran a hand along the stave joinings. "I wish that were the case, Frederick, believe me, I do, but circumstances are what they are."

At that moment another man leaped into the shop from the lane, moving quickly to avoid a rushing wagon. The abrupt entrance caught all three by surprise.

The captain stepped nimbly around the barrels so that they stood between himself and the man who entered. Kitto saw his hand reach for a pistol.

"Mr. Wheale, I hope your progress has been swift!" fussed the round little man who had entered. Kitto turned to look at the customer, then back at the captain. His cool expression had returned.

"Oh, dear," the little merchant said, seeing the captain. "I hope I have not come at an inopportune moment. Please finish your business; I shall return presently." The man spun on his heel to go.

"Not at all, good sir, the master cooper and I were just concluding." The captain stepped toward Father. "If you would be so kind as to stop by my ship, Mr. Wheale, I could show you the dimensions I am working with and get your expert opinion as to my difficulties. I shall be there any time this evening. I *shall* expect you." With a nod, the captain made for the door.

"Captain! Which is your ship, did you say?" Father called after him.

William Quick put a hand on the doorjamb and turned a boyish grin on Kitto.

"Mr. *Wheale*, I shall leave that mystery to your son to solve."

CHAPTER 4:

Into the Evening

Evening had begun. Supper had ended. Sarah cleaned up while Duck pursued his latest passion, which was to stack the round stones he collected from the beach one atop the other until they tumbled down noisily.

"We will leave now," Father announced, standing up from the table where he had spent the past twenty minutes poking at a meat stew. Sarah turned a worried eye toward Kitto, then looked up at her husband.

"Not too late, Frederick," she said. "Press-gangs will snatch up anybody these days."

"Come on, boy."

Father descended the narrow flight of stairs to the shop, his leg knocking a hollow thump on each step. Kitto found it hard not to bound past him in his eagerness. He would get to visit a ship! What a treat, indeed.

After procuring a measuring twine, Father entered the adjacent storeroom and waved for Kitto to follow. He drew the door closed. It was near dark, small shafts of firelight from the cooking fire peeking through the cracks in the boards above them.

"You're old enough to know about this, and old enough to know never to go near it," he whispered.

He walked to the back of the storeroom to a tall cabinet in the corner, reached his hand to the top, and came down with an uneven bundle. He unwrapped the cloth slowly.

Kitto gasped. "A gun!"

"Hush, now," Father said.

Sarah had the strictest rules about such weapons in her home. The wood was scratched and the brasswork mottled with tarnish. Father pulled back the hammer, aimed the pistol at the wall, and pulled the trigger. The hammer slapped down with a tinny clap. He handed it to Kitto, who ran his fingers along the short barrel.

A pistol? With which to visit Father's brother?

"I'll be carrying that. I'll not bother to load it, but having it to bluff with might be handy."

"And what should I carry?" Kitto asked, sure what the answer would be. Father stared at him for a moment. He sighed deeply then opened the cabinet.

"I had been meaning to give this to you someday." Father withdrew from the top shelf another bundle, which he unwrapped. Into his palm tumbled the most stunning piece of craftsmanship Kitto had ever seen. It was a dagger. The guard and pommel were wrought in silver, ornately engraved with swirling curlicues; the handle was smooth, white bone. A fine leather sheath trimmed with silver hid the blade.

"It is magnificent," Kitto said. He withdrew the

sheath and gasped. "My God!" Rather than appear as one piece of metal like all other knives Kitto had seen, the blade appeared to have the grain of wood in alternating lines of silver and black.

"That's Damascus steel," Father explained. "It is a rare technique that only a few smiths master."

"Why had you meant to give it to me?"

Father reached out and took the knife back from Kitto's hands. He turned it slowly, rubbing his finger against the grain lines of steel. Glimmers of firelight sparkled on the steel.

"This belonged to your mother, Kitto."

"My mother?"

"I asked her to carry it always, as protection. I'm afraid it did not do that." Father pushed the knife back at Kitto as if it suddenly repulsed him.

"You gave it to her then? As a gift?"

Father shook his head. "No." He strode toward the door. "Leave the sheath here. Keep the blade 'neath your belt, where it will be ready. And for God's sake, don't lose it."

The father and son walked the cobbled streets, stepping aside for the occasional carriage or cart. An odd pair they made, each with his own limp.

The streets were largely empty. The sun dipped toward Cape Cornwall far off to the west. Kitto walked behind Father. He could feel at his back the dagger Father had given him, tucked tight beneath his belt.

Father stooped toward an open doorway.

"We're a bit early yet for William."

They ducked into the inn and made for a table in the corner. Within a few moments a sour-faced woman trundled over and set down two mugs. Father slid her a few coins.

"There are some things, Christopher. Some things that you ought to know about me. About my past, and about yours."

"Is he really your brother?"

Father straightened, set down his mug, and waved for another. The two sat in silence, Father staring at Kitto intently. The boy squirmed.

"He *is* my brother, this captain. My younger brother by two years. His name is William Quick. I have not seen him for seven years, and I was sure that he was dead. When he walked in the shop, it was like seeing a ghost."

"Why have I never known of him?" Kitto asked. Father scratched at his scalp.

"Because I never told you. You did know him once, when you were a wee bit."

Kitto shook his head. "I do not follow, Father."

Father sighed and rubbed a hand across his stubble. "No. Of course not. Let me tell it right.

"I grew up in Truro. That you know, I believe. I began working as an apprentice for a cooper there when I was a year younger than you are now. My father was a man of the sea and never much around."

"I thought my grandfather was a silversmith," Kitto said. Father raised his hand in a flash of annoyance.

"Do not interrupt, Kitto! The silversmith, James Wheale, was the man my mother married after my father's ship was lost in a storm. I had been apprenticed a few years by then, so I stayed with the cooper, and William was apprenticed to be a silversmith with our new father.

"That arrangement went poorly, and when William was still a lad, he ran away. None of us knew where. Five years passed before he returned, much the young man now. I had finished my apprenticeship but still worked in the same shop in Truro with my master. William's return shook our little family. He and our stepfather never did get along, and in only a few days they nearly came to blows.

"William decided to leave, but before he did, he asked me to join him. He told me he had been to the island of Jamaica. It's an English island, across the great ocean in the New World."

"Yes, I have seen it on Mr. Alden's maps!" Kitto said.

"William said there was plenty of work there for a young cooper, that it was wide open. Not like England, where the guilds kept young men out of trades. I was young and eager for my own shop. I resolved to go with him."

The stout woman appeared and set a plate of bread before Father, then waited for him to fish the coins from his pocket.

"And that is why I was born in Jamaica?" Kitto asked once she had left. "I always wondered."

"Wondered? You could have asked," Father said. "Why did you not?" Kitto shrugged. "Yes," Father admitted, "I suppose I do not welcome such questions."

"And you met . . . you met my mother in Jamaica?" It was the first time Kitto remembered asking about her.

"Yes. She was English. We married, and you were born. Soon after, we decided we had to leave Port Royal—the English settlement on the island. Jamaica was a beautiful place, but Port Royal . . . It was a den of cutthroats and pirates. When your mother . . . when she was with child the second time, she insisted that we leave right away, that the baby be born in England."

Second time?

"You do not mean Duck," Kitto said. Father shook his head slowly.

Another child? A brother . . . a sister?

Father continued. "We did not have enough money to leave Jamaica and have enough left to set up a proper shop in a new city.

"And just then my brother, William, reappeared, in the middle of the night as it happened. He and every privateer from the island had gone off on a raiding party with Henry Morgan, who was the most famous privateer of the island. Do you know what that is, a privateer?"

Kitto shook his head. "Not quite."

"Privateers are men who get permission from a governor to attack the ships of another country. Mostly at that time it meant Spain. The Spanish were the first to the New World, and the richest for it. But they would not trade with the English or any other merchants of the area, and were despised by those who wanted a piece of the treasures the Spanish had plundered there."

"What sorts of treasures? Gold?"

"Yes, some. Mostly silver. The savages living there had mighty kingdoms full of the stuff but no guns. The Spanish whipped them and made slaves of them, then mined the stuff. They've been doing that more than a hundred years now. These privateers struck out at Spanish ships and towns to take what they could. Morgan was the king of the raiders. Privateers lined up to join him. Together they were known as the Brethren of the Coast, and Morgan was their so-called admiral."

"But why did your brother come to you?" Kitto asked.

"William had gotten in tight with this Morgan fellow. But he told me he was in trouble. He and the men with him. They had tried to stop Morgan from double-crossing them during this raid at Panama, and had ended up stealing from Morgan. He needed me for my coopering skills. He offered a huge sum if I were to aid him."

"And you needed money to get your family off the island," Kitto said. "Did . . . did you help him? Did my mother go with you?"

Father fiddled with the heel slice of bread on the plate. "I did help. As for your mum, she . . . she became ill just before we left. She and the baby inside her died."

She died of a sickness? What sickness? Kitto wanted

to ask, but did not. "So you and I left, Father?"

"Yes. On William's ship. On the way one of Morgan's ships caught up to us and attacked." Father thumped his wooden leg on the floor. "That's the truth about this leg, Kitto. Grapeshot cleaned it right off."

Kitto lowered his head into his hands.

"Yes. I know it's a lot to hear. But listen still. We escaped. We hid the treasure and sailed for New York. There I was to make barrels for him while he found a buyer. He needed new barrels to hold the booty. But I was through with all of it. When we reached New York, I took you into my arms and left William standing on the docks. He promised to send me a share—even though I had done nothing to help him—but I never saw or heard of him again."

Kitto spoke hesitantly. "Was . . . was your brother, this captain . . . was he responsible for my mother's death?"

Father's face went stony. He rose in silence.

"We must be going," he said, finally. But Kitto did not move.

"Not just yet, Father," he said. Kitto nodded toward Father's chair, and Father surprised them both by sitting.

"I won't ask to know everything. But this I must. Does your brother's return mean danger for us, for our family?"

"I do not know for certain. But I believe it does, yes."

Kitto stared at the table. "You think your own brother could wish us ill?"

"No. But neither do I think that he looks beyond the horizon of his own circumstances. He needs me for my services and for my silence. Beyond that he has no thought for how his arrival could endanger us.

"This Henry Morgan is now the lieutenant governor of Jamaica! He has both the privateers and the law on his side. He is far more dangerous than William ever gave him credit for. And the men who work for him are equally deadly.

"Morgan would kill us, Kitto. All of us, to keep secret that it was he who tried to steal from the Brethren of the Coast in Panama, not William. Morgan can never allow that to be known."

The barkeep down the aisle held up two fingers. Kitto shook his head and turned back to Father.

"You can trust in me, Father," he said.

The water that glimmered blue during the day was now black in the starlight. Kitto perched in the bow of the rowboat, scanning the silhouetted outlines of moored ships.

In the middle of the boat sat the oarsman, a reed of a man but for two bulging forearms. The man had a long hooked nose that ran incessantly, and when he failed to wipe it against the shoulder of his shirt, the gusts swept droplets off to starboard.

"*Blessed William*, yes! Dropped anchor only yesterday. Came here from New York, so I hear," said the oarsman in a high-pitched voice.

"Do you know anything of the *William* or its crew?" Father asked. "Any information."

"Information? Let us see. . . ." The rowing paused.

"I would make it worth your while to remember," Father said.

"I thought you would, sir. I rowed a batch of drunkards out last night, and one of them was from the *Blessed William*. He and another sailor got to chatting about their captains." The rowboat passed several lengths to leeward of a small barque, where a man on deck with a lantern stood watch.

"And what did they say?"

"The *William*'s captain has a temper, apparently, but the men like him. They must."

"What do you mean?"

"None of the crew seems even to know the purpose of their journey! A bit of a mystery," the ferryman said.

"And the sailors follow him nonetheless?" Father asked.

"They do. They think he's lucky. A right rabbit's foot. All the crew knows is that soon they recross the ocean again."

An irregular wave threw off the man's stroke. He wrestled with the oars. In the distance, still a hundred yards out, Kitto could make out the shape of a ship rocking against the starry horizon, the tip of its mainmast tracing a line between two bright stars.

Shortly the rowboat pulled alongside the ship. The man called, and a rope ladder was tossed down.

Father steadied Kitto as he climbed past the ferryman toward the ladder. "Keep your wits about you, lad."

CHAPTER 5:

The Meeting

The dark hull of the *Blessed William* loomed over them and the tiny rowboat.

"Take a hold, boy." Father held out the rope ladder that had been dropped down to them by unseen hands on the ship's deck. Kitto accepted it timidly. He lifted his bad foot to the lowest loop of rope and stood up on it, swinging free of the rowboat and bumping against the hull of the ship. A fresh layer of tar had been applied to the hull, and it blackened the knuckles of Kitto's hands. He climbed on.

Soon a pair of dark hands seized him by the armpits and lifted him over the rail and onto the *Blessed William*'s deck.

"Thank you," Kitto said. The man before him stood half as tall as the mainmast, it seemed, his features chiseled from a single piece of ebony. While he had seen African men before, Kitto had never spoken to one. The man looked stonily down at him, the whites of his eyes aglow in the starlight. He wore a cloth cap and a gold hoop earring in each ear.

She was an unimpressive vessel, the *Blessed William*: sixty feet stem to stern, with main- and mizzenmast—a small ship for crossing oceans. A half dozen men spread about on the main and quarterdeck. Two held fistfuls of gaming cards over a barrel top, using heavy mugs to keep the wind from scattering them; two others mended a sail at the bow, and two stood before Kitto.

Kitto stood tall and was glad the men did not look down at his foot. "I am Christopher Wheale with my father, Frederick Wheale. We are coopers. The captain visited our shop earlier today." The towering African turned to his shipmate.

This second sailor wore a scraggly black beard that shimmered with the grease of roasted meat. He leaned against a small cannon and ejected a stringy gob of spit over the side.

"Cap'n Quick knows you are coming," he said. Father joined Kitto, and the four stood in silence.

"If Captain Quick expects us, I suggest you lead the way," Father said. The slovenly man glared, but pushed himself to his feet.

The man led them astern, down a narrow stairwell to a closed door. On it, at Kitto's eye level, a small brass figure in the shape of a dolphin was mounted to the planks. The man grasped the dolphin by the tail and rapped it against the brass plate behind it.

"Cooper here, Captain!"

The door swung open, and there stood Captain William Quick, bathed in a pool of candlelight.

"I began to think you would never come, Frederick."

"The thought occurred to me."

Kitto and Father ducked through the doorway. The cabin was just high enough for standing, though here and there stout beams forced one to duck. It measured a half dozen paces by about three. In the middle of the room was a table covered in maps. On one side lay a bed built into the wall. On the other sat an enormous sea chest with a curved top. A tiny window at the rear looked out to the open sea.

"Swickers, send up young Van with a tray and a few glasses."

"Aye, aye, Captain."

William Quick and Father shook hands. "It is good to see you, Frederick, even if you shan't say the same!" He turned to Kitto. "And look at the little one. . . . You grew into a man, you did! I would hardly recognize you if I ran into you down at the wharf." He winked and held out his hand. Kitto squeezed as hard as he could. The captain's grip was like iron.

"Unfortunately, the wharf is where he'd spend all his time," Father said.

"I can't say I blame him," the captain said, still smiling. The three sat, Kitto and Father atop the sea chest, the captain on the bed. Kitto fiddled with the hardware of the chest beneath him. The corners and the lock were adorned with the figures of arching dolphins in pewter. He had never seen its like.

The maps on the table immediately drew Kitto's

attention. He scanned them but could not recognize what they showed. A knock sounded.

"Come in, Van!"

In came Augustus Van Arkel, his blond hair falling across his bright blue eyes. He eyed the strangers.

"Just set it down here."

Van was tall and handsomely built. He had an angular jaw and a chin cut neatly square, the kind of face that gave a girl a catch in her throat. He had a quick mind that had never been bothered with schooling in his thirteen years. That mind had much to dwell on. Van had a secret—two actually—and secrets they must remain.

He set down the tray. It held slices of bread and a wedge of cheese. Kitto startled when a blur of dark fur rose up from behind the young man and over his shoulder. It was a monkey, and it scampered far enough down Van's arm to filch a slice of bread.

"Julius, give me that!" The monkey capered about on Van's shoulders, avoiding his reach.

"Forget the bread, Van, just escort yourself and the beast to the door," William ordered. "And for the love of God, give that animal a bath."

"Aye, aye, Captain," Van said, then turned to leave. Julius waved the bread at the captain and flashed a monkey smile.

"Gentlemen. Let us give thanks for the hand of Providence, that she has brought us together after so many years. To our good fortune!" The captain nodded to them and gestured toward the food.

Kitto looked to his father. Neither of them spoke nor reached for the plate.

"Good health might be a wiser thing to wish for," Father said. William snorted.

"Very well. To our fortunes, may they be healthy, and to our health, may it be fortunate." The captain's smile vanished. "'Tis cursed luck to refuse a toast, Frederick."

"I cannot toast this reunion," Father said quietly. "You will have to understand, William, that your sudden appearance has caused a stir," Father said. "Just moments ago I shared with Kitto, here, some facts about my past. Our past. Facts that I had no intention of sharing. When we parted, William, I told you I wanted no hand in the business any longer. Now here you are thrusting a plate of stale bread in my face and expecting me to open my arms to you."

William gave his brother a sour look. "I'll admit the bread is not fresh baked, Frederick, but at least the cheese is not moldy."

"I do not share your humor."

"No. You never did, either, did you?" William snapped. "I am a part of your past, Frederick, though you would like to forget it! Being brothers ought still to count for something. As for what happened seven years ago, I see that you have chosen to lay blame on me. Easier, I am sure, than laying it where it belongs."

"Our account was settled, William. Now you will leave me out before it is again too late!" Father pounded his fist on the table.

Kitto watched, stunned.

William Quick sat quietly for a moment, a picture of calm, though his face bore no trace of the earlier smile.

"Frederick. Allow me to enlighten you on the way I have spent the last seven years." He set his glass to the side.

"When you stalked off down the gangway in New York—and I lost the cooper I needed—I sought out a certain customs agent I knew. A man who could turn anything of value into gold, and do it quietly. He and I made a bargain, then I sailed south to retrieve the goods.

"Several days out I spied a ship on the horizon. She was a frigate, but not navy. She outgunned and out-manned us, and she was bloody swift! I sailed hard but could not lose her. I tossed cannon and shot overboard, cut the anchor. I had Jenks carve up half the wood on the ship and heave it over."

"Did it work?"

William shook his head. "When she was in range of her biggest guns, she fired over our heads. A warning. We did not heave to, of course. I knew by then who sailed that ship. Only John Morris could sail like that, Morgan's right-hand man."

"I remember," Father said.

"It was then they raised the *jolie rouge*."

"The *what*?" Kitto exclaimed.

"The *jolie rouge*: the bloody flag. A bright red banner. 'Tis a pirate flag. It means but one thing: that they will not accept surrender; that now we would fight to the last man."

"How did you escape?"

"I did something frightfully daft. I sailed directly for Cuba, the heart of Spanish Hades. I hoped we would be spotted, and a Spanish fleet would go after the frigate while we tiptoed off with the wind. And it worked, in a way."

"How so?" Kitto said.

"We picked up two Spanish cruisers. Monsters they were. They had the wind on us and we struck our colors immediately. The frigate, though, managed to veer away and disappear."

"But now you had the Spanish to contend with," Father said.

"Yes. They towed us to Havana, threw us in a dank cell, and left us to the mosquitoes and rats. Eighteen of us entered that gaol, six emerged: myself, Peterson, Isaac, Swickers, Carroll, and Jenks. Any one of those men could have freed himself by telling the Spanish vermin about the booty. But they kept their silence. And when we get back to that island, I will repay them in spades!" William said, clenching his fist.

Island? Kitto wondered.

"How did you manage to escape, sir?" Kitto said.

William cut himself a bite of cheese. "It is a good story, lad, but it is a long one, and our time is short."

"Why so?" asked Father. "Seven years have passed, William. What hurry can there be now?"

William leaned so low to the table that one end of his long mustache curled against his cheese.

"Having escaped the Spanish prison just a few months ago, the six of us got our hands on a little sloop. We sailed north for New York. There I met up with the customs man I knew."

"You told him about the treasure?" Father said.

"Not all of it, Frederick." William winked. "Not *that* part. Just the part about . . ." The captain stopped. He was looking at Kitto, then turned a questioning eye to Father.

"He does not know," Father said.

"No, but I should!" Kitto said. He pulled out the dagger that dug into the small of his back and slapped it down on the table. The silver guard threw a dazzle of candlelight across the ceiling. "If I am prepared to use this—and I am—then I am man enough not to be kept in the dark!"

The room went silent. Kitto watched the captain's expression. It had twisted into one of disgust.

"That knife," William hissed.

"Yes," Father said quickly. "It belonged to her."

"Oh, did it?" William sniped sarcastically.

"To my mother," Kitto said, confused by the captain's tone.

"Frederick, why ever would you—"

"It belonged to her!" Father said, raising his voice. "Now it is the boy's. Leave it alone."

William exhaled slowly and twiddled one end of his

mustache. Kitto looked down at the knife on the table. *What more do they know about her dagger?*

"Go on and show him what you've got, William," Father said.

William reached a hand inside his coat, fishing for an interior pocket. He pulled out a small dark object and laid it on the table next to Kitto's knife.

"Do you recognize it?"

Kitto picked it up. It was a small nutlike thing, pear-shaped, brown, with a hard shell and little hairlike strands on it.

"Smell it," Father said. Kitto lifted it to his nose. There was a hint of something mysterious to its scent.

"Spice?"

Both William and Father raised a finger to their lips. William held out his hand, and Kitto dropped the nut into his palm.

"Nutmeg," he breathed, then returned the thing to his pocket.

"That is all? How valuable can *that* be?" Kitto scoffed. He knew spices were prized by merchants, but he could hardly understand why.

"A few dozen of these here," William said, patting his breast, "would sell for . . . about the dear price your father charges to make an entire barrel."

Kitto gasped. "A barrel for a few dozen nuts!"

"Shhhhh!" both men hissed. William smiled and jounced his eyebrows. "These are not mere nuts, lad. Wars have been fought over these spices. Fortunes have been made by many men. We have sixty barrels hidden away. . . . Sixty!" William whispered. "Maybe *you* can do the arithmetic without a pencil, but I spent years trying to do it in prison and kept getting lost in zeros."

"Oh, he can do it," said Father.

Sixty barrels. Sixty. How much would that be? Kitto's mind spun like a top. The size of the figures boggled him. Hundreds of thousands of pounds at least. *Millions!*

"Is it still . . . will they have survived all the years? Is it safe?" Kitto asked in a rush.

"I wouldn't be here if I thought otherwise," William said. "Yes, they are safe. But the barrels they are in are no good to me. They are Dutch make, and marked with Morgan's seal. There is not a port in all the Atlantic that would pay a fair price for them knowing they had been stolen from the mighty Henry Morgan." The captain twirled the pointed end of his mustache.

"The customs man in New York offered me a ship, but I insisted on the crew. Even so, I had not enough time to do a proper job. *Most* of these men I trust." William thumbed to the deck above. "But that only means I do not trust them all, that any one could be the rat who gave our destination away in New York."

Father's face darkened. "What the devil are you talking about?"

William's eyes darted from the table to his brother.

"That is why we have little time to lose. I spotted a sail two days out of New York. It trailed us the entire voyage east."

Father, who almost never cursed, launched forth with a few choice phrases.

"You have been followed to Falmouth?" Kitto asked.

William nodded. "I could not get a good look at the ship. Perchance that worry is past. As we came round Lizard Point, the other ship finally dropped back. But I fear that my trip has been noticed by someone, and I can only assume who it would be."

"Morgan! Good God, William! You brought Morgan here!" Father spit. His jaw clenched tight and his cheeks trembled.

"No," William answered carefully. "Not likely. Others do his bidding these days, Frederick. John Morris, perhaps. We shall keep an eye out for him." William nodded to Kitto. "You're a wharf denizen yourself. Have you seen any strange characters of late?" Kitto thought of the two men he had seen in the rowboat, but shrugged it off.

"No, sir," he said.

Father closed his eyes and pressed the heels of his hands into his eye sockets.

"Don't be so hasty to hang your head, Frederick!" William snapped. "As I said, the ship held off. If *we* waste no time in Falmouth, we should be able to make off without any further incident."

Father lifted his head and eyed his brother evenly. "William," he said.

"No, don't say it, brother. Do not. My very life hangs in the balance!"

"William," Father continued, "you are my brother.

That does mean something. But I must not allow you to further endanger my family."

"I need new barrels, *mate!*" William demanded, squeezing the edges of the table. "And you're going to make them for me! I did not come all the way across this ocean to be refused again by you. You want to protect your wife and that new little one who scampers into your arms? Then make sail with me, Frederick *Wheale!* Tomorrow I can be ready. You and the boy make the barrels on our journey south."

Kitto sucked in his breath in astonishment. *Have I heard it right? I will sail as well?*

"Are you mad, William? You get me—if that—you surely do not get Christopher!"

"Kitto is not too broad in the shoulders by now, I hope," William said mysteriously, sizing up Kitto with his eyes. "He might still be able to, say, fit through a narrow passage in a cave?" It was a strange thing to say at that moment. Kitto turned to Father to see if he understood, and was sure that he did.

"No. Find another way, William. Find another way!"

William shook his head. "Seven years I spent going over and over this plan, brother. If there were another way, I would not have bothered to come."

"And if I refuse you? What then?" Father demanded.

"Then I will sit in this port a year and visit your shop every day until Morgan himself figures out your real name and comes to your door with the hangman in tow!" William scowled and leaned back against the wall, looking away.

The words were spoken in anger. Kitto wondered if he meant them. Next to him Father's head had gone back to his hands.

Kitto cleared his throat. "Father? You needn't worry. We shall work together, you and I. We can pick up the lumber we need tomorrow and have everything aboard by the evening. We will get Mr. Quick his barrels and be done with it."

Father did not raise his head. "And your mother? And Elias? What of them?"

Kitto thought. "We shall send them off to Truro in the morn, to stay with cousin Henrietta a fortnight." He turned to the captain. "You did not know my father had a new family, did you, sir?"

"I did not," William said.

"Then even if they do reach Falmouth, they will be none the wiser. Mother and Duck will be safe!"

Neither of the men spoke, and Kitto knew it to be a sign of agreement.

"Risk and reward, Frederick. They are uneasy bed-fellows. I'll grant your risk now is great, but so too shall be your reward," William told him.

Father lifted his head.

"You would really do this, William? You would really come here and bring this peril to my door?" Father whispered weakly.

William's voice came out low and menacing.

"Frederick, I just spent a lifetime in a Spanish prison. I am bloody well capable of anything!"

CHAPTER 6:

Brothers

Kitto and Father stayed until late, mostly talking in low voices in the captain's berth of the *Blessed William*. Tempers cooled. Kitto listened to the brothers reminisce about times long past and people they had known. He resisted his urge to ask questions, sure that Father would not want him to do so. Those would have to wait until later.

"We should go soon, William. You had better let us take a peek in the hold so that we know what kind of space we're working with," Father said, pushing up against the table.

"Very well, brother." Kitto followed behind as the two men made their way out to the passageway, then down another narrow stairwell.

"Let me have that," Father said. William handed him the pewter candleholder, its wobbling flame casting an eerie light against the walls of the hold. Father picked his way carefully among a maze of barrels.

"Get that quick mind of yours ready, Christopher," Father called.

"Yes, sir."

Father counted his paces. "Twenty-eight!"

"Twenty-eight, sir," Kitto repeated. Father returned to the waist of the ship and paced from port to starboard.

"Eleven," he called. "Have you got that?"

"Yes, sir!" Kitto's mind manipulated the numbers.

"I did say twenty and eight, did I not?"

"Yes, sir."

Father grumbled. "Ah! I'll count it again." Father paced anew, leaving Kitto and William.

"Will she suffice, do you think?" William asked Kitto. The boy did not answer. "Well, will it?"

"I think it will be large enough," Kitto answered, "if you have told us all we need to know about the cargo." The comment about the size of his shoulders still bothered Kitto.

"Nephew! Such cheek! You say that as if you think I keep secrets from you." The peculiar smile had returned to William's face.

"I do, sir, if you'll forgive me," Kitto said. "Like the dagger, here." Kitto withdrew it deftly and held it out. William turned his head aside.

"Put that thing away, boy." Kitto did as told.

"Does it have to do with my mother? Whatever are you not telling me?"

"It is not mine to say, lad. It is a matter between father and son."

"And what about matters between a mother and a son!" Kitto said with a touch too much of heat. He put the dagger away.

William chuckled. "Quick with the temper, you are," he said. "*Quick* indeed." There was more than a touch of pride in the emphasis.

"And that is my name, is it not, sir? Am I a Quick, like yourself, Captain, and not a Wheale?" Kitto had been burning to ask the question.

William tugged at his mustache.

"Again, it is your father, Christopher, and not I who—"

"I am nearly thirteen, Captain! I have a right to know the truth about my own name." Kitto squared his feet to the captain. "I have a right, sir!"

William raised a finger in warning. "There is more to a man than a name," he said, his eyes flashing. "Remember that. More than a name."

"Yes, sir. But tell me, *please*. I am not a Wheale, am I?"

William stared at the boy for several seconds before answering him.

"You are not a Wheale." He nodded toward the stern. "Neither is he."

"Then why would I be called such? Why would he?" Kitto's heart raced.

"Frederick must have taken the name after we parted ways in New York and he returned to England. For your safety, I suppose, and his own. I only became aware of the change when you told me your name at the wharf."

"So I am a Quick then, yes?"

"Yes," a new voice said. It was Father. "You are Christopher Quick." Father stood a few yards off. He had rested the candleholder on a barrel at the far end of the hold, and the other two had not noticed his approach.

"Don't glare at me, Frederick. The boy has a right to know his name."

"He does. I did not intend to keep it from you forever, Kitto."

"Not right to keep it from me," Kitto said softly.

"Perhaps not. There are worse things."

"Worse? Than allowing the boy to grow into manhood without knowing even his name?"

"Well, now he knows it!" Father snapped. "Thanks to you. So many thanks I have for you, William. Ah! I am glad it is out. One less secret to keep. But, Kitto, you shall say not a word to Sarah, by God!"

Kitto gasped. "She does not know either! But she is your wife!"

"Good lord, Frederick," the captain muttered.

"Stay out of this, William!" Father warned. He turned back to Kitto. "What would I have said, eh? Tell her what I had done? Who I really was? Tell her of my famous pirate of a brother with whom I had cast my lot and cast away my life as well?"

"Hold there, Freddo," the captain said. "I do not care for the *p* word." Father ignored him.

"Should I have informed her of the danger we would all be in one day if that brother were to return?" He thumbed toward William.

"You could have said the truth," Kitto whispered.

"You should have. The truth wears better than a cloak of lies."

"Who are you to preach to me, boy, about truth and loyalty? Have I not stood by you, no matter what the world might think of you? Have I not taught you as best I am able to be a craftsman—"

"*I don't want to be a cooper!*" The words came out before Kitto had time to bite down on them as he had so many times before.

Silence. The sound of water lapping against the hull became distinct.

"I don't want to be a cooper," he said again, quietly this time.

"Of course you don't. You have the sea in your blood, lad."

"Don't talk that rot, William. Take a *look* at him!" Father gestured down at Kitto's foot in disgust. Kitto felt tears spring up. Father snorted and shook his head. "The boy needs a trade. Any fool can see—"

"His foot is bent, Frederick. Just the foot. Or have you forgotten that? It is not a chain about his ankle, tethering him to you."

"I have been there for him! We left Jamaica for him." He looked past William and to Kitto. "We left for you, Kitto. And the leaving is what got her killed."

"You blame him! You blame your son?" William said hotly.

"I did not say that."

William pursued. "Ah! It was for the boy Mercy

48

wanted to leave Jamaica in the first place, wasn't it, so that he wouldn't grow up in that amoral den? It was the boy's fault, wasn't it, Frederick!"

"William, I am warning you. . . ."

"He had the nerve to live when it was she who died!"

Father reached out and grabbed a handful of his brother's shirt. "You are not to speak of her!" Father's cheek twitched in the candlelight.

William glared daggers and continued.

"You look on Kitto every day and see her standing there before you . . . that twisted, shameful foot of his a sure sign of your own guilt. Or is it not that? Maybe what really scares you, Frederick, is to think that were Mercy to have lived, it would be *she* yearning to get away rather than your son here!"

The golden light separating the two men's bodies suddenly went black. Bodies whirled. The men spun about, knocking into barrels and cursing. Kitto watched in shock.

Is this truly happening? What am I to do?

The brothers careened into him and sent him sprawling.

When Kitto found his feet again, he found his anger as well. He withdrew the dagger from his belt and held it out angrily.

"Stop it!" he commanded. "Stop it, the both of you!" he shouted again, the absurdity of saying such a thing to two grown men lost on him.

The struggling figures did not stop. Instead they

tumbled to the floor, elbows flying, punches landing. Kitto could not tell one writhing body from the next. He stuffed the dagger back beneath his belt, enraged.

"How can you *dare* to be so childish?" he demanded of the silhouetted bodies.

There are lives at stake! We are being hunted by killers, and they fight amongst themselves?

A thunderous rumble of footsteps sounded behind Kitto, but he did not turn. Instead he charged forward. When he reached the grappling brothers, he kicked out as hard as he could with his good foot. It caught the figure on top squarely, and the man fell away. Kitto stepped over the man who had been on the bottom, and even in the shadows he could see it was Father.

"You *disgust* me!" Kitto shouted down at him. "Both of you!" He wiped at his tears.

"Captain!" a man called.

The three turned to face the bright light of a lantern. It was held by the towering African, and behind him were a half dozen sailors, pistols and daggers bared.

William Quick pushed himself to his feet and rubbed his jaw where Kitto's foot had struck.

"Easy does it, Isaac. Just the slippery deck that's tripped me."

"Get up, Father," Kitto said. "We are leaving."

If Father resented being ordered by his son, he did not show it. He stood, wiped his trousers and sleeves, then followed Kitto. The men parted before the boy, looking down incredulously on the limping figure.

The captain flexed his jaw and called after them.

"You're getting old, Frederick," William said with a grin. "Your punches don't hurt like when we were lads."

To Kitto's surprise, Father chuckled.

On the upper deck Kitto noted the dark clouds that had rolled in, carried swiftly across the sky by strong winds. A black nimbus passed over the moon and blotted it out. Kitto had no way of foretelling how important those clouds would be to him in just a short time.

At the rail the brothers shook hands warily, as if each suspected the other might strike. William raised a hand in farewell as the two clambered down the rope ladder toward the boat below. It was occupied by the ill-kempt man called Swickers they had met when they first came aboard. Also in the bow was the young man called Van. The monkey still perched on his shoulder, wringing its hands. As soon as Kitto and Father sat, Swickers pulled toward the docks.

The journey passed in silence. The steady breeze cooled Kitto's anger, and now he barely managed to contain the questions he had for his father. Would Morgan's men be able to find them? Would they even want to, or did they only hunt the captain? Did they need to go into hiding?

Occasionally a grunt escaped Swickers's lips, but otherwise only the sound of the wind could be heard, along with the occasional chittering of the monkey, who seemed to whisper secrets in Van's ear.

Without so much as a good-bye, they exited the craft at the dock and made their way. Van and his monkey jumped out first and ran on toward some unknown destination. Once they had reached the end of the dock, they were quickly swallowed up in the shadows. Father and Kitto walked, Father's wooden stump sending a hollow echo through the planks of the pier. On the wharf they passed a group of huddled men smoking pipes and talking in low voices. Father leaned to Kitto without breaking stride.

"Keep your wits about you, now. If anybody troubles us, you run for home and let me fend for myself."

"Yes, sir."

"And don't waste any time on that knife in your britches, neither. Like as not it would be used on you."

They walked along the wharf, then veered down a wide lane. To the left a set of double doors stood partly open. Yellow light poured out of the opening. Above the door hung a sign, a telescope carved in wood. Just after they passed it, the doors flung open. Kitto turned to see two men lifting a third man between them, the one in the middle barely conscious and muttering something unintelligible. The man on the left was gargantuan, head and shoulders above the others. The man on the right was rapier thin and wore a tattered oversize hat on his head that looked as if it had just been sat upon. When the man's face caught the light, Kitto saw that the skin around one of his eye sockets was entirely blackened. A tattoo, perhaps.

The door banged shut. The two men staggered with their burden toward the lane. Without warning, the carried man lifted his head and spewed out a stream of vomit.

"Not my boots, you blackguard!" protested the tattooed man. He hurled the man into his own mess, reared back, and delivered a savage kick. "Let me see if you've been holding out on us?" he said. He and the giant man rummaged through the pockets of the man on the ground. The giant smiled a big brown-toothed grin as he pulled out a silver coin.

"Next round is on him, eh?" the tattooed man said, leering. He and the giant man rose to reenter the tavern when their eyes turned toward Kitto and Father. For a moment Kitto and the tattooed man shared a look. Kitto saw that the tattoo was some kind of spider painted over his eye, lid and all.

"Keep your eyes to yourself or I dig 'em out with a spoon!" the man growled. Kitto turned away quickly, and so did not see the men's eyes linger on them. Kitto and Father hobbled down the street, picking up their pace.

Spider and the man known as Orrick leaned their heads together and whispered in slurred voices.

"Come on." Father pulled at Kitto's sleeve, and they turned down a different street, this one darker than the first. The sound of their steps echoed against the cobbles and the row of stone buildings. They passed small groups of men—sailors, mostly—huddled over games of dice.

Thick clouds darkened the heavens and swept across

the sky. Now and again the moon shook free of its cloak, and for a few seconds all of Falmouth was illumined in a silvery glow. Kitto and Father turned again down another lane, then again, the narrow passages like the halls of a maze. Each time Father turned, he first gave a small tug at Kitto's sleeve. They never spoke.

After several such turns, so many that Kitto had begun to grow uncertain as to where they were, he first heard the sound. It came from a ways off behind them.

"Father!"

"Yes, they are following us. The two from the inn. Do not turn around."

CHAPTER 7:

A Rat in the Alley

The sound of footsteps, still so distant that Kitto could barely make it out, disturbed the rhythmic patter of their own against the stone walls.

Surely it is a pedestrian, Kitto told himself. *Not them.* The outside of his right foot had begun to ache dully, the way it did at the end of a day.

"Are you certain it is the same men?"

Father pulled again at Kitto's sleeve and nearly shoved him toward another lane. When they reached the corner, he peered back through the curtain of blackness.

"It is them, Kitto. I know those men. I recognized one of them," Father said, his breath heavy. *"From Jamaica!"*

Kitto felt a knot tighten in his stomach.

"Morris, that the captain mentioned?"

Father shook his head. "One of his men. A murderous devil, too. . . ."

They walked on. The sound of the footsteps behind them disappeared entirely when they turned down a new lane, but then returned even louder a few moments later.

"They are getting closer!" Kitto willed his legs to swing more quickly. He stole a glance at Father and could see beads of sweat forming on his brow.

Kitto reached his hand to the small of his back and felt for the knife. It had wiggled upward as he walked, and his fingers knocked the handle. The dagger slipped from his belt and fell. The steel clattered against the cobbles. He stopped long enough to retrieve it, and as he did so, he lifted his head to look down the alley, bathed for just an instant in white moonlight.

Kitto saw them. They, too, had turned the corner. He turned again and hustle-stepped to catch up to his father, who had not slowed.

"It *is* them!" He had gotten a quick but good look at the nearer of the men—the one who had threatened Kitto. The figure wore the same oversize hat set at an odd angle. And the looming shape of his companion was unmistakable.

"Turn left down the alley coming up," Father said.

Ahead of them, maybe a dozen paces, a narrow alleyway intersected theirs. The opening in the row of two-story buildings seemed even darker than the one they were on now.

Kitto counted his steps, with each one feeling ever more certain that a hand or sword blade would strike him from behind. But they did not run. Father did not break his stride but hobbled evenly toward the opening. Kitto, taking the cue, tried to do the same.

Once they turned, though, Father tugged Kitto's

shirt hard, and they broke into a full sprint.

They ran, past broken crates and piles of garbage, shuttered shop windows and piles of old bricks. Father's pace was surprisingly fast; he took huge steps forward with the good leg, then a shorter hop with the wooden one, his head bobbing with each stride. Kitto strained to keep up with him. Something dark on the ground ahead scattered into pieces and scampered out of their way before they trod over it; after they had passed, Kitto realized it was a pack of rats huddled over the remains of a dead cat.

"Don't stop, Kitto! For anything! You understand?"

Right after he said those words, Father slipped. The forward hop with the stump did not find a purchase and slid forward. Father's arms flew up and he careened to one side, feeling as he fell a sharp pain in the muscles of his good leg.

Kitto stopped. "Give me your hand!"

Father flung an arm about Kitto's shoulders, and soon they had regained their footing. Before they ran anew, though, they turned and looked back down the way they had come, now the better part of a hundred paces behind. Two men emerged from around the corner where the alleyway met the cobbled lane. Kitto saw that the smaller man held something in his hand, which he kept low to his side. The towering man's shadow stretched half the distance between them.

The smaller one shouted a curse and pointed at them. Kitto and Father sprang forward, the thumping of Father's stump resounding loudly. Father groaned in agony with each step. Kitto saw Father's pained grimace and it was at that moment he understood for the first time what fear was—raw, chilling fear. He could taste it in his mouth and feel it squeeze his chest like a giant hand. They turned down another alleyway and ran on.

"Cursed stump!" Father groaned between clenched teeth. "I'm giving us away, Kitto! Let us split up; they're sure to follow me!"

"No, sir, we stay together!" Kitto whispered back. The men behind quickly reduced the distance separating them to a mere fifty yards. On Kitto and Father ran, pell-mell now along a bending alleyway that barely kept their pursuers out of sight.

Then Kitto spied it. An alleyway approached, this one intersecting their own at right angles, one part to the left, the other continuing on to the right. The light against the ground was different down there. *No cobblestones!*

"This way, Father!"

Sure enough, as soon as they entered the alley, the sound of the stump faded on the packed dirt. It was so narrow they had to run single file, Kitto in front.

They had made it only forty paces down the alley when Father went down again. The thud of his chest against the ground stole his air from him. He groaned. Kitto lifted him by an arm, but when they were half up, they both lost their balance and fell one atop the other against the side of a building. Kitto lay pinned beneath

Father. They each craned their neck back toward the intersection.

Two darkened shapes appeared. The larger man bent, his hands on his knees. The thin man held his arm out straight. It was certainly a pistol he held. From the distance, Kitto could hear their breathing, ragged and heavy. Kitto held his own until tiny points of white light danced before his eyes. Father's weight felt crushing. Above him a black sky of storm clouds rolled in on a strong wind. They were so thick no light could penetrate them.

"Which bloody way!" the smaller one rasped, his hands on his knees. The larger answered only with his labored breath.

"The Beak will feed us our own backsides if we lose them!" Kitto felt Father's body stiffen when he heard those words.

Somewhere far down the other alley, a large rat, lolling about in a pile of rubbish at the side of the alleyway, stirred an empty bottle. It rolled against the cobblestones.

The men turned toward the sound and ran off, in the opposite direction of Kitto and Father. Father exhaled slowly. He pushed himself up.

"The Beak!" he whispered. "That is John Morris. Here in Cornwall! God help us!"

Kitto did not bother to question him. Instead, the two of them struggled to their feet and ran off into the darkness toward home.

*   *   *

One hour later the young man known as Van stepped through the low doorway, ducking low so that the monkey perched on his shoulder would clear the door frame. The inn was dark. The air hung thick from pipe smoke that slowly curled in the candlelight. He made his way past the tables toward the back, where sat two men. The one with the tattoo over his eye and curly orange hair kicked at the chair so that it slid out from beneath the table toward Van. He sat quickly, feeling the weight of the men's stares.

"You're late," Morris told him.

Captain John Morris had coal black eyes and black hair that always seemed neatly combed. He had helped liberate the island of Jamaica from the Spanish, sailed with the legendary Captain Myngs, and when he was a much younger man, his prospects had been bright. His face was horribly disfigured, though. Two curved lines crept up from either side of his mouth: purple, bumpy scars that had darkened from exposure to the sun. He had suffered these as a boy at the hands of a cruel sea captain who had strung him up for days against the mast for the crime of failing to polish a strip of brass. Together the scars formed a leering grin.

Morris's second disfigurement was his nose, or what was left of it. The last inch had been cut off with a sharp cutlass. What remained were two symmetrical ovals, like those of a skull. John Morris had William Quick to thank for that wound.

Spider grinned a mouthful of bloodred teeth and reached to his plate for a bone to gnaw on. Van shuddered at the sight of those teeth. They belonged on a vampire, not a man. Julius hopped down onto the table and extended a thin black hand toward the heel of bread on Spider's plate. Spider stabbed out with his fork. The monkey dodged the tines and silently bared his pointed teeth. Spider returned the gesture, and Julius retreated to the safety of Van's shoulder.

"You have information?" Morris asked.

"Aye. If you have something for me," Van answered, trying to sound more cocky than he felt.

"Spider?" the captain said.

"Aye, Captain."

The tattooed man reached beneath the table for his boot. A moment later he produced a tiny sewn pocket of leather, held tight by a strand of hemp. He slid it across the table.

Morris's eyes again scanned the room, but there were only two other patrons and neither took notice.

"There's your forty pieces, Judas," Spider said with the wide smile.

Van glared at him. "I never promised my loyalty to Captain Quick." He snatched up the bag and pulled it to his lap. "And this ain't no forty, neither." He loosed the string and inserted a finger to count the pieces.

"You do not leave with that satchel until I am satisfied," Morris said. He dabbed neatly at the remains of his nose with a soiled napkin. His nose leaked fluid constantly, and required that he carry a kerchief.

"You'll be satisfied."

"Let us have it then."

Van took a deep breath. "Quick plans to sail tomorrow. He will probably wait until dark if the wind and tide allow it, which he believes they will." The young man transferred the satchel to his own belt, making sure the bag hung on the inside of his trousers.

"They have found the cooper. He has agreed to do the job."

Morris sent a chilling look toward Spider, who hung his head in shame. "Yes. We know about the cooper already. And the *Blessed William's* destination?" Morris said.

"He hates the Spanish with great feeling, so they'll forgo the Canary Islands and water at Cape Verde."

"A major slave port. Does Mr. Quick intend to purchase?"

Van shook his head. "No money for it. None of us crew gets paid until we're back in New York. Somewhere along the way he'll come up with the money he promised. He had better."

"Are the men whispering belowdecks yet?" Spider asked, his eyes slit.

"If you mean mutiny, no. But no sailor keeps a dogwatch happily, knowing he might never see the first copper for it," Van replied.

"So if it comes to a fight? . . ." Spider pressed.

Van shrugged. "Captain Quick's got a way about

him. The men might just fight for him, paid or not."

"A crew of twenty-seven?"

"Twenty-nine, counting the cooper and the cripple."

"Then let them fight all they want. And the boy . . . he goes with them?" Morris asked, his eyebrows arching.

"He met with them tonight."

"Then he might know too much," Morris speculated. "He shall require some attention," he said to Spider, who smiled and picked up his bone. Julius flashed his teeth again, hungry for the bite he would not be offered.

"Maybe I do to the boy's foot what I did to Captain X's hand all them years ago," Spider said, licking his lips. Morris was not listening. He was staring intently at Van.

"You know something more." Morris could read hesitation in Van's look.

Van nodded warily. "I found out . . . where they live," he said haltingly.

Spider's jaw stopped working the bone. "The cooper?"

"That *would* be helpful. Tell me."

"Ten more silver."

Spider scowled and threw his bone at Julius. The monkey ducked and the bone flew over Van's shoulder and fell to the floor at the foot of a man hunched over a pint of bitter. The man turned an irritated face toward them, but when his eyes met Spider's, he turned away.

"Robbery!" Spider protested.

"Give him the ten," Morris said. Spider turned an incredulous look at his captain, but reached to his belt for another satchel.

Once Van had retrieved the stack of coins, he told them what he knew.

"Very good," Morris said. "That will make our work easier." He leaned his head toward Spider. "We shall have the cooper Mr. Quick needs."

"What do you need a cooper for?" Van said. Morris's brow furrowed, and Spider's lip curled to a snarl.

"You will live longer, young man, if you train your ears not to hear that which might cause you pain." Morris fixed Van with a stare so pointed it made the young man squirm.

Spider pointed with his fork. "You get his meaning, Judas?" Van nodded.

Morris sat back. "Now. When we take the ship, Van Arkel, I shall trust that you know in what direction to thrust your sword?" Morris asked.

"Aye," Van managed. "Just so long as your crew does not mistake me."

Morris reached into his coat and withdrew a red cloth.

"Have this on your head without fail when we attack, and you'll have nothing to fear," he said.

"And when shall I expect it, this attack?"

"Perhaps two weeks' sail after Cape Verde," Morris answered. "That way it shall be very unlikely another ship might witness the excitement."

"And my other half, as agreed, once the ship is taken?" Van persisted.

"Much is said of me, young man, but never is it said

that I go back on my word. You will get the sum—*if* you earn it—and I will happily double it should we get what we are after in the end."

Van tucked the red head scarf beneath his belt as he stood up from his chair. He turned and left.

No one bothered to say good-bye.

CHAPTER 8:

Impending Doom

THE FOLLOWING DAY

"Gentlemen, wake up! We'll be leaving shortly." Father stood in the doorway to Kitto and Duck's bedroom. His face was gray. He had not slept. When the men from the *Blessed William* arrived before first light that morning, he had met them at the door with pistol in hand, opening the door before they ever knocked. He had loaded up the seamen William had sent with the tools of his trade and a wagon full of rough boards suitable for barrels.

"Give us just a minute, sir," Kitto answered, sitting up in bed. Father left. Kitto had made a decision the night before, and now it was time to act.

"Duck, wake up. I've got something important for you." When the boy heard that, his head popped up.

"Oh, yeah? What have you?"

Kitto stepped out of bed and reached behind the headboard. He came up holding the dagger Father had given him, the naked steel looking deadly even in the morning light. The sheath was still downstairs in the workroom. Kitto turned it longingly in his hands, marveling at the beauty of its craftsmanship. He hated to part with it. Never had Father made him such a gift. But it must be done for Duck and Sarah's protection.

Duck's eyes widened. "You ain't supposed to have something like that!" he said.

"Hush. Yes, I am. Father gave it to me. Yesterday."

Duck scowled. "I didn't get nothing."

"Well, now you are. I'm giving it to you."

"You are?" Duck's face brightened.

"It's a loan. I want you to hide it in your belt and give it to Mum once you two get to Truro," Kitto said. Duck held the dagger in his hand and made a few gallant sweeps with it.

"Oi! What a beauty!" he marveled. He dropped his arm. "Kitto, are you going to get me in trouble with Mum over this?"

Kitto shook his head. "She'll understand. Just tell her I gave it to you for her to hold safe until we see you again. Remember, it's a secret, right?"

Duck nodded solemnly. "Cross me heart." He took the dagger over to the window, unlatched the shutter, and swung it open. Kitto made up the bed out of habit, although he knew no one would sleep in it that night. Duck was silent over at the window, studying the dagger with his tiny hands.

Kitto stepped back and inspected the unwrinkled

blankets once he had finished. *I will not sleep in this bed tonight,* he thought. *I wonder how long it shall be until I lie here again?*

"Ooh! Kitto! I think I broke it!" Duck's eyes were wide with fear. Kitto stepped over and snatched away the dagger.

"What did you do?" The silver pommel at the very bottom of the handle had turned askew so that it no longer aligned smoothly.

"I didn't mean to! Please don't be cross. I'll fix it!" Duck reached for it, but Kitto pushed him away.

"Stop it," he said. The pommel had not just turned. It had also withdrawn slightly from the handle. Kitto could see some kind of wood affixed to its underside. He worked the pommel back and forth gently and tried to draw it out. Gradually it edged out farther.

"Looks like a cork to a bottle or something," Duck said. "Seems a bit cheap to have a knife handle that's hollow." Kitto said nothing but continued to pull on the silver knob. Suddenly it popped out completely, and something small and whitish tumbled out of the bone handle and fell silently to the floor.

"What's that?" Duck picked it up, and Kitto plucked it from his palm.

"Hey!"

"Hush! Just let me see what it is." It was a small piece of parchment, a scrap really, rolled carefully into a cylinder shape. Kitto unraveled it between his fingers.

"What's it say?" There was something written, a

single word in faded black ink. Kitto leaned toward the window for better light.

"Ex . . . que . . . melin," he read aloud haltingly.

"X K melons! That don't mean nothing," Duck said.

"Exquemelin," Kitto said again. He shook his head, bewildered. Was it someone's name, perhaps?

"Want me to ask Daddy?" Duck offered. Kitto chewed on his lip.

"Not just yet." He wound up the scrap and slid it back into the handle's hidden chamber. "Let's just keep this between us for now, right?"

"I'm good with secrets. You know I am," Duck said. Kitto knew just the opposite to be true, but there was little to be done now. Maybe later he could ask Father about it. He carefully reinserted the cork end of the pommel, working it slowly so as not to tear the soft wood. In a moment the pommel nestled perfectly into place.

Sometime later Kitto and Duck stepped outside the doorway of their home and into the gray brilliance of morning. The carriage had arrived. Sarah and Father finished up in the house.

"When will I see you, Kitto?" Duck asked. He looked up at Kitto with wide eyes. Above them towered the driver, staring off down the empty lane. The horses stirred the loose dirt with restless hooves. Kitto got down on one knee and pulled Duck to him.

"Soon," he assured, "and I'll have many stories to tell. But in the meanwhile, I need your help."

"What?" Duck asked. He would do anything.

"I need you to keep an eye on Mum," Kitto whispered. "Take care of her and such. Being the man and all. Can you do that?" Duck nodded, puffing up his chest. Then the little boy's face puckered.

"But . . . who keeps an eye on me, then?"

"God will."

"Not really."

"Really."

"But where is He watching from?"

Kitto tapped Duck's chest. "From here."

"And if that don't work, I've got this dagger here—" Duck reached back to where Kitto had secured the weapon beneath his shirt and belt.

"Don't you pull that out!" Kitto said. Duck scowled. "And if you run into trouble, don't go pulling a knife on anybody."

Duck cast his eyes downward. "I am scared," the boy said.

"You'll be all right."

Sarah and Father stepped through the doorway and into the lane. Kitto stood. He had grown in the last year, and he stood nearly the same height as did Sarah.

"Good-bye, Mum. I shall see you soon," Kitto said.

Sarah reached out and took Kitto by his shoulders.

"Nearly a man, you are," she said, and pulled him close. She whispered in his ear. "The way will be dangerous, Kitto. Terribly dangerous! But every day a hundred times I will throw my thoughts up to God that He may guide you." Sarah pulled away and held him by the shoulders again.

"Do not be in such a hurry to be a man, Kitto. Make only the best of decisions again and again. Your father will do a poor job of looking after you, I am afraid. You must look to your own safety as if I were there to pester you myself." Her voice quavered.

"I will take care, Mum. Please do not cry," Kitto begged. There was a limit as to how much he could keep inside.

"Sarah. The carriage awaits," said Father.

Sarah withdrew from the embrace and dabbed at the corner of her eyes with her finger. Then she took Kitto's face in her hands.

"Hear me now, Kitto. I am not a wise woman, but I know one thing to be true, as true for you and the foot God has given you as anyone." Duck stared up silently at them. Even he could see the intensity in his mum's expression.

"If you can see a thing in your mind's eye—*really see it!*—then you can make it come true. Anything. But you must believe with all your heart and put your very soul to the task. That is the great power that God has given you. Bear it with you, and no obstacle, no matter how mighty, will ever thwart you for long."

Sarah stepped back, her eyes turning toward Duck, who had leaped against Father's legs and held tight.

"Now get this one from me, Sarah," Father said. Duck would not unwrap his arms until Sarah pried them free and ushered him up into the carriage with a swat on the bottom. Duck sniffled as he climbed.

Sarah followed. As she stepped up onto the metal stair, a coarse hand covered hers on the railing. She turned. Father stood, looking uncomfortable. He seemed as if he might speak, but no words came. Sarah smiled faintly.

"I shall miss you too, Frederick," she whispered. "You take care of Kitto and yourself as well. Send for us the first possible moment." Father stood mute. Sarah climbed up and called to the driver, who clucked to his horses. The carriage jerked into motion.

Duck turned in his seat to wave. It was the last time he would ever see his childhood home. The clatter of hooves resonated down the street.

Kitto held his hand high. Father stood rubbing his jaw.

The brothers kept waving to each other as the carriage grew smaller and smaller.

As they passed the corner, neither Sarah nor Duck noticed the three men lurking there: the wiry man with the frightening tattoo and the ridiculous hat, the giant man with narrow-set eyes, and the dark man with a raw hole for a nose and two livid scars extending from either side of his mouth.

Kitto shoved two shirts and a pair of trousers into the old canvas sack. It did not take long for him to gather all that he owned in the world. He was leaving Cornwall, leaving by ship, and the prospect so thrilled him. His first sea journey! Had it not been for the harrowing episode the night before, he could have enjoyed the moment without reservation.

Across the room Father was a picture of energy. He busied himself with his own sack.

"We shan't be back here, son. No knowing when those men will find out where we live and come looking. With the barrow we can push the last tools the long way down Killigrew Road, then cut back over to the wharf. It is there we shall have to be the most wary."

Father turned and went down the stairs two at a time. Kitto scanned the nearly empty room, now knowing it would be the last time he would ever see it. There was little to miss. A simple table and benches, a stone hearth. Sarah kept a plain home. The few decorations she had were packed in her own trunk on their way to Truro. Over in the corner stood a stack of stones a foot high that Duck had worked on that morning. The gray, angular rocks balanced in an unlikely column. Kitto stepped forward to knock it down, but then reconsidered and withdrew his clubfoot.

Father's wooden leg thumped up the stairs. When he rounded the corner, Kitto saw that he held something in his hands, something wrapped in a familiar cloth.

"It's not worth its weight in tin if you are much more than ten paces, but it will do." He set the pistol down gently on the table. They both looked at it, then at each other.

"Do you know how to use it?"

"Use it? Well, sir, I . . ."

"Well, do you or don't you?"

Kitto nodded meekly. "At the docks a man showed me once," he said. "Just how to fire it. But . . . do you mean for *me* to carry it?"

"I do," Father answered. "That and the dagger I gave you."

Kitto felt his face flush at the mention. "I . . . I gave it to Duck." Father's brow knitted fiercely, so Kitto spoke fast. "To give to Mum once they were out of town! She would bring nothing to protect herself—as you well know—and . . . she might wish she had brought something."

Father considered silently for a moment, then nodded. "You are right. Good lad. The pistol shall suffice. And I've got an old cutlass I shall lay in the barrow for any trouble on the way. I can use it well enough. Be careful with that pistol, Kitto. It is loaded now, and primed, so take care."

"Yes, sir. But, Father, can we not . . . Surely, if these men are villains, we can seek out help? The constable's men? Would not the law come to our aid?"

Father shook his head. "If these *are* Henry Morgan's men—and they must be Morgan's—then the law is on their side. He is the king's man, Christopher. The lieutenant governor of Jamaica. We are just a cooper and a boy. Nothing more. If we run to the constabulary, I'll hang on the end of a gibbet before sunset." He pointed again to the pistol. "Take care not to shoot yourself with that thing."

"Yes, sir."

"And don't use it until you've no other choice. One shot is all it's good for, then it is useless. Loading takes too long in a fight. Do you know how to load it?" Kitto shook his head.

"I will show you now." Father reached for his shoulder and patted it, but found nothing there. "Ah! Left the bandolier downstairs." He turned back to the stairs, leaving Kitto staring at the polished wood.

The staccato thump sounded again as Father hurried down. Kitto took the pistol into his hands. The wood was a dark reddish brown, flecked and notched with scratches and nicks and dents. It felt very solid, very real. Kitto lifted his arm and sighted down the barrel at the stack of stones Duck had balanced in the corner of the room.

At that moment from downstairs there arose a tremendous crash, a splintering of boards and the breaking of glass. The entire house shuddered; the stone pillar Kitto pointed at with the pistol tumbled to the floor.

From below came the sound of an anguished howl. *Father!*

Kitto's body went stiff like an oak plank.

They are here! They have found us!

Father bellowed again—this time in anger—and now he heard the grunt of another man and the ringing of steel. Kitto's eyes darted across the room. A window set in the wall overlooked the herb garden and back lane. He could be out that window and down in a heartbeat.

Kitto's whole being told him to make for that window, but the sounds of crashing, and the ringing of steel—they stopped him cold. Goose bumps stood out along his arms and down the back of his neck.

Another huge crash shook the floor beneath him, and he heard the tinny clanging of tools being strewn about.

Kitto stumbled toward the top of the stairs. He looked down the long stairwell. It turned at the bottom, and Kitto could not see what went on in the workroom below.

"Orrick, not the pistol!" an unfamiliar voice rasped. "You're not to kill him!"

Kitto slid more than stepped down the first two steps, the fear churning inside him. One hand clutched the railing, the other the pistol. His knees felt as if they might buckle beneath him. Sounds of wood splintering, steel clanging, ceramics smashing—all these reverberated up to him. Kitto took two more steps, and when he was nearly halfway down the stairs, a broken chair skittered across the floor and banged into the bottom step.

The pistol shook uncontrollably at the end of his arm.

Go down! You must go down! a voice inside his head commanded. Kitto managed two more stiff-legged steps. The smashing sound suddenly diminished. Now he heard only the gasping of a man struggling for a breath.

Fear for Father's life fully penetrated his panic. Kitto thundered down the last half dozen steps. His shoulder slammed into the wall with a crash, and the great commotion in the room instantly ceased.

The room was a scene of destruction. The workbench had been flipped and lay in the middle of the room, its contents scattered across the floor. Chairs were overturned or lay in pieces. And in the center of the room facing Kitto, Father half stood and half was lifted from the ground by an enormous, thick-armed man behind him. One of the man's massive arms wrapped around his neck. Father's face was bright purple, eyes wide and bloodshot.

Just to the side stood another man. He brandished a cutlass in one hand, a dagger in the other, and a pistol butt protruded from his belt. A wide, livid scar curled up each cheek from the corners of his mouth, and there were two hideous holes in his face where his nose should have been. He turned his ebony eyes on Kitto. There was something terrifying and repulsive about the man, and fortunately for Kitto, he had trained the barrel of his pistol immediately upon him; Captain John Morris would have taken his chances on Kitto with the dagger had he not.

"Easy, lad!" Morris rasped. He had a voice like fingernails on a slate.

Kitto's pistol wavered.

"Let—let my father go!" he choked out.

Morris calmly calculated how long it would take him to drop his dagger and draw his pistol. Too long. The boy's arm extended way out in front of him, the pistol dancing about.

"Keep your head about you, boy. Nobody needs to die today," Morris whispered.

Kitto's words came out in fits and starts, as if he were in the midst of crying. He swung the barrel toward the huge man holding Father. "Let . . . him down. Let him . . . down! Now!" he screamed out. The huge man turned to Morris, uncertain of what to do.

Morris raised his cutlass hand toward the larger man and nodded. "Orrick, give the poor fellow some air." They could not afford to have the boy shoot the cooper by accident! They needed the cooper. . . .

The large man loosed his grip. Father toppled to the ground onto his hands and knees, sucking wind. He sat back on his heels, half turned so that he could see Kitto standing at the first stair with the pistol.

"Keep it on *that* man!" Father croaked, pointing to Morris. Kitto swung the barrel again. Morris straightened from his crouch and dropped his arms to his sides.

"I have business with your father, lad," Morris said in a tone as friendly as ever any patron had used in the shop. "This has been a misunderstanding, this . . . hostility. No reason for it. Put down that pistol and we shall conduct our business like gentlemen."

Kitto desperately wanted to believe him. His eyes flashed to Father, then back.

"Do it now, boy!" Morris ordered.

"Pull the trigger, Kitto!" Father shouted. "For God's sake, shoot him!"

CHAPTER 9:

The Thick of It

Their eyes met, Kitto's and Father's. *Does he truly mean for me to kill? Can I kill?* Everything that Kitto understood about right and wrong, good and evil, seemed to swirl in front of him. He could not tell one from the other, and he was paralyzed.

The large man grabbed Father by the hair and yanked him up to a kneeling position. Again Morris held up a hand to steady Orrick.

"Don't be a fool, lad!" Morris warned. "We are men in the crown's employ. King's men. We knew your father would try to flee, so our entrance had to be . . . rough. But that is past now." Morris gestured to Father on the floor. "He has been subdued and will be brought to justice."

"Justice!" Kitto spit. "What do you know of it?"

Morris's eyes narrowed. "I believe you know something of your father's predicament, eh? But you have been misinformed. The law is on our side. See to this; I am putting down my weapons." The scarred man bent, laying the cutlass and dirk on the floor between his boots.

"You have been outmaneuvered, boy. Other than become a cold killer, you have no choice but to submit."

"I have one shot, sir!" Kitto said, surprising himself. The fear was ebbing, forced out by a tingling sensation of power that was his rage.

Morris sneered. "Then take your shot, you little whelp. Take it and to the grave go us all!"

Kitto took a deep breath. His aim steadied and his finger flexed on the trigger. Captain John Morris felt the peculiar sensation of fear; a look had come upon the boy's face: a look of fierce determination.

Father saw the look too. And in his mind's eye he saw the image of his clubfooted son dancing at the end of a hangman's rope. He could not have that.

"Kitto!" Father gasped, and twisted with great violence beneath Orrick's grip, throwing an elbow into the man's groin. Orrick let out a sucking sound and his hand loosened.

"Run!" Father screamed, and ducked as Orrick attempted to grab hold again. Father rolled to one side, leaped to his feet, and dived for Morris and the pistol at his belt. Morris stepped back just in time. The two men careened together into the wall.

The pistol was out now, both men's hands upon it. Father ended up on Morris's back, and the dark man staggered beneath the weight. They began to spin crazily, smashing into walls and furniture. The barrel of the pistol waved about wildly yet somehow did not discharge its shot.

Kitto anguished. *I cannot run, Father! I cannot leave you!*

His own pistol swept back and forth between the struggling figures and the giant Orrick, who now stepped clumsily about the wreckage on the floor, trying to engage in the fight without stepping into the line of fire. Finally Orrick reached down and picked up a large hammer with a heavy squared head.

Now Orrick was a brute; he was quick neither of hand nor of mind. In the excitement he had entirely forgotten Morris's warnings: that the cooper was needed alive, that he might prove useful should Captain Quick not. Orrick remembered only the command of "no pistols"; he had a hammer. His massive arm cocked back, ready to bring it down any moment on Father's head.

The grappling men crashed into the wall by the front door, kicking the pail of fireplace ashes on the floor. A cloud of gray floated up. Their spinning ceased, each vying for control of the pistol.

Kitto watched through the rising haze of ash as the barrel leveled at his own chest. Morris's strength was winning. He lifted his eyes to the boy in front of him. His finger inched from the back of the pistol toward the trigger.

Father understood what Morris intended. Kill the boy and discharge the shot. Then the fight would be over.

"No!" Father wailed, and felt a surge of desperate strength. He pulled downward, and so doing, slid from

Morris's back. The barrel edged downward, away from Kitto. Downward and inward.

Father knew his strength would not outlast the older man's, not at this awkward angle. He knew he had but one chance to save Kitto's life.

The barrel turned ever inward.

The explosion, when it came, filled the room and lit it for an instant in a flash of brilliant light. For a moment the two men still stood, gripping the weapon. Then Morris fell aside, slumped against the wall and began to slide down it, his hands clutching his side. Orrick saw his moment; he stepped forward and brought the hammer down with crushing force. It struck Father on the crown of his skull, shattering it and killing him instantly—though already Father was a dead man, as the bullet, having first passed through Morris's side, entered his own through the midsection and lodged there.

Father fell straight to the floor, limp and lifeless.

A blindness of rage overcame Kitto. Every part of his body went rigid. He squeezed tight the hands that balanced the pistol between them. Another flash of light. Another explosion of sound.

Then there was sudden silence. Kitto lifted his eyes to the huge man in time to see the purple-black hole in place of his left eye. A trail of blood spilled out of the wound. The giant man tottered, his head flopped back, and he fell. He was dead before his body struck an upturned chair, splintering it to pieces.

The room shook with the impact, and then all was still.

Kitto stood there, wide-eyed and unmoving. A thin stream of smoke issued from the pistol. Then his hands loosened, the pistol fell, and he rushed to Father, whose body had fallen facedown over that of Morris, who lay on his back breathing heavily.

"Father!"

His eyes were open and glassy. Kitto looked down at Morris, who stared back out of the corner of his eye, the effort to turn his head too great.

"He is dead! You have killed him." Kitto's voice was barely more than a whisper. Tears wet his cheeks and dropped down to darken the collar of Father's shirt.

"You murderer! He is dead."

Morris stirred, turning his head to look more directly at Kitto. One nostril bubbled with blood. Morris felt himself weakening from the wound in his side. His face had blanched, and the two scars at his mouth shone pink and formed a haunting smile.

Morris reached with his left hand beneath him. He felt something. His fingers closed on the leather handle of the dirk he had set down earlier.

"You should have done like I said, boy." Morris eased the knife out slowly.

"You have killed him," Kitto said through his tears. "Killed him!" Kitto stroked the back of Father's head, the hair wet and cool with perspiration.

"It did not have to be this way," Morris said. The

tip of the knife Morris held dragged slightly against the floor.

Kitto heard it.

Morris howled with rage and heaved with everything he had. Father's body slipped from him as his arm swung the knife in a fatal arc toward Kitto's throat.

Kitto was quicker. His head snapped back and Morris's arm swept past, the glinting steel missing its mark by an inch. Kitto tumbled backward.

From outside came the clattering of horses' hooves down the lane. Morris lay facedown, panting.

The constable? King's men? More killers? Kitto's mind reeled. He looked to Father.

"Yes, take a good look at his death mask, boy. You'll soon wear one yourself."

The sound of hooves grew louder, the pace slowing as the riders neared.

Kitto turned, stumbled over the legs of the upturned bench, then scrambled for the back of the shop. He threw back the iron latch, stepped out into the back lane, and ran.

The haunting voice called out behind him.

"You are dead, boy. Dead! Do you hear me? Dead!"

A cock crowed in the distance. Morris fell to his side and allowed himself to slip into unconsciousness.

Kitto ran and ran. Tears streamed from his eyes, and blindly he turned down alleyway after alleyway without a thought to where he was going. Finally the intense burning of his clubfoot from the distance he'd traveled brought him to a halt. He bent over, his breath heaving, and threw himself against a stone wall, sliding down to the ground.

Father! Kitto saw the blank look on Father's face, staring up. *He is dead. Father is dead.* Kitto wrapped his arms about his shoulders and wept so hard his shoulders shook and he felt he might die from lack of air. A long time he sat there, clutching himself. An hour, perhaps? It might have been longer. Finally the waves of despair passed, and Kitto was able to lift his tear-streaked face toward the sun that now peeked over the low roof of the building opposite him.

A foul smell he had not noticed before overcame him. He turned. Several feet away, lying in the middle of the alley, were the matted remains of a dead cat, a black cat. Kitto recoiled, then recognized it as the very one he and Father had leaped over on their terrifying race home last night from the captain's ship.

The captain! My uncle! The thought struck Kitto to alertness. His uncle was in great danger. If Morris had come after him and Father, then William would be next. He must warn them!

Kitto pushed himself to his feet. He recognized the alleyway where he stood now, and knew that it was not far from the wharf. Fortunately, he had run in a direction away from the main flow of foot traffic, so that now it would not be difficult for him to make it the rest of the way without being seen.

Cutting down alleyways and peering around corners,

Kitto angled his way toward the far end of the wharf. The sound of the surf lapping against the seawall was a welcome sound. He was edging his way along the side of the fishmonger's stall to steal a look out to sea when he heard voices. Familiar ones.

Desperately Kitto looked about for someplace to hide, but there was nowhere. Simon Sneed and his merry band rounded the corner.

"Oi! Look at this!" A huge smile alighted on Simon's face. "What I tell you, boys, eh? I knew he'd be skulking about waterside. Didn't I?" The other boys grinned too.

"Ten pounds we'll get!" one of them exclaimed.

"Maybe even more," said another.

"We'll split that prize, we will," Simon said, "though it seems only fair that I get a double share since it was my idea to look about down here."

Kitto had no idea what they were talking about. "You don't know what you're doing, Simon. I am on a desperate errand."

"So I hear. Very desperate, indeed. It's all over town, cripple, that you're a killer. Got your own father and some other poor bloke."

Kitto stiffened. "That's a lie!" The larger boys formed a half circle around him, the wall of the fishmonger's stall at his back.

Simon's sneer crept back onto his lips. "I'm sure it is. You ain't got the guts for that kind of thing. But we don't care. All we know is there's a reward on for your capture."

"And we're going to get it, too!" shouted a large boy with brown teeth.

"Yes, we are that," Simon said, "but first there's a score to settle, ain't there? Seems to me the constable wants him one way or the other, dead or alive if you get my meaning." Simon stepped forward and grabbed Kitto by the shirt. He pushed Kitto up against the wall.

Kitto felt the panic rising inside him. He had to escape. He had to get word to his uncle.

Simon leaned close and blew a breath of foul air that smelled of mildewed potatoes. "I'm going to enjoy this more than the money," Simon said. He reared back, made a gargling noise in his throat, and shot out a gob of spit. It struck Kitto across one eye and cheek. Kitto winced. He tried to wipe the spittle, but Simon held him.

"No, you leave it there. Now I'm going to rub it in with me knuckles." Through one open eye, Kitto could see Simon draw back a fist. He steeled himself for the pain.

"Let that fist fly, little worm, and I'll knock the teeth from your head!"

All eyes turned. Around the corner had come a tall boy with a monkey crouched on his shoulder. It was Van. Kitto recognized him from his uncle's ship.

"You ain't from these parts. This has got nothing to do with you!" Simon growled.

Van stepped toward the circle of boys. When he got to the first, a strapping lad as big as he was, he gave him a hard shove so that he could make it closer to Kitto. The boy stumbled aside.

"This one comes with me." Van took Kitto by the elbow, but Simon did not release his grip.

"Like blazes he does," Simon said. "He's a killer. Constable wants him, and we're taking him in."

Van gave Simon a dead-eyed stare. "It don't matter a whit to me if the king himself wanted him. My captain's given me orders, and not you or any other of these runts is going to get in my way." One of the boys edged closer to Van. The monkey on Van's shoulder arched his back and hissed, baring sharp teeth.

"He's all talk, lads," Simon said loudly. "And he's trying to steal our reward money. There's six of us. We can take two in as well as one." The crowd began to close in on Van and Kitto.

Van's hands whipped behind his back. When they whirled out again, they held two small daggers. One he pressed to Simon's throat beneath the chin. He pressed the tip of the blade into Simon's skin until it puckered.

"Aye, your six could take us. But you won't be one of the six collecting that prize money, will you?" Van said. Simon's Adam's apple bobbed up and down as he swallowed, his eyes wide.

"Come on then, sir," Van said to Kitto. Kitto moved toward Van.

"Sir!" Simon exclaimed, shocked out of his fear. "He's just a cripple!"

Van glared at Simon in disgust. "Just a cripple! You have no idea who he is."

Kitto stepped away from Simon, but before he left the circle of boys, he wiped the spittle from his face, reached out, and wiped it against Simon's shirt.

"That belongs to you, you pig," he said.

Van and Kitto stepped away. Now that the blade was no longer at his throat, Simon seethed.

"You're helping a criminal, and that makes you one too!" he shouted at Van. "Let's go, lads. Let's get the constable on them both!" he said, and the boys ran off in the direction of the quay.

"You all right?" Van said.

Kitto opened his mouth to speak, but no words came. His eyes welled up with tears.

"Aye. I heard about that," Van said. "Captain Quick sent a few of us ashore to find you. We got word about . . . about what happened." Van gulped and hoped the boy did not notice. "The constable's men are on the hunt for you," he said. "They won't be long once little Robin Hood and his band gets word to them." Van peered around the corner. He held two fingers to his mouth and let out a shrill whistle. A large man stepped into the walk, and Van beckoned to him.

"That's Swickers," Van said. "He's got the rowboat at the ready."

Kitto hardly heard. He stared down at the ground without expression, a dazed look on his face. Van reached out and squeezed his arm, and Julius ran over onto Kitto's shoulder. Kitto did not look up. The monkey chattered softly in his ear and petted Kitto on the head.

"It's going to be all right," Van said, and so saying he felt his stomach flip.

What have I done?

CHAPTER 10:

Aboard the
Blessed William

"Greetings, nephew. I see young Van here got to you before Morris did." William Quick stood before him, his hair pulled back and tied in a sailor's pigtail, a haggard look to his face. Kitto had just made it up the ladder at the side of the ship. Van and Julius scrambled up behind him.

"My father," Kitto began, but William held up a hand to stop him. He turned to the wiry man standing at his side. "Alert me of any approaching vessels, Peterson," William ordered.

"Aye, aye, Captain."

"Come," William said, and turned to walk toward the center of the deck. Kitto bowed his head and limped off after the captain. The crew on deck watched him go.

The two descended a narrow stair and an equally narrow and dark passage until the captain reached the stern cabin.

"Best close that door," the captain instructed. William Quick sat on the bed by the table and gestured toward the sea chest. "Sit down," he said.

Kitto felt a great rolling inside his gut, as if the *William* rode on a heavy sea. "My father . . . ," he began, his voice cracking, but the captain raised a hand quickly.

"Van!"

The door opened immediately, and the young man from the deck popped his head in. The monkey on his shoulders bobbed its head up and down, its long tail wrapped around the young man's neck.

"Captain?"

"We'll need candles. And some bread and cheese. Did we manage to get any cheddar before we weighed anchor?"

"Two wheels, sir."

"Good man. Bring the lad a wedge and something to drink. Fetch a bucket."

"Aye, aye, Captain."

The door closed behind Van, and his steps could be heard down the narrow hall.

The captain's cheery tone vanished. "We shall have to be careful, Kitto, ever more careful now." William Quick waited several moments in the dark silence, listening. Kitto sat dumbly. He felt a tremendous lethargy, as if his blood had thickened to a sap.

Lost in a fog, Kitto barely noticed when Van returned, setting on the table a bucket of cider and a wooden plate of cheese and bread. Two lit candles were also placed on the table, filling the room with a gentle light.

William kept his eyes on his nephew. His nephew! It

was hard for him to get used to the idea. So much time had passed. So much changed, and so little. After the long dragging years in the prison and now this—in the thick of it again, like old times.

Unblinking, Kitto sat. *I should not be here. Not without Father. I cannot do this, not alone. Father!*

In his mind's eye he saw the blank look on his father's face, lying on the floor in the shop. Dead.

Father!

William waited until the door latched again, then reached across the table and gave Kitto's cheek a bracing pat.

"One look at you and I see it is true what I heard. My brother is dead?"

Kitto nodded.

"And is it also true you killed him?" The accusation shook Kitto fully awake.

"Maybe I should put the same question to you, sir!" Kitto snapped.

William's eyes flashed.

"Have some bread and cheese, boy," William said. He cut a wedge from the cheese and held it out. Kitto shrugged it away.

"Word spreads fast in this little town, if you know where to lean your ear. I sent every man I could spare to find you. But I thought I would never see you again. Why did you come to the wharf?"

"I came to warn you," Kitto said.

"Warn me?"

"If the men knew of my father . . . and killed him . . . then you, too, were in grave danger."

William's eyebrows flickered. He was impressed. "That's more than you owed me. It is a noble gesture."

"No, sir. Not noble." As Kitto spoke, his thoughts became clearer to him. In his ride out to the ship, he had formulated a plan. "My father is gone now. What little wealth he left behind will be seized. My family has nothing. I am the man of the house, and I . . . I am lame."

Across from him, the captain squirmed in his seat. *Does he anticipate what I am about to ask?* Kitto wondered.

"I am here to take on the task that brought you all the way to Falmouth, uncle. *I* will be your cooper. And when we retrieve those riches you have spoken of, *I* will take my father's share and make a home somewhere far from here for Sarah and my brother."

The captain stared evenly at the boy. There was a hardness in the man's gaze, but a touch of pride, too. Finally he spoke.

"What about this Sarah you speak of? And the little one. Do you know . . ." The captain stopped himself. "What *do* you believe happened to them in all this trouble?"

Kitto peered closely at William, searching his veiled eyes. "They went off this morning to Truro," Kitto answered. "To stay with a cousin for a spell until we— until I—return."

William nodded but said nothing. He pushed a wedge of cheese around with his finger.

Kitto was a keen student of his fellow man. Since he was old enough to walk about town on his own, he had learned to read people's expressions to see how they reacted to his crippled figure: a guilty aversion of the eyes, a setting of the jaw, a patronizing smile. The captain's face was telling him something now.

"You know something, sir."

William's fingers stilled for a moment, then resumed fiddling.

"I know we are in danger. Little more," he said, his finger twitching faster. Kitto reached out and plucked the cheese from the plate and tossed it to the floor.

"I *know* what they are saying ashore. That *I* killed my father. I *know* I am wanted by the law. I am in this as much as are you, and I deserve to know all that you do."

The captain stared at his hands on the table. "Yes," he said, and nothing more.

William Quick loathed indecisiveness in general, and indecision was most despicable when it was his own.

"Tell me!" Kitto demanded.

William stared at the boy without speaking. Suddenly Kitto understood.

"My brother and Sarah? They are . . ." He felt an unbearable tightness at his throat, like a strangling hand.

CHAPTER 11:

A Partnership

Kitto reached out to steady himself. The captain grabbed him by the shoulders.

"No!" he said loudly, giving Kitto's shoulders a shake. "They are not dead." William sat back and pulled roughly at his mustache. "They have been made prisoners . . . or maybe I should say hostages."

"By the constable?"

William shook his head and said, "One of my men saw them escorted onto a ship, the *Port Royal*. They were unharmed, but he did not believe they went of their own volition."

"*Port Royal*! What ship is that?" Kitto asked, his voice full of anxiety. William held up a cautioning hand and glanced toward the door.

"Port Royal is the primary destination in Jamaica, the heart of Henry Morgan's world." William nibbled a wedge of cheese.

"She is the one who trailed your path across the ocean?"

William nodded, his head barely moving. "Tell me.

The men who came to your house, what did they look like? Was there one with a scar on either side of the mouth, and a? . . ." He made a circular motion with a finger around his nose.

"Yes. Yes! He was there! He was awful."

William closed his eyes in defeat. "Morris! Bloody rot," he whispered.

"He is as bad as he seemed, then?" asked Kitto.

"Bad? Hmm . . . Bad," William considered. "No, I would not use that word. He is much worse than bad. He is a killer. But, sadly, he is not the man you killed?"

"No. There was another man. A giant man. I heard him called Orrick. It was he who smashed the hammer, and then I . . ." Kitto remembered the quick buck of the pistol and the crimson trail. Kitto could not begin to accept what had transpired. *Did I do that? Did I truly do that evil deed?*

William grunted. "I knew him, though not well. You think him dead?"

"Yes, sir." Kitto wanted desperately to know more about his family, but the captain gave the impression that he did not like his thoughts interrupted.

"You have never killed a man before."

"No!" Kitto protested.

William tipped the bucket toward their cups. "When a man dies and the world becomes a better place for the rest of us, glasses are raised."

"Cheers," he said. They each drank, Kitto but a sip. He winced at the tangy bite.

"But what about my mum? And my brother, Duck? You have said nothing of them. What do you plan to do?"

William sat in silence. He did not look up at Kitto.

"We *must* do something!" Kitto stared off a moment. "But wait! He is wounded!" he nearly shouted.

"Who?"

"That Morris fellow. He and my father wrestled for the gun. When it went off, the bullet struck him, too!"

"Ha-ha!" William pounded the table with his fist, rattling the cheese knife. "Well done, Frederick! You are certain?"

"It is the only reason I was able to escape," Kitto said, realizing it for the first time. "Father saved my life."

William held up a finger. "It is not yet saved. Was he wounded badly, do you think?"

"Not mortally, I am afraid. Afterward he took a swing at me with a dirk. He almost did me in right then."

William sat back and smiled, candlelight dancing in his eyes. "Oh, for the foul airs of the tropics just now!" he sighed. "In Jamaica a little scratch can kill a man. Maybe we shall get lucky, Kitto." William's face fell. "What am I saying? John Morris is more pocked with holes than a block of cheese in a rat's nest! I made one of those holes myself."

"You did?"

"Aye, the nose. You could not have missed that!"

"Like two black holes," Kitto said.

"That was my handiwork." William smiled sweetly. "That was the day we left Panama. A good day, that one.

I wish now I had chased him down into the jungle and finished him off."

Kitto clenched his cup in anxious frustration. "But, Captain! What about Sarah and Duck? We must go back for them, Morris or no! We can't abandon them to that monster!"

William took a deep breath. "About that, Kitto, we can do nothing."

Kitto gaped. "Nothing? Nothing!" His body went so rigid that William thought he would hurl his cup. "I cannot do nothing about it, and you cannot either!"

"Quiet down, for God's sake! Yes, we do nothing. There is nothing we can do." He pried the cup from Kitto's hand and set it aside.

Kitto raised himself up. "I *do not* accept that, sir! I cannot do nothing about it, and . . . and curse you if you do nothing either!"

William shook his head in astonishment. "Simmer down, lad! Lord, did your father tolerate such insolence?"

Kitto slumped, his anger dissipating. "Not so well."

"As for your family, we can and will do nothing in a manner of speaking, but in another way we will do all we possibly can."

"I do not understand you," Kitto said. William refilled his cup from the bucket.

"There are only two reasons Captain Morris would seize your family. The first is he thinks they might know the location of the plunder—that Sarah might know. But that is unlikely; most men keeping such a secret would

not share the finer details with a woman. So probably it
is the second reason."

"Being?"

William scraped a thumbnail against the pewter cup.
"I spent seven years in a Spanish prison on the island
of Cuba. For a while—I do not know how long—my
captors suspected that we knew something of the items
looted from Panama. By the time my ship had been captured, remember, it had been emptied of its booty—so
they only had their suspicions. They tried to get it out
of me."

"What did they do to you?" Kitto asked.

William sighed. "Oh . . . just the usual sorts of things
really."

"And you held out against them?"

The captain snorted. "No one holds out indefinitely.
I fell into a . . . trance, shall we say. And it worked."

"What was that?"

"I slipped into madness. Went batty. I wept, cried
out for my dead mother, I screamed until I was hoarse. I
cracked just enough that I forgot what it was they were
asking of me. Had I not, then surely I would have told
them. But then I would not . . ." The captain did not
finish.

". . . would not be here today?" Kitto said, complet-
ing the thought. William nodded.

William's eyes glistened. Was it tears?

"But Frederick would be here, wouldn't he? Had I
just died along with the others in that prison. . . . A mar-

ried man with a family. His life traded for the likes of mine." The captain reached over to pour himself more from the bucket, but Kitto's hand beat him to it and pulled the bucket away.

"You cannot blame yourself for the desire to live, Captain. Now finish your tale, please, sir. You never did tell the Spanish?"

"To be truthful, I do not remember. But I do remember them being unhappy with me. And I remember having the sense that they had given up. As for the *goods*," William leaned in closer, "whether they remain where your father and I left them I shan't know until I see them there myself. Or should I say, when *you* see them," he added cryptically.

"What do you mean by me?" Kitto asked. *There it is again. That hinting of something more than just the nutmeg.*

William waved a hand in dismissal.

"Not the time. In whatever condition we find the items, they will need to be moved to fresh barrels before I can bring them into any port. Can you truly do the job without your father? They don't need to be the best barrels, mind you. We shall only have them in our hold a short while before we reach a suitable port for exchange."

"I can do it. I might need some help, but I shall get it done."

"Good lad! I have no stomach for skirting the English coastline for a cooper who can keep his mouth shut. Not when word gets out that the Pirate Quick is alive and well. You will have all the help you need." William straightened.

"But I have lost my train of thought here. Your family. Morris snatched your family for a reason. I suspect that it was not Morris's intention to kill Frederick. You, certainly, but not him. He seized Sarah and your brother to use as leverage to get your father and me to talk once he had us in custody. Now that Frederick is dead, however . . . their value as captives is greatly reduced."

"He *will* kill them, then, or already has?" Kitto held his breath.

"Perhaps." William considered it. "Yet I doubt it. When the time comes, he will use your family to his advantage, to get us to give up the treasure. So until we are in a position to make some sort of a trade, we must avoid the *Port Royal* at all cost. Once we have the treasure—the spice, I mean," he added hurriedly, "we will negotiate."

"And you will do that? Trade the spice for my family?" William cut a wedge of cheese.

"Certainly not."

Kitto's nostrils flared. "So you would let them die, then? And keep your money?" He felt his cheeks redden.

"Don't arch those eyebrows at me, lad. I did not say that! But if you think I will hand over such riches, you are a fool. That would mean death as well, at least for me. Perhaps you have heard of the island of Madagascar?"

Kitto shook his head.

"It is off the east coast of the African continent, tucked out of the way of all decent people. Pirates run that island, Kitto. Treacherous and bloodthirsty pirates. They come and go from its shores and take any ship they can chase down. And I happen to owe one of them quite a bit of money. Ridding myself of Henry Morgan and John Morris would only delay my inevitable death. I need to clear my name in Madagascar, too."

"But my family? You will see to it they are brought to safety?"

"I will. You have my word on that, Christopher Quick." The sound of the name startled Kitto. "But my word will not be worth the air I expend to share it with you if the *Port Royal* catches us before we have our prize. If they catch us first, they will simply torture and murder every member of this crew one by one if I *do not* tell them, and kill us all in one go if I do. We must avoid them at all cost."

"And can we do that? Avoid them?" Kitto felt the anxiety tightening in his throat again.

"They have a larger crew, better guns, and a faster ship. We barely had time in Falmouth to scrape the first layer of barnacles from our hull."

"Then they will catch us?"

"Over my dead body." William flashed his crooked smile.

CHAPTER 12:

Making Sail

TWO DAYS AT SEA

Kitto stood at the rail of the quarterdeck, moonlight washing the holystoned planks in a pale light. He felt too anxious and too excited for sleep. And then there was the mild nausea as well. A ship at sea is never still. It rocks and sways, pitches and yaws. Kitto was not ill, but he was not far from it. Several days would pass before his body had adjusted entirely.

He had lain awake for hours in the hammock assigned to him by the steward, Adams, trying not to think about Sarah and Duck. His tireless brain gnawed on the gristle of his circumstances: this new uncle, this new life, this new name. He thought about Father. He tormented himself. A thousand times he replayed that moment in the shop when the gun shook in his hands and fear paralyzed him. Could he have stopped it? Had he only shot Morris right away . . . had he only shot the giant man a moment earlier, his father would be alive.

Suddenly the captain was at his side, humming a sea chantey and looking quite cheerful. William could not help his good mood. For seven long years he had schemed in his gray prison cell. Now, finally, he was moving forward again, the nautical miles passing beneath the hull.

"No rest for the weary, Master Cooper?" William asked.

"Can't manage it, sir. Maybe I'm not accustomed to swinging."

William cocked an eyebrow. "Swinging? Oh, the hammock, you mean. Careful how you use that word. 'Swinging' has a different interpretation for someone in my line of work." The captain lolled his head to one side and hung out his tongue, a mime of a hanged man's expression.

"Come, Kitto, let's go to my cabin for a bedtime story. I have one you'll like."

The two exited the quarterdeck and headed down the stair. High above them, perched on the mizzentop spar, a lone figure watched them go. Van withdrew the spyglass he had filched from the captain's berth, opened it, and peered through it toward a watery expanse to the north. Julius, clinging to the ropes beside him, looked out too.

"There she lies!" Van whispered. She lay so far off that only the tip of her black mast peeked over the curvature of the earth. Van had no reason to feel as confident as he did, but he felt certain she was the *Port Royal*, cautiously trailing them as she had done from New York to Falmouth.

"There's our ticket, Julius," he said softly. Soon another payment would line Van's pocket, and then with luck a third as big as the first two.

Then he could go home! He could find her at last and never would they be parted!

Van collapsed the telescope and hid it in the long inside pocket he had sewn into his shirt for concealing things.

"Come on, Julius." Together they climbed skillfully down the ropes and made their way below. Ducking under the swinging hammocks, Van found his own, scrambled into it, and lay still in the dark, fingering the silver pieces in the little leather satchel.

An unshakable feeling of guilt gnawed at him. He tossed and turned in his hammock a long time before sleep took him.

"You are adept with the numbers, are you not?" William asked Kitto. Kitto hunched over the chart, the curling ends secured with a bowl of spent pipe ash and a candlestick.

"My best subject."

William seemed pleased. "Good. Tomorrow I will instruct you on the use of the backstaff. That instrument solves north–south reckoning, but as east–west goes, there is no easy trick for using the sun or stars to determine position. For that we will use algebra."

"Here is England, of course, and Falmouth," he said, laying a finger on the southwestern end of the island. "We are about here, according to today's backstaff reading." He slid his index finger down the map. "Winds predominate in a southerly direction all through this area," he said, sweeping his finger southward from England and just to the west of the African coastline, "then curl west about here"—he swept his finger toward Kitto's left—"crossing the endless ocean and passing right through the Windward and Leeward isles of the Caribbean Sea, then tending more northerly past Spanish Cuba, etcetera, and northerly up along the coast of the American colonies, and back up toward England."

"Making a big circle?"

"Precisely."

"Why not just cut straight across then?" Kitto asked, dragging his index finger in a straight line from England to the Windward Isles. "It would save hundreds of miles."

"Maybe even a thousand," William agreed. "Except for the fact that this center of the circle is too unpredictable—shifting currents, waning breezes."

Kitto reached out to touch the parchment. It felt soft and thick. There were familiar coastline shapes and countless place-names scratched in a tight, minuscule cursive. Fathom soundings were marked near the shores, showing depths of waters. Sweeping arrows indicated current patterns.

"You fancy charts, do you?" William observed, eyeing Kitto. "Should we find our pockets full at the end of this voyage, there is nothing to say you could not school yourself in the science of cartography."

Kitto flushed.

"Me? A cartographer?" he said, liking the sound of it.

"There's a sore need for good charts. Captains pay handsomely for them. Governments pay even more handsomely. It beats sweating in some dusty workshop making barrels."

Kitto bristled. "There's nothing wrong with being a cooper. It is a *fine* trade!" Kitto huffed. William answered with a great laugh that reverberated in the small room. Kitto scowled fiercely—he did not fancy being laughed at—and when William saw the expression, his laughter rose up higher.

"You have a peculiar sense of humor, sir!" Kitto pouted, and stared down at the map while the laughter subsided.

"I apologize, lad," William said, still grinning. "I have been absent long, and I have not had the pleasure of watching family traits reveal themselves. That temper of yours, that pinching of the eyebrows there when you grow irritated; that you picked up from your father. But that look in your eyes . . . the way they narrow and your cheeks get all red. . . . It bears an exceptional similarity to your mother, Christopher Quick."

Kitto gulped.

"My mother?"

William nodded. "I knew her," he said.

"Did you . . . was she a likable person?" Kitto asked

with hesitation. He held his breath and awaited the answer.

William stared at him evenly for a moment before replying. "Your father was madly in love with her."

Kitto waited for him to continue, as his question had not been answered, but the captain merely gazed aside. Kitto understood.

"Uncle, you are a man who says more in the spaces between his words than with the words themselves."

The comment startled William. His eyes flashed, then he stood up abruptly and crossed the cabin.

"That's a dangerous mouth you have there, boy."

"Yes, sir. I know. But you did not care for my mother, did you?" Kitto asked quietly.

"No. I did not."

"Why not?"

"I did not trust her."

"And why is that?"

"She was too pretty." The comment threw Kitto. He gave a perplexed look.

"Too pretty?"

William frowned and shook his head. "I do not mean to be disrespectful. Frederick is . . . was, I am sorry . . . a decent man. But he was neither rich enough nor—quite frankly—handsome enough to justify the affection Mercy Carter appeared to have for him."

Kitto gulped. "Carter? That was my mother's last name?" His heart pounded in his chest.

"You did not know? Not even that?" William asked.

Kitto whispered the name a few times to himself, as if doing so might trigger his memories. None came.

"I did not know," Kitto said. "But I don't understand. You say my father loved her. She loved him as well?"

"One would assume."

"You think she did not. Was it so impossible?"

"Impossible, no. But given what—or rather who—she had waiting in the wings, I am more than a bit skeptical."

"And? Who was that?"

William winced. He was getting into this subject deeper than he had intended.

"A wealthier man. With better prospects and better looks."

"You, do you mean?" Kitto asked.

William guffawed loudly. "Me! What compliments you give! No, not at all." He paused to clear his throat.

"The man was Henry Morgan, the buccaneer prince himself."

CHAPTER 13:

Family Tales

Kitto's jaw dropped.

"Henry Morgan? The same who . . ."

"The one and only. Morgan frequented a rooming house where your mother worked as a cook and maid. He was taken with her. Quite taken, in fact. But he was a married man. Frederick came along, and Mercy became involved with him."

"So my mother was not a . . . a companion of Morgan's?"

William twirled his mustache before answering. "No. Yet Morgan always seemed to be about. Of course, Frederick was too blind to notice. He was so very happy. I wager you know your father well enough to know how rare such happiness could be for him. But there was something about Mercy that gave me pause."

"What was it?" Kitto asked.

"She had not a copper to her name, but she possessed a quality that made you believe her fortune was on the rise." William shrugged. "Maybe it was just her residence, or the . . . profession of her protector, that made me doubt her sincerity."

"Her protector? Do you mean Morgan?"

William shook his head. "Heavens, no. Morgan would not protect his own mother from a pack of dogs. I mean the Grand Dame." The captain paused. The boy was young. When would be the time to tell him about his past?

"Your mother worked at the rooming house . . . cleaning and such. The Grand Dame—she was the one who owned the place—she took a liking to Mercy and had taken her in a year earlier. They were married soon, she and your father. He had barely known her a month. Some time later she was with child."

"That was me?"

William nodded.

"And Morgan, where was he in all this?"

"He seemed to fade away, but after some months he would come by the Grand Dame's place. I was there once when he did. This was soon after you were born. Morgan asked after Mercy, about her health. Even dropped off a gift in a box." William paused.

Kitto sensed his hesitation. "What was the gift?"

William scowled. "You have seen it. The very dagger you had with you the other night."

"Morgan gave that to her?"

"Now you understand my surprise at seeing your father had both kept it and given it to you," William said.

Kitto felt so confused. If only Father were here to answer his questions. He felt tears rising and swallowed hard to keep them down. He cleared his throat slightly.

"I found something in the dagger," he said quietly.

William stopped twirling at his mustache. "What do you mean?"

"The pommel came loose. Inside was a small note of parchment."

"Let me see it," William instructed. Kitto explained that he had loaned the dagger to Duck for his and Sarah's safety.

"It said 'Exquemelin' on it. That was all. Does that mean anything to you?"

William broke into a grin. "Exquemelin! Ha!" He smiled broadly and rubbed two fingers affectionately over the curious black mark on the back of his hand. "Surely it does. He was a good friend of mine once. Haven't seen him since Panama."

"Why would his name be on that slip of parchment?" Kitto wondered aloud.

William took a long and thoughtful breath. "A puzzle," he said. "As far as I know your mother and he had never met." He shrugged. "Maybe Morgan put it there. Who knows?"

"Did my father know that Morgan fancied my mother?"

William nodded. "He loved your mother and he couldn't see anything else. He believed her."

"But you did not?"

William grimaced. "I should, of course. She clearly adored you."

Kitto felt his heart leap. "She did?"

"I stopped in one day, soon after you were born," William said. "I am no parent myself, but if I ever were, I should want my wife to mother as yours did you. She bobbed you up and down, made all the silly faces and cooing noises. She handed you over to me for some reason or other. I had never held a baby before and had not the first notion. Mercy had a good laugh at my expense, but her joy about you was so infectious I joined in too. She was a happy woman then, even all cooped up in the house while your father was off scratching out a living."

Kitto felt hot tears spring to his eyes. William saw them and lowered his eyes. "She loved you as a mother should, and it was obvious to anyone who saw it."

There were a few moments of quiet while Kitto quelled his emotions.

"But still you doubted her," he said finally.

William twirled the end of his mustache and stared at Kitto thoughtfully before continuing.

"Sixteen seventy. That year ring any bells?" Kitto shook his head.

"That was the year the Panama campaign began, when Morgan gathered the Brethren to decide which Spanish settlement to sack." William tugged at his mustache. "I was having a meal one day at the rooming house, swapping yarns with seamen, when we heard cries of distress from out by the beach. Three of us ran out. It was Mercy who had cried out, your mother. She was up to her ankles in the surf, the picture of anxiety. Deeper in the water was a man, his back to us, and beyond him was a young child—you.

"From Mercy's cries I assumed you had come upon some trouble in the surf. The man must be helping you back in, I assumed. Your mother made a rush out into the water and the man turned. It was Henry Morgan. He grabbed Mercy's arm and threw her roughly back toward the beach; she fell into the wash, screaming. A wave crashed over your head, and I realized you could not wade in because Morgan was blocking you. He was drowning you."

Gooseflesh ran up Kitto's arms. "Go on."

"My companions turned tail when they saw it was Morgan. But I was not going to stand there and watch my nephew drowned. I drew my pistol and hailed him. He turned on me with this crazed, dangerous look. I thought we would have it out right then and there, but he surprised me by just storming off. Mercy ran out and fetched you."

"Thank you," Kitto said finally. William poured himself cider from an earthen jug.

"Did she tell you why he was trying to drown me?" Kitto asked.

"No. She was beside herself. The Grand Dame had gotten word about the ruckus by then and came running over to us. But before the old lady got there, Mercy pulled me to her."

William reached out and grabbed Kitto by the forearm.

"'William!' she said to me. 'I must speak with you. I have something I need to tell you. No one must know. Especially not Frederick.' We agreed on a place to meet the next day, and that is when she told me about Panama. She told me about Morgan's plan to aim the privateers in that direction."

"Did she tell you about the nutmeg?" Kitto asked.

William nodded slowly. "She told me Morgan knew about a Dutch vessel captured by the Spanish bearing a hoard of nutmeg in Panama's harbor. She said Morgan intended to steal the spice in secret, keeping it just for himself, Morris, and their inner circle of brigands."

"But how on earth could she have known such a thing?"

William was quiet. "There is only one answer to that, lad."

"Morgan told her?"

"He must have."

"But why would he do such a fool thing?" Kitto puzzled.

"What makes a man do fool things?" William said cryptically, and arched his eyebrows.

"You think he was in love with her? My mother?"

"I do."

"But why . . . why would she tell you?"

"I assume she thought I would bring Frederick in on it, and thereby get them the money they needed to leave Jamaica. She wanted to raise you in a more wholesome place."

"And you agreed to do it?" Kitto said.

"I did. Right then and there. I had a few debts with that unsavory pirate in Madagascar I mentioned. I had experience in the trade of spices; I knew how profitable they could be."

Kitto's eyes narrowed. "So you did intend to steal the spice."

William's eyes flashed in anger, but then the look faded. He shrugged. "I went with all options open. We sacked Panama. I happened to blunder upon the Dutch ship minutes before Morgan and Morris. They killed the man I was with and tried to kill me, but I made it out. I fled into the jungle and gathered my men. Together we trailed the nutmeg through the jungle. Morris went with the spice, only a handful of men and slaves with him." William chewed at the inside of his cheek and stared off for a moment, as if the thread of his story had slipped from his grasp. *Or is it something else*, Kitto wondered. *Is there some part of the story that William does not want to share?*

"You and your men overtook Morris?"

William nodded. "We did. Morris escaped into the jungle—though not with all of his nose." William jounced his eyebrows with pleasure. "I did not pursue him. We took the treasure and sailed for Jamaica."

"And got my father?"

"Yes," William nodded. "Before we had overtaken Morris in the jungle, he had burned Morgan's brand into the side of each Dutch barrel. A fancy letter *M*.

There is not a customs man or merchant west of the Canary Islands who does not know that mark. I could never move the spice directly with that on the barrels. Frederick agreed to help. Within a few days we set sail."

"But my mother?" Kitto asked quietly. "She never made it aboard that ship. . . ."

William gave his head a slow, nearly imperceptible shake.

"Tell me what happened. Please, sir."

William twirled the tip of his mustache. "Your father showed up carrying you without Mercy, brandishing that dagger of yours in front of him like a madman."

"And what did he say?" Kitto pressed.

The captain let go of his mustache and pushed at his upper lip to reveal a narrow gap from a missing tooth.

"See that hole? I questioned your father and the next thing I knew I was sprawled against the starboard rail spitting teeth!"

"But why?"

"Mercy was dead. Your mother was murdered."

Kitto cast down his eyes. "Morgan must have discovered that she had betrayed him, then killed her, or had her killed." William nodded.

"Your father's name was on the arrest warrant for the murder, though. More of Morgan's tricks! We set sail in a hurry. At the end of the first day, a ship appeared out of the west."

"Morgan?"

"The admiral himself, yes. In a faster ship. Just

before they let fly with the cannon, he raised the flag."

"The Union Jack?" Kitto wondered.

"No. A black flag with the hand of a skeleton in white." William propped his elbow on the table and held the back of his right hand toward Kitto. There was the black square tattoo Kitto had seen the first day he had met the captain.

Kitto peered at it. "I see no skeleton hand," he said.

William lowered his hand. "Good," he said. "I had it covered over while I was in prison. It is called simply 'The Hand.' Morgan and Morris's most trusted men bore the mark. If you bore it, no man would dare cross you, no customs agent clear to New York would refuse a bribe."

"And *you* were one of those men?" Kitto asked, bewildered. William scowled and tucked his arms to his chest.

"I was young and foolish! And poor. Deadly combination. I looked up to Morgan like a father, and he betrayed me. . . ." William let his voice trail.

"The other ship was faster, you said," Kitto pressed. "How did you get away?"

William chuckled. "Desmond Jenks, our carpenter, can shoot a cannon better than I spit tobacco," William said gravely. "They peppered us with grapeshot, and then good old Jenks bargained his soul with the devil and managed to strike their mast not just once—*thrice!*— three times in nearly the same spot! Her mast toppled and while they tried to clear their lines we got away."

"And my father?"

"He lost his leg. A few others got worse."

"And now you are a hunted man?"

"Yes, I am. Hunted the world over."

CHAPTER 14:

A Cooper's Boy

THREE DAYS AT SEA

"Threescore barrels is what we need," William said. He and Kitto stood in the carpenter's workroom, located near the bow of the ship on the main deck. A small grid of sunlight shone through the hatch above them onto the dusty floor.

A workbench was set against a wall, spanning the room's generous eight feet. Above it, all manner of saws, chisels, hammers, hatchets, adzes, planes, and drills hung against the wall, made fast by a series of leather belts. Along the other wall lay the stack of wood, thin slats of oak piled as high as Kitto's head. He felt a quivering in his stomach as he contemplated the size of the job.

"There's another pile down in the hold," William said, watching Kitto. "What else will you need?" he asked.

Maybe I have made a mistake, William thought. *It's too much for just a boy.*

Kitto took a deep breath. "If sixty barrels are needed in all, then I shall need an assistant." He ran a hand along the smooth handle of the adze that he had watched Father use a thousand times, the varnish worn away.

"An assistant?"

"Aye," Kitto answered, trying out the sailors' manner of answering in the affirmative.

"Ah, yes. I know the perfect man! He is a fast learner and a hard worker. And . . . he comes with an assistant himself."

Kitto blinked in surprise. "Two assistants then? Well . . . that's wonderful!" William was grinning when he stepped through the doorway to call to Swickers.

"Aye, Cap'n?"

"Send the American my compliments and have him report directly to the carpenter's berth."

"The American? Oh, yes . . . aye, aye, Cap'n."

"Oh, and Swickers? Have him bring his assistant with him."

"His? . . ."

"Yes. His assistant."

"Ah! Yes, Cap'n!" Swickers shuffled down the corridor.

"I shall also need a lantern, maybe two," Kitto stated.

"You've got this hatch here, that's light enough. I don't like fire to be casually located around my ship. There's nothing more dangerous to us on this floating powder keg than to have one lantern mishandled."

Footsteps approached, and through the doorway

strode the young man. He knuckled his forehead, draped in straight blond hair. The monkey on his shoulder saluted too.

"You called for me, sir?" Van asked.

"Augustus Van Arkel, meet Mr. Christopher Quick."

"Already have, sir," Van said, and held out his hand. Kitto stood to take it after a moment's hesitation. Hearing his true name still took him aback. They shook. Van had an iron grip.

"A pleasure to meet you, all proper-like, Mr. Quick, but I must warn you that if you call me Augustus like our good captain here, I shall have to knock your teeth in, if you please."

William rolled his eyes. "As you can see, Augustus has bit of a problem mastering his tongue, though he has had plenty of practice in the navy. How many times have you met with the cat-o'-nine-tails, young man?"

"Not enough fingers and toes to keep count of that, sir. You would have to count the stripes on my back," Van answered with a broad smile. Kitto liked him immediately.

"He is a real pistol, is he not? From America, too, which explains the foul tongue."

Sailors are always a bit rough in the mouth, but even among seamen, Van stood out. He could swear fluently in Dutch, French, Portuguese, and even knew a handful of foul words in Spanish and Italian. About every third sentence Van uttered featured body parts not discussed in polite company.

"I am from Rhode Island, sir. God-awful backside of this world. Allow me to introduce Julius," Van said, plucking the creature from his shoulder. He thrust Julius toward Kitto, and Kitto accepted him, holding him warily. Julius growled.

"Your assistant," Kitto said ruefully.

"Best to pop him up on a shoulder, sir. He does hate being held like a sack." Kitto pulled the animal toward his shoulder. Julius scrambled up, and Kitto could feel the pressure of his bony feet. Then something moved through his hair.

Van tried not to laugh. "It's your curls, sir. He's very curious about curls. He'll tug all day at them. I think it bothers him they're not straight." It was a peculiar feeling, being groomed by a monkey. William reached out and gave Julius's tail a sharp tug. The monkey squealed and swung a paw out at the captain, wrapping another arm around Kitto's head for balance. His clawed fingers dug into Kitto's eye socket.

"Ow . . . ow . . . ow!" Kitto pried the paw away gently.

William snickered. "I am sure the two of you—or rather, the three of you—will be fast friends in no time. Van, you have made a step up in the world. I now promote you to cooper's assistant!"

Van leaned toward the captain. "Such a promotion means more pay?"

William eyed Van with irritation. "Do a good job of it and I will keep Swickers from hurling your monkey overboard. Kitto here is not only our cooper but also my nephew. Make sure you show him the unfailing respect and courtesy you have always shown me." William's sarcasm was thick.

"I shall be the picture of gentlemanliness, Captain Quick, sir."

Julius chose the moment to hop from Kitto's shoulder to the top of his head, where he could more closely analyze the fascinating curls. Kitto craned his eyes upward. A hairy arm reached down before his eyes and inserted a finger into one nostril.

"Julius! Don't be rude!" Van slapped away the hand. Julius hissed. "Er . . . sounds like interesting work, sirs. And I shall be able to get so much more done, Captain, without having to serve on the watch," Van said, trying not to smirk.

"Like blazes you will," William retorted. "You can serve a stint on deck like the rest of the crew."

Kitto piped up. "Captain, this is a large job. I cannot have my assistant running off to make a watch call when we are in the middle of a barrel." Darkness blocked Kitto's vision. It was Julius, hanging his head over Kitto's to stare eye to eye with him upside down.

William grumbled an oath and looked down at his boots, running through the ship's schedule in his head. Kitto and Van shared a confederate glance.

"Fine!" William relented. "Van, you are relieved from watch just until the sixty are completed; I'll inform Carroll and he'll figure out how to make do. Now wipe that smile from your face." Van tried but failed.

"Aye, aye, sir! Cooper's man it is. You will not be sorry."

"I already am." William strode off through the doorway.

Van reached out a second time and took Kitto's hand. "Well done, cooper!" he said with a huge smile.

"My pleasure. Van, it is?"

"And Kitto, sir?"

"And Julius." Kitto pointed up. A hand snatched at his finger, and he felt a hard wetness.

"Julius, no biting!" Van scolded. Kitto snatched back his finger. "He's really pretty harmless, you know, as long as he likes you," the older boy confided.

"I shall try to make myself agreeable."

Van plucked Julius from Kitto's head and tossed him onto the workbench. Immediately Julius picked up a small adze.

"Oh, dear," Van said—but of course he said something far worse, for the monkey had hefted the tool and began waving it over his head.

"Best to duck, sir!" Van advised, pulling Kitto down. The adze flew across the room, struck the wall, and clattered to the floor.

"Julius! Behave!" Van leaned confidentially toward Kitto. "He's got a bit of a temper, sir. But he's not mean at heart."

Kitto took a moment to observe the young man anew. Van was large for his age, stood several inches taller than Kitto, and had somehow managed, despite the seaman's diet of salt pork and hardtack, to grow into a wiry, muscled thing.

"Pleasure to make both your acquaintances, I think," Kitto ventured.

"Same, sir," Van said, stepping forward to snatch from the bench a large spike that Julius had begun to fondle. Julius screamed and performed a series of backflips on the workbench. Kitto found himself laughing out loud for the first time in days.

"Yes, he does that when he's upset, sir," Van said.

Kitto bristled. "If you 'sir' me, Van, I will have to ask the captain to return you to the watch."

Van nodded thoughtfully. "I know lots of colorful names, sir, if you like." He grinned.

Kitto smiled back. "I think 'Kitto' ought to do it."

"Very well, Kitto."

"Come on. Let us begin, Van. We have much to do."

From that moment on, Kitto and Van—and Julius— were inseparable. Kitto gave his new friend an intense though brief instruction in the craft of coopering, and in the few hours they spent outside the workroom, Van took the role of master. Kitto picked up a dozen different names for the ship's sails, the correct terms for rigging, the translation of the many orders called out and repeated back across the windy decks. Van, for his part, hung on Kitto's every word in the workroom like they were recitations of prayer, his piercing blue eyes watching everything with the keenest concentration. Van did not intend to sail the seas forever. Once he had made his fortune—even a modest one—and was able to return to Newport to make a home for himself and his sister, he would need a trade that kept him in one place.

The two of them fell into a smooth, intense rhythm of work. Mostly Julius kept himself entertained by inspecting the chips of wood that fell onto the floor, turning them in his hands with a shrewd look. Julius found Kitto's clubfoot interesting too, and quite comfortable to sit upon. The first time he did it, Kitto and Van were standing shoulder to shoulder, holding a ring of staves in place for binding. Kitto got a surprised look on his face.

"Julius! Be off with you," Van said, poking him with his toe. "Sorry, Kitto, he doesn't . . . he doesn't understand."

Kitto sensed Van's discomfort. He was used to people squirming when his deformity was thrust to the forefront of attention.

"He's no bother. Leave him. At least it's doing one of us some good."

Van liked that answer. He had lived a hard life and brooked no self-pity in his friends.

But a friend was not what Augustus Van Arkel was looking for, he reminded himself. He knew what he had done in Falmouth. That meeting in the tavern with Morris and Spider was never far from his mind, nor was the heft of the silver coins he kept hidden.

It was not a heavy satchel, but sometimes when he worked alongside the crippled boy, it seemed to hang with the weight of a stone.

CHAPTER 15:

Approaching Cape Verde

FIFTEEN DAYS AT SEA

Now more than two weeks into the voyage, all hint of seasickness had abandoned Kitto. Only when the wind truly freshened did he feel slightly queasy. A meal of salt pork and peas sat heavily in his stomach. There was little to be said for the daily rations other than that they filled the hole of his hunger.

Kitto would have liked to spend more time up on deck to marvel at the intricate orchestra of activity that kept a ship sailing, but he had no time. He and Van worked long hours, Van continuing to prove himself both talented and tireless. They had finished more than a score of barrels already.

Kitto climbed the stairwell onto the quarterdeck, taking a break from cutting a set of staves. He reached out to steady himself as the deck pitched beneath a swell, and looked about for William. The quarterdeck was toward the stern and above the officers' berths and captain's cabin. It bobbed slightly less than did other parts of the ship, and hence was the spot where William usually took up with his brass spyglass.

The backstaff that the captain had been using to teach his nephew celestial navigation was tucked under William's arm. The wind fluttered the sleeves of his white shirt and swept back his long locks, revealing a squared forehead. He held the telescope to his eye, his attention riveted.

"Devil take that man!" William swore, his lip snarling. He and Kitto were alone on the deck except for Jenks several feet away, bent over the starboard rail taking measurements.

"What is it, Captain?" Kitto asked, staring himself but seeing nothing. William looked down at Kitto for a solemn moment, then returned the telescope to his eye.

"Cullen!" he shouted. When no reply came, William yanked away the instrument and bellowed out for the unlucky sailor. Cullen was a young man with unusually long feet he often tripped over. He nearly did so now as he rushed to his captain's bidding.

"Aye, Captain!"

William thrust the spyglass at the man. "Have Peterson up there give us a read on due north. And next time I call make certain you hear."

"Aye, aye, Captain." Cullen scurried off the quarterdeck, down toward the center of the ship, his bare feet slapping the planks. He passed the telescope on to a man working the rigging at the base of the mainmast.

William spun on Kitto. "Why are you not below with your barrels?" he demanded.

"I thought we'd continue our navigation lesson. What is it you see?" Kitto asked.

"The devil," William growled. "We *are* in a major shipping lane, though. . . ."

"Is it a ship?"

"Yes. Could just be traffic to Cape Verde," William muttered.

"I do not know Cape Verde."

"It lies off the western coast of the African continent. A Portuguese island. They have used it a hundred years or more as a port for its most lucrative trade." He raised a hand to shield the sunlight.

Kitto hesitated. "I was up the mast the other day," he confessed. "I thought I might have seen a ship myself, in about the same direction." Van had badgered him into the harrowing climb, and Kitto had gone so as not to seem the coward.

William's head snapped toward him. "You did? Why ever did you not tell me, Kitto?"

"Well, I," Kitto stammered. "I was not sure, and Van said it was just a trick of the sun on the water."

"Van Arkel? He was up there with you?" William asked, the knob of skin between his eyebrows puckering.

"Yes, sir. I was not sure, but Van looked and said it was nothing."

The captain narrowed his eyes, then turned away.

"No matter, I suppose." He rapped his fist against

the rail. "Can't ply any more sail than I already have." He turned. "But next time you see anything unusual, you keep your mouth shut and you find me," William snapped.

Kitto's cheeks burned. He did not answer. William's eyes searched the horizon vainly.

"If there is a rat on this ship, it is *not* Van, sir," Kitto ventured in a whisper. "He's a good mate, and I trust him."

William turned on him. "Then you are a fool, which is your right, except for the fact that it could cost all of us our lives!" William said hotly, then lowered his voice. "Peterson, Swickers, Jenks over there, Isaac, and Carroll. Those are the only men who rotted those seven years away with me in that Spanish hole. *They* kept their mouths shut. *Them* I trust. No one else has earned that privilege! Now you watch what you tell that boy."

"Aye, aye, *sir*," Kitto said with a bite. William glowered, then snorted and broke out in a toothy grin.

"Kitto, you take orders about as well as I do."

"Sail ho!"

The call came from Peterson, high up on the platform of the mainmast, his voice muffled by the wind.

"What say you, Peterson!" William shouted up with his hands cupped around his mouth.

"Square-rigger, sir, three points west of due north. I can just make out the top of her mainmast!"

"Bloody rot! What would it take to buy a bit of luck!" William fumed.

"It is them, then?" Kitto asked, feeling both a strange

admixture of fear and a hope. *Are Sarah and Duck out there? Would Morris have kept them alive?*

"If I had to bet on it, I would wager that it is. Fleet vessel she is, I can tell you that," William said. He turned to Kitto. His features softened. "Listen, lad, about your brother and Sarah. . . ."

"Yes, I know," Kitto said, turning toward the stern, his face reddening.

"Morris is no fool, though. He would keep them alive as long as they might prove useful, but we will not know for some weeks still. They will likely need to water in Cape Verde as much as we do. I should think they would wait to engage us until after we had headed out to sea again and were far enough along not to encounter any other traffic. To attack us tonight would risk the attention of the Portuguese." William turned abruptly and strode over the quarterdeck to where Jenks poised with a large saw, about to begin his cut.

Kitto looked out into the pink glow of the afternoon sky. *Dear God in Heaven, please protect them!*

William addressed the carpenter. "Have that emplacement ready by nightfall and it's double rations for you, sir."

Jenks smiled and knuckled his brow.

"Aye, aye, Captain Quick! I figured if I kept working slow enough you would make me an offer."

"Do shut your hole, Mr. Jenks. You're a bad influence on my nephew. He needs no encouragement."

* * *

At the end of the day, long after Kitto had fallen asleep, Van lay awake in the hammock next to him. Sleep would not come. The boys' bodies were oriented head to toe, as was custom in a ship so that more bodies could be squeezed into the tight confines of the crew's berth. Van's foot dangled outside the hammock, rocking back and forth. Julius curled up in the crook of his arm.

Van tried to think of his sister. Sometimes that helped but not tonight. Instead, he reached for the pocket of silver hidden inside his trousers, as he had done several times that day. Yes, of course that was a ship that Kitto had spotted out there. And soon enough the boy sleeping beside him would learn that he, Van, was the traitor, someone who sold his mates for a handful of silver. And what *would* happen to the boy? The one Van was growing to like despite himself?

"Blast!" Van hissed aloud. He could not afford guilt. His sister could not afford it. He had a goal—a mission. Nothing would stand in his way.

Nothing and no one!

Van hefted the bag in his hand, careful not to jingle the coins.

"My Judas money," he whispered aloud. Julius stirred, cocked his head up at Van, then settled back into sleep.

CHAPTER 16:

Slaver

SIXTEEN DAYS AT SEA

Kitto awoke the next morning, his head still thick with sleep. The hammock next to him swung empty, as did all the others down the line. Sunlight leaked through the many tiny shafts between the swollen timbers of the deck above his head.

It had been a long night. He had lain awake in his hammock, the strands of rope curling up around him, cocooning him in dark thoughts. He struggled to keep his mind from Sarah and Duck, imagining how they suffered. When he succeeded, then the images of his father splayed out on the floor filled his head, and the grief washed over him so raw and fresh it overwhelmed him.

Had he known that Van, too, could find little sleep himself that night as he had for the last several, the two might have kept company. Instead, each lay stewing in his own gloom.

Kitto dropped to the deck and made his way carefully

through the berth, stepping over chests and duffels crammed with personal belongings. He made for the workroom, thinking he might find Van there already. When he found the room empty and silent, it suddenly struck Kitto how quiet the whole ship was. And how gently the boat rocked! The lack of motion was almost dizzying to Kitto. He stumbled for the stairs.

As soon as he set foot, breathless, onto the deck, he saw it.

Land!

A large island loomed ahead of the *Blessed William*. It was fringed with bright green; brown hills rose up in the distance. A few smaller islands had passed already along the starboard side. There were several other ships to be seen now, some smaller fishing boats closer to the shoreline, and one large ship less than a league ahead and sailing in the same direction as the *William*.

Kitto took a deep breath to see if he could smell the land. The aroma that struck him was thick and pungent and foul. He winced and looked about for an explanation. That was when he noticed the solemn looks on the faces of the crew. It was hardly what Kitto would have expected. *Shouldn't we be celebrating?* Looking for Van, Kitto spotted William instead near the bow, the ubiquitous spyglass raised.

"Cape Verde, sir! That is where we are?"

William turned. "Aye. Cape Verde. And even more foul than I remember it."

"Sir?"

William pointed beyond the bow. Kitto could see the large ship ahead of them. William gestured over the stern. Two similar ones trailed in the distance.

"None is *the* ship, is it?"

"No. But can you not smell it?"

Kitto breathed in again, and again was struck by the same unsettling odor.

"Is that the way Cape Verde smells?"

"It is, at least for the last century or so." The captain peered again through his instrument.

Maybe we lost the Port Royal *during the night*, Kitto thought, again both hopeful and fearful at the thought of meeting with the mysterious ship. Kitto scanned the deck for Van and found him leaning over the starboard rail. When he made his way to him, Julius hopped from Van's shoulder to his own, holding Kitto by his ears.

"Well, Van, we've made the first leg of it!" Kitto announced. Van turned and looked at him without expression, then turned back.

"What? What the devil is wrong with everybody on this ship?" Kitto demanded.

Still, Van did not answer him.

"Van. Please. What is wrong?"

"Look at her," Van said, nodding toward the ship ahead of them, making its way toward the wharf at the end of the island ahead. "Do you know what she is? What she carries?"

"No," Kitto answered, irritated. "And why should it matter, anyway?"

"She is a slaver. That's what this island is, Kitto. A depot for human cargo, where people are traded for gold." Van spit over the rail.

"I did not know you felt such a passion about the subject," Kitto said. He had never given slavery much thought, as removed as he was from it in Falmouth. He wrinkled his nose at the stench.

"Is it the slaves that smell?" Kitto said.

"You would too if you and hundreds more were packed into a space large enough for only a few dozen and left there for days and weeks on end. The captains cram them in, Kitto. Like cod stacked in a crate. The food they get is worse even than what is given to the pigs, when there is any at all. They die, Kitto . . . happens all the time, and it's days before any seaman figures it out. Days. Bodies are starting to rot before they finally throw them overboard."

A particularly strong aroma passed on the breeze, and Kitto made a sour face. The *Blessed William* was slowly passing the slaver along her starboard side.

"Good God, it is awful!" he exclaimed, giving his nose a squeeze.

"You never forget that smell, Kitto. Not when you live with it day after day."

"You sailed on a slaver?"

Van braced his hands on the rail. "I did once. I was eight. I didn't know it was a slaver when I signed on, or what I would have to do."

"And what was that?"

"I fetched buckets. The ones they'd make their mess in. I would haul them to the upper deck and dump them, and the captain would go wild with temper if ever I spilled any of it. And I helped bring down the gruel. Handed it out in wooden bowls, no spoon or nothing. Twice a day this little bowl of oats or cornmeal. On their lucky days they would unchain a few of them and take them up onto the deck for air. I remember them holding their hands over their eyes to block out the sun."

"These were men, these slaves?"

"Sure, but children and women, too, Kitto, by the plenty. Wee lads not half our size. Ahh!" Van lowered his head into his hands and scratched away at his scalp.

Julius hopped back over to Van, chittering in his ear and wrapping his thin arms about Van's neck.

"How awful!" Kitto said quietly, staring out at the ship they were passing.

Van nodded. "The worst part was the sound. Moans and cries, like an entire forest of animals caught in a huge steel trap. I had eight years then. Eight. I about went batty that trip because I could never fall asleep for all the horrible noise, and when I did the nightmares were even worse."

A silence grew between them. Orders for sails to be reefed were shouted across the decks.

"I wish there were something to be done," Kitto said quietly.

"Nothing but fill our barrels and be off," Van answered. "That's all we can do."

* * *

"Gentlemen!" William called. He stood at the rail of the quarterdeck looking down on the gathered crew.

"As promised, you will receive a small sum from Mr. Peterson before exiting. Per our agreement, your true earnings each will receive when we return to New York, and if all goes well, a generous bonus shall line your pocket as well."

Kitto stood on the main deck beside Van at the port rail. He scanned over the gathered crew, seeing the eagerness written on their faces. Most of them would squander all they were about to receive in a few short hours on games of dice and Portuguese food.

"Be warned!" William continued. "We leave on the outgoing tide tomorrow morning, which should be at the start of the second watch. Be here, by God," William commanded, shaking a fist, "or it shall cost you three days' wages, and your good stead with this captain!"

William unclenched his fist and leaned over the rail, his voice lowering.

"It is no secret that a ship has been trailing us. I do not know which vessel it is, but she might just make port today, here, and if she does, our departure could be hastened. Keep your mouths shut about what ship you are from, and keep your ears trained for news. It is the best way to guarantee the healthiest stack of silver in your pockets when this journey has ended."

Kitto looked out over the gathering. It was a motley crew. Beards had grown long and tangled, odors had sharpened, and skin had tanned. Kitto felt a tingling in his feet. He so wanted to get ashore. He had never set foot outside of Cornwall before, never been more than a dozen miles from his home—not counting his earliest childhood, of which he remembered little. The prospect thrilled him, but then guilt and grief washed over him again.

In an instant I would give this back and never leave Falmouth. I would be a cooper and have my father alive and Sarah and my brother safe. Kitto stared out at the empty sea off the port rail.

William finished his address and a spirited cheer of "huzzah" was called.

"Where shall we go, Van?" Kitto asked. "What is there worth seeing here?"

Van tilted his head back to take in the sun. His tanned skin was growing more nut brown by the day, and his long, straight locks covered his ears and forehead.

"I ain't going. I hate this place. Besides, Julius here is too fond of bright jewelry. Last port we were in he about got my head blown off slipping a gold bracelet into my trousers." He reached to scratch Julius beneath his chin.

Kitto's face fell. "Oh. Well, I shall stay too," he resolved, swallowing a keen disappointment.

"You do not have to stay, Kitto. I have made port here before and it is not much to see, but it is good to get off the ship. Just stay clear of the slave auctions. You can follow the captain about. No doubt he will enjoy what he finds." Van nodded toward William, who stood still on the quarterdeck facing astern, scanning the horizon.

"Why? What will he do there?"

"You do not know? He's a card man. A gambler! And a right good one, too. That's how we all got on this ship. In New York I watched him turn a wee pile of silver this tall to a small mound in no time."

"Is that right?" Kitto gazed up at William. "I've never seen a card game," he thought aloud. He had heard of such things, but dice was the sailor's pleasure. Sarah forbid her boys to play or even to associate with those who gambled, but Kitto had squatted beside small groups of men at the wharf casting the bone dice and cursing their luck.

The ship edged closer to the wharf. Kitto could see the docks teeming with sailors and the ragged lines of ebony-skinned men and women lashed together by ropes. He stared, enthralled by the shouts in strange languages, the odd dress, the brown hills in the distance—all so different from Falmouth. A golden beach stretching for miles in either direction sparkled in the sun, wrapping the island in a glittering ribbon.

"Mr. Peterson, the anchor, sir!" William called.

"Aye, aye, Captain!" Peterson relayed the order. The heavy clinking sound of the links slipping through the hawsehole resounded throughout the ship.

CHAPTER 17:

Fate and Greed

Kitto followed Van down the stairs and toward the workroom. His disappointment at not being able to explore Tarrafal—the chief port of the Cape Verde Islands—had faded. At least from the deck he could best keep watch for the ship that might still carry Sarah and Duck.

"Kitto!" Both boys stopped and turned.

William nodded to Van. "He shall rejoin you in a moment, Van. Come with me a moment, Christopher, if you please." He beckoned with a hand, and Kitto turned and followed him back to the captain's berth. They entered and William gestured for Kitto to close the door.

"Listen, lad. I hate to deny any sailor his chance to go ashore, what with it being a long journey and all. . . ."

"I plan to stay on board, sir," Kitto interrupted. "Van and I both. We shall get more barrels done that way, and I shall keep a close watch for the ship. If I see her, then Van and I shall come to fetch you right off."

William appraised him with a gentle smile. "Thank you, lad. I will go ashore after sundown once we have taken on fresh water, to gather the news. I do not see how the events of Falmouth could have reached here before we did, but it would not be the first time the speed of gossip outpaced the wind."

"Will you play at cards?" Kitto asked.

"Who is telling you of my bad habits?" William answered, the crooked smile glinting.

"Van says it's how you raised the money for the crew."

"Ha!" William chuckled. "Don't believe all you hear, lad. There would be no smiling sailors departing this ship today if they all relied on my gaming for their wages." He reached toward a small chest that lay against the wall, flipped open the lid, and removed a blue silk bag.

"My lucky deck, this one," William said. "Have a look." He flipped it through the air to Kitto who snatched it one-handed. He worked his fingers at the string that held it closed.

"You've seen cards, of course."

"Never," Kitto answered.

"Truly?" William stood abruptly, his eyebrows arched. "Frederick never played with you?"

"My father?" Kitto laughed. "No. We were too busy for play." Kitto's mind flashed to the memory of working alongside his father in the shop. Shoulder to shoulder they would work, nearly on top of each other yet knowing the work so well their hands never got tangled, as if they shared a single mind and a single body. Kitto felt a pang of deep sadness that all that was gone.

"Frederick was a fine cardplayer," William said. "He

taught me Picket, Gleek! Games I have won and lost fortunes playing. He played the devil out of the bluffing games."

"My father gambled?" Kitto was astonished. Nothing could seem more out of character. He wondered what else he did not know about his father.

Kitto finally worked the string loose, and out slid the deck. It had a Celtic pattern for a border, and a depiction of a unicorn rearing up on its hind legs in the middle. He ran a finger over the image, then began to flip the cards over to see the pip side. William snatched the deck away.

"Let me try something." He whiffled the deck, expertly shuffling it. "You have heard me speak of luck, have you not?"

"I have. But always you seem to curse it when you speak of it."

"Yes. What of fate? Are you familiar with fate?" the captain asked.

"That the life of a person is . . . already decided for him?"

William grunted. "A paralyzing notion, fate. And then there is will, the decisions we make that lead us to action. Those two notions, fate and will, are like two sides of a coin, each supporting the other. Understand?" Kitto nodded.

"Now," he continued, "you have known people to whom everything seems to come with little or no effort, yes?"

"I have." Kitto thought of Duck's easy manner.

"That is fate playing the heavier hand. Others never get a break but for those they make, and people remark at how impressive a person has turned out, eh? That is will.

"So were I to do this"—William swept his hand across the table, leaving behind a trail of cards facedown in a smooth arc—"and I asked you to select a single card, it is a perfect test of the two. Fate would say you will be drawn to a certain card. But at this moment you could choose any, exercising your will."

"Am I to take one?" Kitto said, and William nodded.

Kitto eyed the deck. He felt something like a glow to be in his uncle's company. They had spent only a few snatches of time together since they left Falmouth, what with William busy with the ship's workings and his own demons. The men loved the captain, and Kitto was beginning to feel an affection for him too.

The cards spread neatly in a line, each easily retrievable from the next. Kitto reached out. He let his hand drift over the cards.

"In the prison in Cuba there was a gypsy who took this very deck of cards—this special deck known as a *tarot*—and laid the cards out before me like I did you," William said. "Over some months he taught me that each card has a meaning, and that the one you choose now tells about your place in the balance between fate and will."

Near the end there was a card that had turned just slightly in its orientation, as if its foot were sticking out. *I shall pick the lame card, as I am a lame fellow,*

Kitto thought, and plucked it from the pile.

"I think luck gets too little credit in this game, sir," Kitto said. "A piece of paper cannot read a soul." He flipped the card over and tossed it faceup onto the table. William's eyebrows arched.

"Oh, really?"

Kitto looked at the card. There was a drawing, in fading colors, of a hand emerging from a cloud. The hand held a sword aloft, and encircling the tip of the sword was a garland-draped crown. At the bottom of the card were inscribed the words ACE OF SWORDS.

"What does it mean, then?" Kitto asked.

"Maybe it is just luck." William shrugged. "This card indicates great success, triumph. Quite an impressive card indeed to pull out of the deck at such a juncture in your life."

"Triumph?" Kitto snorted. "Show me where you see that in me!" If there were one word to describe his lot in life, that could hardly be it.

"You are here, are you not? You wanted to see what life on a ship would be. . . ."

"Not at this cost I did not wish it!" Kitto protested.

"Fair enough. Maybe your triumph is yet to be."

"Humph!" Kitto heard himself exclaim, but he felt unsettled. Some power lay in those cards; he could not deny it.

"So what then? Is it a good soul I have, or a rotten one?"

William shrugged. "No card can tell all that. In some

card games the ace is the best card in the deck, in others the worst. There are games wherein you remove all the aces before you even play."

"Now that sounds more like my life, sir," Kitto said sourly. "Removed from the game before it begins."

William held the ace of swords up at Kitto. The boy stared at the sword and the hand that bore it.

"Not since I have known you," William said. He reached out to sweep up the deck again.

"Wait!" Kitto said, spreading his hands atop the cards. William looked up at him quizzically. "Now it is *your* turn, Captain. You take a card!"

The captain's face clouded. "No. I do not desire—"

"'Tis only fair, uncle! Pick a card. Give us a view of the stuff from which you are made."

William had a dangerous look. "Very well!" He made a selection instantly, flipping a card and tossing it down between them. Kitto craned his neck to get a view.

The bottom of the card read, THE MOON. There was a golden orb with the profile of a man's face within it. It floated over a valley where two animals—a wolf and a dog perhaps—bayed up at it, and the foreground was water from which emerged a clawed creature like a crab. On either side of the card, in the valley, two towers stood.

William grumbled. "Well, I have known that for weeks already, but it does not hurt to see the cards agree." William scooped them up, but Kitto snatched the moon card before it was gathered.

"What does it mean?"

"It means there are hidden enemies about, and danger in all directions."

Later that day Kitto left Van hard at work with a barrel and went up on deck. The hot, thick air of the workroom was starting to make him queasy. He saw William standing on the quarterdeck, dressed in a fine red jacket and black tricorner hat. William peered intently through his spyglass. Kitto hobbled over to the quarterdeck stairs and climbed them two at a time.

"What is it?"

"Peterson seems in a terrible hurry," said William. Kitto looked out toward the wharf. He could see the rowboat. "But Peterson has never met a molehill he could not call a mountain." William lowered the spyglass, collapsed it, and pulled back his jacket to slip the instrument into a leather loop. Kitto could not help but notice the large pistol at the man's hip.

"Good thing the water boat has come and gone. We could leave tonight if we had to."

Kitto held up his hand against the glare coming off the water. Peterson heaved at the oars. Kitto felt his stomach churn. This could not be good.

He cast his eyes down at the rail. "Uncle . . . ," he began, his courage wavering.

"Yes?"

"If the ship has arrived . . . if we discover that my family is aboard, I do not think I could again abandon them no matter what the danger or sacrifice."

William Quick's nostrils flared.

"I thought, Christopher, that you understood. The safety of your family lies . . ." He looked about briefly. ". . . it lies in the *spice*. With it we have the power to bargain with our enemies; without it we can do no more than beg!" he hissed.

"But we do have something, sir!" Kitto persisted. "Something to bargain with." He chewed the side of his lip. "You have it."

William glared. "What, my head? It is the only one I have, thank you."

Kitto shook his head. "The spice is on an island, and as you have taught me, every spot on the globe has a specific name in geographic coordinates: longitude and latitude. That is what they want!" Kitto said. William's eyebrows curled more menacingly.

"And I should just give those figures up, eh?"

Kitto stared at the floor. "It might save their lives," he muttered.

William took a deep breath. He bent forward and pressed his thumb and forefinger to the bridge of his nose.

"Kitto, it is easy to speak so lightly of riches when you have always had them."

"We have never been rich!"

"You have never wanted. Not truly. But your lot has changed. You are a cripple, Christopher Quick. You have only enough schooling to write and think a bit, but not enough to become a man of science. Your mother has little besides her beauty to recommend her, and even that is diminished in the eyes of a potential suitor by the presence of that scampering little brother of yours. What man takes a wife with nary a pound to her name, with one wee lad tugging at her hem and another tripping along behind her?"

Kitto stiffened as if he had been slapped. "You are *cruel*, sir!"

"Perhaps I am," William answered, looking away. "But only because life has made me so. Life is harsh, Kitto! It does not pick up the downtrodden from the gutter just because they deserve sympathy."

Kitto gritted his teeth. "It's your greed! Greed! That's what stops you!" A few of the sailors stopped what they were doing to listen in on the conversation, surprised to see anyone—let alone Kitto—fight openly with the captain.

"Without that treasure there is no freedom for me." William tapped a finger hard on Kitto's chest. "Or for you, or for Sarah, or your wee brother. Now that you have been associated with me you are marked for death like all the rest of us." William turned back to the rail and looked out at the shore. Peterson still rowed, not yet within earshot.

"Kitto, after Panama had ended and I had disappeared, Morgan spread the word that it had been I who cheated the other Brethren of the Coast. The haul out of Panama was meager, and the buccaneers were very irate about the little silver in their pockets."

"He blamed you?"

"Aye, he did. Easy enough to do with me gone." William spit over the rail in disgust. "Every pirate west of the Canaries believes I stole that treasure."

"But . . . why does this crew sail with you, then? Why not just turn you over to Morgan and get a handsome reward?"

"Why? Greed! Your pet virtue. They know the stories, and I have told them just enough to suggest the tales are true. I did steal it! It was not my intention. I only wanted to prevent myself from being cheated. But it has amounted to the same thing. The members of this crew risk having their pale necks stretched in the tropical sun, all for *greed!*"

Kitto had nothing else to say. He knew his cause was lost. He stared down at his hands, then at the foot curling against the holystoned planks.

"So you see, boy, it's not quite so plain as you make it. These men have risked their necks to join me. Some are like the only family I have got, and their lives are no less dear to me than your mum's and brother's are to you."

Kitto stood crestfallen, his eyes still on the deck. "So is there no way out of all this then?"

The glint returned to William's eyes. A warm and confidential smile played across his face. He placed a hand on Kitto's shoulder.

"Why, sure there is, lad. I just need a lucky ace or two."

CHAPTER 18:

The Stakes of the Game

"Captain, sir, a word please, sir!" Peterson scrambled up the rope ladder. He was a tall man with dark hair that had begun to gray. He might have been handsome once, but his years in prison had taken their toll, and now he looked older than his thirty-one years. Peterson reached the deck and bent over his knees, trying to catch his breath.

"Where is your stamina, man?" William scolded. "Come give us the news!"

Peterson pushed himself upright and cast an eye at Kitto. "It might be best . . . to speak in your quarters, sir," he managed between breaths.

"Nonsense! Peterson, you of all people know the level of the boy's involvement. He's a right to know how our tangled web is spun."

Kitto felt a cold tingling travel up his spine. He held his breath, terrified at what Peterson might say.

"Very well, Captain," Peterson said reluctantly. "After arranging for the water boat, I went into that Donkey inn."

"The Burro," William said. "I lost half a fortune there once over a game of dice. What of it?"

"I trolled about there a bit to hear what's the news. Several slavers in now. There is this one fellow. He just come ashore minutes before. On the crew of *Crucible*, he says." Peterson paused to take a deep breath and to throw another wary look Kitto's way.

"*Crucible . . . Crucible,*" William muttered, staring off with slit eyes.

"Aye, you know it, sir. *Captain Mawbry,*" he whispered, as if there were anyone who might overhear.

"Mawbry!" William barked. "Bloody rot! He did not see you, did he?"

"No, sir, he was not there. The sailor only mentioned him."

"Who is Captain Mawbry?" Kitto asked.

"My nemesis is what he is," William said. "He's a slave trader, owns a small fleet of ships by now. He would sell his own mother if she'd bring a good price."

"And what of him?" Kitto demanded. "What has he to do with us?" There was something imperious and sure in the way Kitto stood there and addressed the first mate. Peterson answered him.

"He and the good captain have some history."

"History and enmity," William continued. "Each shared over a gaming table. He stole some money from me many years ago. I had borrowed deeply from a cut-throat pirate who ran the island of Madagascar, around Africa's tip. I trusted Mawbry to deliver to the pirate the money I owed. Instead, he kept it, came up with some excuse about how it got stolen from him, and I ended up locked away in that pirate's dungeon."

"That's where we first met, sir," Peterson chimed in with a hint of boyish pride.

"Continue, man," William said.

"Aye, sir. So he tells me he was on duty when this dark-hulled brigantine approaches and sends out a boat. The man who gets off onto his boat has eyes like two nuggets of coal, a gaping hole for a nose, and a nasty scar either side of his mouth."

Kitto felt his feet go cold. "Morris!" he squeaked. William raised a finger for him to be silent.

"Aye, Morris. This bloke—Iverson is his name—says this man, the captain, kept his hand pressed to his side like he was favoring a wound."

William winked at Kitto. "Fine work, lad. Very fine." Kitto flushed crimson.

"This Iverson—he's all torn up. First time on a slaver, it was, and he'd no notion what he was in for." Again Peterson cast a wavering look at Kitto.

"Meaning?" William demanded, growing impatient.

"Iverson says this ugly captain had with him a boy, a wee lad of five or six, he says, bound about the hands and mouth. They hauled him onto the deck by a rope."

Kitto felt a sudden constricting feeling in his throat, as if it had suddenly gone bone dry. Neither he nor William said a word.

"This lad, the ugly captain wants to be rid of him.

Mawbry tells him he has no need for a cabin boy, certainly not one who needs to be hauled out of a boat by a rope. The man says he's not offering a cabin boy. He's looking to sell him off as a slave. That he's got no family but criminals and he's caused nothing but trouble—that because of the boy he'd lost a member of his crew—and that the tyke could be stuffed in the lower decks," Peterson said, his voice lowering to nearly a whisper.

The tightness in Kitto's throat gave way to a tremendous heat. His pulse thundered in his ears and his hands started to shake. William and Peterson faded from his vision into a dark haze until a rough hand seized his shoulder.

"Not yet, son!" William barked. "You keep that temper of yours tethered."

"Selling Duck as a slave!" Kitto spit, his face crimson. "Tell me, Captain! Will you finally do something now? For if you do not, then you will lose me as your cooper!"

William raised a finger in the air between them in warning. "Check your temper, now, Kitto. Now. Of course I will do something. We will!" William lowered his voice. "But we will only succeed with cool heads and hands. Do you hear me?"

Kitto turned away.

"What more did that pathetic sot say?" William demanded. Peterson continued apologetically.

"They made the trade. Mawbry had said there was

some African king who collected oddities, and who would fancy a white slave boy. I kept this Iverson fellow talking, and he told me the ugly captain says also that . . ." Again Peterson's eyes flickered toward Kitto. "Says that there might be another such boy he would deliver in the morning, a bit older and harder to break he might be, the man says. And crippled in one leg. Would his African king fancy such a slave as well? the man asked."

Kitto's knuckles were white on the rail. "Let that murderer try to lay hands on me!" he spit toward the island. "Let him!"

"Steady, lad!" William intoned. "This is *good* news. We know now they intend to make their move sometime this evening. Is there anything more, Peterson? Anything about the woman?"

Kitto sucked in his breath, but Peterson shook his head. William sighed.

"No, sir, nothing about that. But he did say his captain, Mawbry, was going to make an evening of it tonight at the Copo Dourado."

"The Copo, eh?" William smiled. "Well, well, well." There was something sinister in his look. "The fanciest gaming house in Cape Verde. Mawbry has done well for himself. Good. He can be easily distracted by a competitive card game. I shall have to give him one."

"Yes," Kitto nodded. "You keep him entertained and I take some men to go get my brother." He said it with such authority that it took a full second for either man to react.

"Does your mother not hate me enough by now, Kitto?" William asked with sarcasm.

"Whatever do you mean by that, sir?"

"Do you expect that I would say grace over setting that temper of yours loose on such a dangerous mission? Be reasonable!"

Kitto kicked his bad foot into the rail. He clenched his teeth tightly, and hot tears found their way to his cheeks. William watched him, then drew a slow and deliberate breath. He exhaled.

"Did you hear that, Peterson?" William asked, still staring at Kitto, who did not move to wipe away his tears.

"What's that, Captain?"

"That deep breath I just took."

"I heard it, sir."

"That's why I am captain, Peterson, and not a dead man."

"Yes, sir."

"I shall take Van with me to the Copo Dourado. You put together a small band, Peterson—no more than five. The *Crucible* will not be well guarded, since she's all but empty of her cargo. Five trustworthy souls, Peterson. No more. Take Isaac and Swickers for sure, then two other pugnacious types. Fighting types, Peterson," he said, explaining his vocabulary. "But it needs to be a quiet operation, you understand."

"Aye, sir, for the ship that pursues us will be anchored close by." Peterson looked as if he might be ill.

"Precisely, Peterson. Your command of the obvious is quite compelling."

"Thank you, Captain."

"And, Peterson, about that five. Should it include any members of this crew not yet over the age of twelve, I shall . . ." William went on to describe in brief detail a form of torture he had heard of once that involved heating a blacksmith's tongs. Peterson blanched.

"Aye, aye, sir. Your meaning is plain, Captain."

"It is wrong." Kitto whispered. "Wrong to keep me out." Here it was again, the same old pattern that he had lived with all his life. Since the moment he could walk—but not do so as well as the others—it had been the same. Always an excuse made for why he could not be with the others, why he could not play ball with the other little boys, why he was never given chores at home that sent him far, why his father believed he should be a cooper and not something else. Here it was again, his uncle this time, overlooking him because of his crooked foot.

"I am crippled, but I am not useless. 'Tis *not* fair!"

William regarded him stonily. "Fair describes a good woman, Kitto. Not life."

CHAPTER 19:

The Mission

"It's infuriating is what it is!" Kitto pouted. He sat at the edge of his hammock, his legs dangling. His black curls had grown out in the past weeks, and they draped over his eyes. Julius, squatting in the hammock next to him, rubbed his furry skull into Kitto's elbow.

"Oh, come on, Kitto, you can hardly blame the man," Van said. He stood over his seabag. From it he kept pulling knives and daggers of all sizes and concealing them in his boots, underneath his belt, strapped to his leg.

"I do blame him! And I don't need you sticking up for him either," he said. He watched Van drop his trousers and tie yet another small knife to a leg.

"What the devil are you doing, Van?" Kitto asked.

"I know what I'm doing; it's what I'm getting into I do not know," he answered.

Van pulled up his trousers and cinched his belt. He reached behind his back beyond Kitto's line of vision and checked on the small bag of silver coins strung there. Just to be sure. There was the pang of guilt again. He brushed it off.

"I will wish Peterson luck for you, Kitto," Van said. "He'll get your brother back here and safe."

Kitto nodded. "You just be sure to keep that slaver busy. I have already told the captain I will not leave the island without Duck." Kitto was resolved, utterly committed. He would see Duck freed tonight or die trying.

Kitto stared down between his feet at the floorboards below him, strewn with articles from Van's sea duffel. There was the foot again. For the ten thousandth time he cursed it silently. Were it not for the foot . . . William would want Kitto to accompany him, and not Van. Or even appoint him to go with Peterson to free Duck. But no. Instead, Kitto would thump about the decks, waiting for the men to come home.

Van punched his shoulder.

"Staring won't make it go away," Van said. In all his life very few people had dared speak lightly of Kitto's foot. His head shot up in astonishment tinged with anger. But there was a gentle look in Van's wide eyes.

"What of it?" Kitto accused.

"I know you think that's why you ain't coming tonight. Your foot. But that's not it."

"How would you know?" Kitto demanded.

"You're his nephew, Kitto. He can't risk you getting hurt. You're family. What is more important than that?"

Kitto's resentment at being left behind still lingered, and it tainted what he said next. The instant it passed his lips he regretted it.

"What would *you* know of family, anyway, Van?" The

words cut through the gloom like fine-honed daggers.

In a blink Van sprang. He grabbed Kitto by the shirt-front with one hand and reared back with the other to strike. Julius shrieked and did a backflip on the hammock, landing unevenly and tumbling to the floor.

"Watch your mouth, you miserable turd! I know plenty about family. More than you ever will! I have had it and lost it! Who could know more about what it means than I?" Van gave Kitto a violent jerk, then released him. Julius screamed again and leaped at Van's leg.

"Bloody *monkey*!" Van kicked out at him.

"Van!" Kitto exclaimed, shocked to see Van's anger aimed at his dearest companion.

"The beast bit me." Van inspected a mark on his shin. It had not broken the skin. Julius hovered in the shadows with his head tucked. "Fine, you traitor. Stay with him if you like!" He angrily stuffed his gear back into his duffel.

Julius shuffled forward and wrapped his arms about Van's leg. Kitto sat there feeling as if he had just been kicked in the stomach. Van slung the duffel over his shoulder and turned to storm out.

"Van, wait!"

Van stopped, his back still to Kitto. The empty feeling in Kitto's stomach rose up to his throat and choked him. Tears sprang to his eyes and spilled over. He wiped them away roughly and sniffled. *Such a baby I am turning into*, Kitto scolded himself.

Van turned just enough to see Kitto. He frowned and shook his head.

"Aw, Kitto! Why did you have to go and say a thing like that?" Van dropped the duffel and flung himself across his hammock. "Might have been the cruelest thing you could possibly say."

"I am sorry. I just am so . . ." Kitto shook his fists in the air and spilled more tears. "It's just the one thing I can't stand, Van! Helpless! Feeling helpless! Being helpless! I *have* had a family and never knew what it meant, not really, not until now and my father is dead and my brother and stepmother I might never see alive again. . . . And all I can do is nothing! Everybody else gets to pitch in, but not me, and all because of this blasted foot!" Kitto kicked out at Van's duffel. "I should cut it off and be done with it!"

Van plucked Julius from his leg, rubbed noses with him, then set him into Kitto's lap. Julius buried his head in the folds of Kitto's shirt. A tear dropped from Kitto's eye and landed on the monkey's back. Julius's head popped up and scanned the room, then burrowed again.

"Just don't cut your foot off in our workroom, cooper. Bloodstains make me itchy."

"You know what I mean." Kitto sniffled, and absently scratched Julius behind the ears.

"Nobody likes to sit about when there's work to be done," Van said. "But it ain't your foot that keeps the good captain from putting a pistol in your hand. That Sarah of yours is the problem."

"My mum? What about her? How do you even know of her?" Kitto asked, astonished at the mentioning. He wiped a last tear from his cheek.

"I am the cabin boy, remember? Or was. I delivered the hot cider the night our good Captain Quick first met you and your father, and apparently . . . your mum, too."

"Yes, that is right," Kitto remembered. "She and Duck came in that day, but just for a moment."

"It was a moment William Quick could not get out of his head," Van said.

"You're putting me on!" Kitto protested.

"I'm not either!" Van said in earnest. "I had to lift him into his bed that night. 'Oh, Van,' he says, 'I'm the unluckiest of men.' I tell him, 'Not at all, Captain, sir.' And he says, 'No, it's the same old curse. The first time I lay eyes on a woman . . . the very first time, by God. I die. . . . I am lifted like a butterfly on a summer breeze, stretching my wings in the light of her smile. . . .'"

"Van, stop!" Kitto blushed deeply. "You are having me on, you are!"

"I am not either, I swear it!" Van raised a hand in oath. "He says, 'Nothing like it has ever happened before, and here she is married . . . and to my brother!' And then his head hit the pillow and it might have been solid lead and wouldn't have mattered a whit. No one saw more of him until well into the next day, when that famous scowl of his was as dark and dangerous as the day he first spotted that ship following us out of New York's harbor."

Kitto shook his head. "Really? He said all that?"

"I swear it's true."

Kitto did not know what to think, but it was oddly comforting to believe that his foot had not entirely exempted him from the night's ventures.

"How strange. I never would have known it, even having been there when he met her," Kitto said.

"So like I was saying, it ain't your foot. If you go and get yourself killed, the captain would never be able to so much as face your mum again."

Van slapped him on the shoulder, the hard feelings between them cleared. "Forget tonight," he said. "Before this journey ends, we shall all have a chance to show our mettle. You save yours until the time is right."

Kitto pushed himself off the hammock and dropped nimbly to the deck.

"You should go, Van. And do watch your step with all those hidden blades; I'd hate for you to ruin a fine pair of trousers."

"I will. And try not to be so nice to Julius. He's the only family I've got."

"Van Arkel!" boomed a voice.

William Quick stood in the doorway, his fists balanced on his hips. How long he had been there neither of the boys knew.

"Aye, sir. Captain!" Van squeaked, caught off guard.

"Get up on deck. The boat awaits us. Have you a dirk, something to protect yourself with?" If the captain had heard the conversation, he did not show it.

"Aye, sir. And then some."

Van scampered off. William remained in the doorway. His face lay in the shadows, and Kitto could not make it out clearly.

"There will be time yet to show what you're made of, lad," William said, nearly echoing Van's words. "When that time comes, you will know it."

Kitto said nothing. William turned and walked away.

Part of Kitto's brain must have been silently formulating the plan already, because when the captain uttered those last words, Kitto knew suddenly just what he would do and how he would do it. He drew a sharp breath. Julius sensed something amiss and looked up at Kitto with his head cocked. Kitto winked at the monkey, and to his surprise Julius winked back.

Kitto counted just eight men left aboard the *Blessed William*. He stood on deck and made himself look busy by kicking over a neat coil of rope and winding it again. Peterson stood at the bow, huddled with Swickers and Isaac, the three of them devising a plan for the evening's action. A man named Whitney plucked a violin at the stern, along with Simmons, the gunner's mate, who sat on a barrel smoking. That left three: Ferris, the cook, busy in the kitchen, Jenks, the carpenter, and Carroll, the quartermaster.

Kitto coiled the rope and waited. He knew precisely what he would do. Julius sat atop the apple barrel and watched him without interest. The sound of laughter burst suddenly from the stair leading below deck. Jenks and Carroll emerged, Jenks smiling broadly.

"You'll not *really* hold me to that wager, will you, Desmond?" Carroll asked. "We're just playing as gentlemen, like?"

Jenks's smile vanished. He turned around to glare at the quartermaster.

"Bloody hard one, you are!" Carroll complained. "Ah!" he shook his head. "I know better than to bet me grog!" The two men found a spot along the rail where they could crouch and cast the dice up against the bulwarks.

No better chance shall come, Kitto thought. He held out an arm to Julius, who jumped for it, landed awkwardly, then climbed up to his shoulder. Together they slipped down the same passageway the two men had just left. It took Kitto a moment to adjust to the dim light. Only a few minutes of sunlight remained, and little of it penetrated belowdecks.

"Let's be quick about it, Julius!"

Kitto shuffled along to the doorway with the metal dolphin affixed to it. He gave one last look behind him, sent up a silent prayer to the heavens, then tried the handle.

The latch gave way. William had not locked it! Kitto pushed open the door quickly and stepped inside, closing it behind him. Julius hopped to the floor, then up onto the captain's bed. The ship had drifted about at the end of its anchor so that its stern pointed toward the setting sun. Pale golden light lit the swirling motes of dust that Kitto's arrival had stirred.

"First, the key," he whispered aloud, and stepped toward the cabinet from behind which he had seen William retrieve a set of keys during his second visit to the ship. He slid his fingers along the rough plank of the cabinet's spine until they struck something. Kitto lifted the iron ring from the nail on which it hung. Three keys dangled from the hoop.

Julius chattered loudly and did a backflip on the bed.

"Hush!" Kitto scolded, then returned to his task. "Now, which cabinet, I wonder?" He ran his eyes about the room. He decided it must be the large one beneath the captain's mattress. He slid himself between it and the table and crouched down to the lock. Meanwhile, Julius sprang for the counter and tugged wildly at the handle, growling.

"Quiet, Julius!" Kitto scolded. He pushed at the lid, but the lock held fast.

"Please, please, please be one of these keys," he whispered. He tried the first key, his hands shaking. The first was too small—probably it opened the captain's cabinet. The largest key he tried next. It slid smoothly into place.

Kitto turned the key and heard the telltale click.

An hour later Kitto stood at the rail a bit apart from the rest of the men and looked down at the tiny rowboat alongside the ship, Julius on his shoulder. Swickers sat in the boat, using the oars to keep her alongside the

Blessed William while Carroll lowered a roped bundle of pistols from the deck.

"Wish us luck, lads!" Peterson called up to Whitney and Ferris, who would remain behind to guard the ship. "Swickers wagers there'll not be more than a few men, so if we can just get onto the ship without event, we should be fine."

"How many will that little boat hold?" Kitto called. Everyone turned to look down the rail at him. It was a curious question, coming from one who would not be joining them. Isaac, who leaned over the rail several feet away, narrowed his eyes.

"Seven, I suppose," answered Peterson, "depending on the sea. But it will just be five of us. Captain says no more than five men, and even that is a bit spare to leave aboard ship here in these waters. We'll like to get robbed ourselves," Peterson said. He gestured to Carroll.

"In you go, man."

Carroll lifted a leg over and began lowering himself down the rope.

Whitney raised his fiddle to his cheek and began to play a mock funeral dirge.

"Don't dampen our spirits, Whitney!" Peterson barked. The music stopped. "Captain said to make it look like common thievery, so we take anything that looks interesting besides the lad. Should be easy enough." Peterson did not sound convinced.

Jenks climbed over next, and while the men watched him, Kitto reached casually behind his back.

His untucked shirt hid the butt of the pistol he had taken from William's cabin. Isaac still watched him, but Kitto did not think the large man could know what he intended.

Peterson motioned for Isaac to go down. Isaac swung his leg over the rail where he stood and catwalked a few feet over to where the rope was tied.

"Bring back souvenirs for us all," Ferris squawked, nodding quickly as he always did whenever he spoke.

Peterson turned to Kitto. "Is there anything I should say to him, in particular, lad? Your brother, I mean. Something to make him trust me? He might be a bit frightened, you know."

Kitto pushed away from the rail. He stood to his full height, his feet spread to a width just beyond his shoulders. Julius chose that moment to hop atop Kitto's head. It did not do wonders for his dignity.

"No. *You* should say nothing," Kitto said. Thankfully, Julius leaped to a rope above.

Kitto reached behind his back. The pistol slid out cleanly from beneath his belt. He aimed it at Peterson's chest.

"What the blazes?" gaped Peterson.

"*I* shall tell him his brother has come to save him!" Peterson's jaw dropped. "Now, step aside, Peterson! I am coming aboard."

CHAPTER 20:

Painted Black

Whitney, who had raised the fiddle to his shoulder, flinched in surprise when the pistol appeared. His instrument squeaked. Isaac, who had just begun to lower himself, stood again on the outer ledge of the rail. His head rocked back and he began to laugh. It was a deep, rich laugh, his mouth full of neat white teeth. Whitney and Simmons, too, began to giggle, as did Ferris, who snickered and nodded his head very rapidly.

"Where'd you get that bloody thing?" Peterson demanded, greatly annoyed.

"I borrowed it from the captain's quarters. Now step aside, sirs, all of you. I'm going down into that boat." Isaac's laughter settled into a broad smile. Without hesitation he swung his leg back over the rail and in an instant was standing next to Peterson.

"You'll do no such thing," Peterson growled. "Now stop this ridiculous . . ." Peterson stepped forward quickly toward Kitto, intending to snatch the weapon away. Kitto pulled back the hammer with his thumb and it gave off a very audible click. Peterson froze, and the remaining laughter went silent.

"But I've got my orders, lad!" Peterson croaked. "You're to stay. Captain would be in a rage if I took you!" Peterson felt a cold bead of sweat run down between his shoulder blades.

Kitto surprised himself by managing to keep his hands still.

"Peterson, I am warning you, either step back or the rest of us get to see what you would look like with a third eye," he said, the pistol steady in his hands. "It's not the first time I shot a man."

"So I've heard," Peterson grumbled.

Whitney could not resist the temptation. He raised his bow again and began to play a dramatic melody.

"Pipe down with that thing!" Peterson bellowed at him. "Come on, lad, I have my orders," he pleaded. "Don't get me in a fix." Peterson's timid eyes were large and afraid. He did so hate to be in trouble with the captain.

"It's not your fault, Peterson. I held a pistol on you. You had no choice. And you've got plenty of witnesses to back you up," Kitto told him. *"Doesn't he?"* Kitto turned the pistol on the three seamen standing nearby.

"Aye!" "Certainly!" "Does that!" Ferris and Whitney and Simmons chimed in nervously.

"You see? You have no choice and nothing to worry about."

Peterson's look hardened. He shook his head in disgust. "Your apple did not fall far from William Quick's tree, I'll say that." He wiped his brow with the back of his hand. "Go on down, Isaac, and make room for the Killer Cooper."

"Good show, lad!" Simmons cheered. Whitney struck up a lively jig, and Isaac slapped the rail smiling before going down.

In a few moments the boat was full: six of them, not including the monkey. Kitto had tried to shoo Julius back up the rope when he climbed down, but Julius bared his teeth and would not yield. Kitto sat alone in the bow, the pistol across his lap, Julius clutching his clubfoot.

The men in the boat had curious, meaningful smiles on their faces. There was a hint of mockery, yes, but also something more than that. Men of action respect action, and even if it were a tad ridiculous to see the puny boy holding a seasoned ship's officer at gunpoint, Kitto had just risen several notches in their estimation.

Except for the occasional quip from Peterson, who spoke out of nerves, the party traveled in silence. Swickers pulled into the wind, a steady, balmy breeze out of the north that carried on it the scent of salt and fruit trees and fish. The men passed between them a tin of tar paint, dabbing at it with a soiled cloth and smearing black onto their faces. Jenks handed the tin to Kitto, who did the same, and Carroll then produced a large black square of cloth from his pocket.

"My good luck rag," he said. "You wear it." Carroll folded it in half the way the men did and handed it toward Kitto. "Pull it over your head." Kitto did so, and

Carroll helped him to tuck it in tight so that his skull was now solid black and smooth.

"You're a proper pirate now."

"Aye, pirate," Peterson grumbled. Most of the other men had covered their heads as well. Only Isaac applied neither the tar nor the head cloth.

Darkness settled quickly now that the sun had fallen. Within minutes the light had waned from dusk to night.

"She should not be much farther," Peterson said for the fourth time. They had passed a dozen ships by now, most of them slavers. Swickers gave them as wide a berth as he could.

Swickers stopped rowing for a moment to rest. "We'll need to board quiet like," he said breathlessly.

"Lobbing a couple grappling hooks onto the decks won't be so quiet," Jenks observed. A coil of rope wound around his neck and beneath one arm. At one end of the rope, hanging to his waist, was a large hook made of cast iron that looked exactly like those used to pluck large fish from the sea.

"No hooks. Or at least no throwing them up to the ship," Swickers said.

"Then what is our plan?" Carroll asked, running the flesh of his thumb along the cutting edge of his cutlass.

"One of us shinnies up the anchor line carrying a hook," Peterson said. "When he gets to the deck, he sets the hooks and throws the lines down wherever he can do it without being seen."

Now Swickers grunted. "We all get aboard without a

cry raised, it'll make for quick work. They ain't likely to leave much of a guard."

"So who's the lucky bloke who gets to go first?" asked Jenks. "My vote goes to the monkey. And if Carroll can't do it, we could try the one there at young Quick's feet."

"Not me. Not unless I lose at drawing straws," Carroll protested, patting his protruding belly. "I don't shinny so well as I used to."

"I shall do it."

Again all eyes turned to Kitto. He had not even been sure that he had said it aloud, but he had. Everyone stared at him with a mixture of mockery and respect.

"Captain William would not like it," Isaac said, shaking his head.

Peterson spoke up, surprising them all. "Maybe not, but he's this far, ain't he?"

"I am, and I won't be much good in a fight," Kitto said, looking from man to man for opposition. "I am a good climber, especially on a rope. The foot will hook around and keep me from falling." The men looked down at his crooked limb.

"Captain William—"

"Shut up, Isaac!" Peterson snapped. "The boy volunteered. We all heard it. Kitto goes first."

It was settled. Kitto felt his heart pounding.

"Can you set a hook?" Swickers asked, craning his neck around to take another look at Kitto and not so impressed by what he saw. His tangled beard glistened in the faint starlight.

"On the rail should I put it?"

Swickers nodded "Aye. That's the best spot. And really give it a shove into the wood. Should it give when we're climbing, it'll make an awful row when we hit the water."

Isaac pointed. "Is that the ship?"

There were two ships, both obviously slavers, anchored within a hundred yards of each other. They lay a good ways off still. The nearer ship had a lantern lit on the main deck. A shadowy figure could just be made out beneath it, puffing on a pipe.

"God's blood!" Swickers muttered, squinting.

"What is it?" Peterson asked.

"The two ships being so close. No guns." Swickers scowled angrily. "Tuck them in your belts if you like, gents, but if shots is fired, we have the crew of two ships to contend with."

Kitto looked down at the pistol he still held in his lap. It would have done him little good anyway. He extended the butt end toward Carroll.

"Will you hold this for me? It's the captain's." Carroll nodded and accepted the weapon. He held the hammer up to the starlight to inspect it.

"Oh, don't worry," Kitto told him. "I never bothered to load it yet."

Peterson flinched. "This whole time and that pistol ain't even loaded?" he hissed. Jenks snickered.

"Have you got a blade?" Carroll whispered to Kitto. "Something with a guard?" The burly man withdrew a dirk from his own belt and handed it toward the boy.

"I'm not much with a sword, I am afraid," Kitto admitted, hesitating.

Carroll pushed the dirk toward him. "This un's got a wide guard. It'll stop a blow or two if your life depends on it. Take it," he said, and gave Kitto a slap on the shoulder that did not fill the boy with confidence.

"If you need to stick a man from behind," Swickers offered, "get him low. About here." He fingered a spot on his own back. "Go too high and he'll still be able to scream."

Kitto's spine tingled. Could he kill a man in cold blood? Stab him in the back? Could he do it if he had to? Kitto began to regret volunteering, but he scanned the blackened faces of the men in the boat. These men had nothing to win and everything to lose by boarding that ship. He had to be the one to go.

"Thank you," he said to Carroll, taking the weapon in hand. It was not a delicate instrument; its handle was thick and heavy, with a large, round metal butt. Kitto tucked the dirk into the front of his belt, then tightened the belt.

"Swing around the stern," Peterson ordered. "Let us make sure this is the right ship." Swickers rowed a wide arc out toward the open sea and edged his way in. When they were still too far off to see the woodwork of the ship, he stopped. Carefully he lifted each oar from its oarlock and wound a cloth around the inside of the metal hardware.

Caroll saw Kitto's quizzical look. "Keeps the locks from chattering when we get in close."

So this is it then. Kitto found himself shamefully hopeful that the ship was not the *Crucible.* Butterflies fluttered in his stomach.

Duck is on that ship, he told himself. *Think only of Duck . . . of getting him to safety. I must get him off that ship no matter what happens.*

Sure enough, as they got closer, the curlicues in the woodwork of the ship's stern became plain, as well as some fancy lettering in all uppercase letters spelling CRUCIBLE, along with a quotation in what looked to be Latin. A strange, muffled sound emanated from the hull. All six of the boat's occupants strained their ears.

"One man," Isaac whispered. "Singing." Kitto nodded, just able to make it out. It came from within the ship and not from the smoking man they had spied earlier on the deck above them.

Swickers reached to the floor. His hands withdrew a coil of rope with a large black hook attached to the end. A grappling hook. It was cast iron, black and heavy. Swickers passed the coil forward to Carroll, who held it up for Kitto to slip a head and arm through. Kitto adjusted the coil and Carroll wrapped the hook tight in the strands of rope.

"You sure you know what you're getting into, boy?" Peterson hissed from the stern of the boat. Peterson had begun to have misgivings about sending forth a boy on such a mission, and a lame boy at that. What would the captain say!

The darkness had deepened like a dense fog. With

their blackened faces, the men could hardly pick one another out. Jenks shook an encouraging fist in Kitto's direction. Carroll grasped him by the shoulder and gave him a squeeze.

"Climb right up the line, set the hook, and we'll be up there quick as rats," Swickers whispered.

Each of the men, Peterson even, had been in engagements when it had been his turn to make the first move. They knew the hollow feeling in the pit of Kitto's stomach.

Think of Duck, only of Duck! Kitto closed his eyes for a moment. *See it in your mind and make it real!*

Swickers maneuvered the boat so that it floated alongside the anchor cable, which stretched tight against the flow of the tide. The cable leaned at a sharp angle up to a hole in the hull that was near to, but not on level with, the ship's deck.

Quickly Kitto worked the laces of his boots. None of the men spoke. Peterson's eyes sparkled in the starlight as he looked up at the shadowy hulk of the ship's stern looming over them. Not a hundred yards away to the port side of *Crucible*, the other ship lay dark against a backdrop of starry sky.

In a moment Kitto rose barefoot, carefully stepping forward toward where Jenks held on to the cable. As he passed each of the men, he felt a bracing pat on his backside or on his shoulder, votes of encouragement. Kitto leaned out and took hold of the cable. Its thick links felt damp and slimy with algae, but another foot higher the metal was dry and smooth.

Kitto was about to swing up when Isaac's hand shot out and grabbed his leg. All eyes went to Isaac's silhouetted frame. He pointed upward. They all looked, and then they heard a shuffling of feet on the deck planks directly above them.

The sound of the gentle waves lapping at the side of the small boat seemed to echo against the ship's towering stern. Every man held his breath; Swickers slowly withdrew a pistol and aimed it up at the ship's rail above them.

A man's arms came into view.

It was at that eternally long and silent moment that Julius decided he had had enough of the little bobbing vessel and scampered up Kitto's poised body onto the cable. Before Kitto even had time to react, the monkey was beyond his reach, half up the anchor cable, looking back at him and smiling.

CHAPTER 21:

Attempt at Rescue

The sailor above must have been standing at the stern rail. He would only have to lean over it to see the rowboat and its occupants plain as day.

The arms moved. The men heard a rapping sound, and then a glowing clump of stuff slowly tumbled down through the air and landed with a slight hiss in the water no more than a yard from where Kitto balanced.

Ash from his pipe.

All eyes moved back and forth between the bodiless pair of arms above them, and the silhouetted form of Julius, who had stopped to groom himself halfway up the chain. Above, the man coughed, then spit. From within the ship the singing voice hit a crescendo. The man on deck chuckled. The arms withdrew and they heard the distinct sound of footsteps receding.

Peterson let out a sigh. Isaac withdrew his hand from Kitto's leg.

"Close one," Jenks said, the same smile plastered on his face. "Lucky for us he didn't drop his trousers as well."

Peterson leaned toward Kitto. "That cursed monkey could foul the whole thing! Cast him down if you must." Kitto nodded, though he knew he could never do such a thing.

Without further word, Kitto rechecked the coiled rope around his neck and shoulders, then hoisted himself up. He wrapped his legs and feet around the thick chain. His bent foot actually made it easier to grip the slick metal, and in just a few seconds he had hauled himself up nearly half the distance. Julius crawled back to him casually and nuzzled his head into Kitto's curls.

Then it happened.

The sound of footsteps sounded anew, accompanied by a rattling sound like the dragging of a chain. Kitto's body went rigid.

"Right up here . . . *now*, boy! Did I not say this brass-work had to sparkle? Did I not?" There was a smacking sound and then a wail and thud, the sound of a body dropping to the deck.

Boy? Could it be Duck?

"Yes, sir! Yes! To sparkle! You like things that sparkle!" It was a boy's voice, but with a thick accent that sounded vaguely like Isaac's. It was not Duck.

Again there was the sound of a person being struck.

"Don't you mock me, you savage! Lucky you're Mawbry's pet, or I'd teach you a lesson with the cat. Take this cloth and get the job done. I'll set right here until you do."

"Yes! You sit and watch me sparkle! You are good at watching, sir!"

Kitto felt alarm. *What can I do now?* He most certainly could not come over the rail above where the anchor cable went through the hawsehole into the hull of the ship. That was precisely the spot where the voices were located. He stole a glance down at the boat below. All the faces stared back up at him, the whites of their eyes like floating crescents against the dark sea.

I cannot turn back. Think of Duck! I must go on!

Ever so slowly, Kitto put one hand above the next on the cable and pulled himself up carefully, sliding his feet along. Hand over hand, a few inches at a time, he continued, and it was not long in this manner before he could reach out and touch the hull, sticky with tar. The boy could only have been a few feet away now, for Kitto could hear the heavy breath of a small body and a faint rubbing sound. Fortunately, Julius stayed with him, a few links beyond his reach.

Just above Kitto's head was the deck and the woodwork supporting the rail. The foot of the rail was not set right flush to the deck, so there was a lip of wood that went around the edge of the ship. Slowly Kitto stretched a hand out toward that lip to test it.

Yes, he thought. *It is just wide enough to slide along toward the middle of the ship.*

But Kitto's arms already ached. It had been a slow climb up the anchor cable, and now that he was at the top, the idea of holding himself by only his fingertips daunted him.

Believe with all your heart, he thought, remembering Sarah's words. Kitto shut his eyes and saw himself in his mind's eye sliding along that thin lip of wood, holding fast and true and having the strength to pull himself up and over the rail.

I will make it, by God, I will!

Julius sprang from the cable and landed on the woodwork below the rail, his tiny fingers finding unseen holds. Kitto reached out with his left hand and curled his fingers over the lip of wood. The wood was bone dry against his fingers, and his grip was sure. He could hear the sound of the man singing belowdecks again, clear enough to hear that it was not the King's English the man spoke.

When he was sure he had a good grip, Kitto unwrapped his legs and feet one by one from the cable. His body swung suddenly toward the hull and he held out his toes to soften the inevitable blow.

Bump!

His toes and knees struck against the planks of the hull and made what seemed to him a terribly loud sound. No one appeared above him but Julius, who looked down at him with his head tilted askew.

"Such is my luck to catch this watch!" the man's voice grumbled above. "A little dice game! What's the harm? Black Mawbry had no call to raise such a stink!"

"You're very good with the gambling, sir!"

"Shut your hole."

Kitto slid his hands one by one to the left, several inches at a time, his body wriggling beneath him. He passed beneath Julius, and the monkey's tail tickled the end of his nose. With the curling away of the hull beneath him, there was no place to put his feet that provided any assistance. His shoulders burned and his fingers ached.

How will I reach the rail? The rail itself was supported by a small wall that rose more than three feet above the deck. Even if he had the strength to haul himself up to the level of his hands, he could never reach the top of the rail to be able to hoist a leg over.

Kitto's heart hammered, his breath came out strained and ragged, and the first wave of panic washed over him like a bucket of springwater. He looked desperately back toward the anchor cable. It was impossibly far away now, too far for his tired fingers and arms to hold out.

Left with no other choice, Kitto kept on, sliding farther and farther along the foot of the rail as fast as he could manage, praying for some solution to appear to him. The man's voice began to fade. Now Kitto's shoulders burned fiercely and his locked fingers began to lose their feeling, but there was no break in the rail, no crack or hole up ahead into which he might jam a hand and be able to hoist himself higher. Julius reached down from his perch and crawled onto the top of Kitto's head, adding to his misery.

Kitto knew now. He would have to drop. He could not do it. He dangled motionless from the lip of wood, and looked down toward the water, black and shimmering like the scales of an immense sea serpent. Julius chattered happily in his ear, and then Kitto felt a sudden jolt of pain at the back of his skull. Julius had reached down and unwrapped the hook from the coil and was letting it swing on the end of the line. The metal rapped him again.

Bloody monkey! he cursed, but a moment later the idea struck him like a blow.

The rope! he thought. *The grappling hook!*

It would likely make a terrible noise, but he had no time nor strength to consider another solution. Kitto let go with his right hand and wrenched off one coil. His body swung precariously, and Julius squealed, retreating back to the security of the rail above. Desperately Kitto wriggled his hand to uncoil a few lengths of slack. Were the slightest rising wave to lift or drop the ship suddenly, the fingers of his left hand holding him up would slip. None came.

The hook hung down several feet. Kitto had strength in the hand suspending him for just one throw.

Had he been able to look down toward the water at the stern, he would have seen the crew utterly enthralled at his trials. Carroll had nearly stood in the boat with fists clenched. Peterson had reached out and squeezed Isaac's arm, and Jenks held his hands together in prayer—despite his devout Godlessness.

From within the ship, the volume of the man's singing reached a new peak. The voice belted out with great passion.

"Shut your hole, you stinking Portuguese ape!" Kitto heard the man on deck complain.

He heaved. The black claw of iron was flung up in a wide arc. It flew into the air and disappeared beyond the rail. Julius craned his head around to watch it go. There was a very distinctive *whunk!* when it hit the deck.

Belowdecks the man's singing continued. Kitto yanked back on the rope. He expected shouts any second. The alarm would be raised. Surely it would.

But no shouts sounded. Kitto worked feverishly, his fingers burning.

Please, God, I beg of you! Let the hook set!

The sound of the iron sliding along the deck greeted his ears. Surely it was too loud! Surely the man on watch would hear and come to investigate. By now Kitto did not even care. His arms burned like fire, and he could not feel the fingers of his left hand though they held all his weight. He did not understand why the muscles did not yield. He jerked and yanked on the slack of the rope, frantic with fatigue, his breath forced out between clenched teeth. He heard another *thunk!* sound when the hook rapped into bottom of the rail on the other side. Still there was nothing upon which the hook might find purchase. Kitto reached high and wrapped his right hand and wrist around the rope several times so that he had a fast grip, then gently as he could muster he began to pull back on the rope so as to slide the hook upward along the inside of the rail face and give it the best possible chance of setting into the wood lip of the rail itself.

Then, without warning, Kitto's fingers slipped.

There was an awful and endless instant of weight-lessness, of utter surprise, of staring wide-eyed up at Julius and the bewildered monkey staring back. Then Kitto felt the world give way beneath him.

Duck! Duck!

The air rushed up, and the rail rushed away.

It seemed to Kitto later, when he would recall that moment, that he fell a long way, but it could not have been for more than the time it takes to gasp. Then came a ferocious, violent jerk. Kitto's arm was yanked upward as the rope went taut and the grappling hook held. A series of popping sounds issued from his shoulder; it was the sound of his arm being wrenched from its socket. His body came to a halt in midair and hovered, spinning slowly. Excruciating pain shot through Kitto's body and reached to his very toes. His mouth opened wide to scream, but no sound came. He spun there for several seconds, blinded by agony.

How Kitto proceeded to scale that line with just one good arm and his teeth the men in the boat would never know. Jenks later swore that he wet himself while he watched, and Isaac bore fingernail marks where Peterson had dug into his forearm.

It was an impossible feat. Impossible. But Kitto did it. There was a voice in his head, partly Father's, partly Sarah's—partly God's—and it spurred him onward. His hand kept reaching, kept pulling, ever higher on the rope, his jaw clenching down on the line. Julius grabbed a fistful of his hair to help once he was high enough, and then miraculously Kitto reached the rail.

He slipped soundlessly to the deck.

Breathless, Kitto slumped against the rail, mostly concealed in the shadows. Julius hugged him about the neck. Kitto looked up at the grappling hook that had saved him. A single sharpened prong pierced the very edge of the rail. Despite his agony, Kitto could not help but smile, then silently laugh. His laughter gave vent to his nerves, and before he knew it his shoulders were shaking and his eyes blurred with tears of relief. Julius nuzzled his fuzzy head against the tears and then recoiled when he felt the sticky tar.

Get ahold of yourself! the voice commanded Kitto now, and he wiped the sweat and tears from his face with the back of his sleeve. It also came away tarred. Gingerly he reached up and tossed the rest of the rope over the rail.

What Kitto did not pause to see was whether the rope had dropped far enough so that his comrades could reach it. As it turned out, the rope bunched. It did not lower down to the water as it should have. Instead, it hung a few feet below the rail in a bundle. Kitto could not see Peterson stand up in the rowboat waving to alert him.

The men from the *Blessed William* could not help him now. Kitto alone would have to save his brother.

What with the curve of the ship Kitto could not see the two figures nearer the stern, but he knew they were there. He pushed himself to his feet, red-hot tendrils of pain reaching out from his shoulder, and stepped into the shadows. His right arm hung slack; he could not so much as raise it an inch.

My good arm, too, he thought. Kitto reached around into his belt and withdrew the heavy dirk that Carroll had given him, and proceeded to walk amidships to where he might find a stairwell. He was careful not to drag his clubfoot along the deck planks. Julius climbed up his backside to his perch on his shoulder. Kitto turned around to see if Peterson or the others had followed, but he was alone.

Soon Kitto found the stairs and made his way down them, his steps silent except for the occasional creak of a board that was easily lost in the natural creaks and shifts of a large ship. The singing grew louder. Kitto made his way down a hall, toward a light. It must have been the main mess, judging from its size. The light of two lanterns cast a hazy glow down part of the corridor. Kitto slipped forward, the singing growing ever louder, and peered around the corner.

There sat two men. Slumped, more like. The first sat at a bench with his head flat on the table next to a dark green bottle and a pewter cup. Asleep. The other had his back toward the door. He practically lay back in the chair at the head of the table, his head lolling, eyes closed, his arms gesturing widely as he sang. In one of his hands he held his own cup, and every few sweeps of his arm some of the amber liquid sloshed out of it and onto the floor.

Kitto turned from him and made his way back into the shadows.

Swickers had said the main hold for the slaves would be in the lower deck, so Kitto went back toward the stairwell and looked for an entrance leading farther down. He found it and began down the stairs into the blackness.

The smell was overpowering, of human waste mixed with salt and lime that had been used to purge the ship after its last load. He would never forget that smell. Not ever. Kitto wrinkled his nose at it and tried to breathe through his mouth, but the odor still nauseated him.

At the bottom of the stairs there was only inky blackness and silence to greet him, but he sensed that he was in a large space. He took a few tentative steps forward, casting an eye back toward the stairs.

"Duck!" he hissed into the blackness. "Elias Wheale! Duck, are you here! It is I, Kitto!"

CHAPTER 22:

Duck in Chains

"Elias Wheale!" Kitto called out again, using Duck's proper name. He stepped forward into the blackness.

His feet struck against something metal—a chain perhaps—and it skittered across the floor. Something stirred several feet away, as of a person rousing from sleep, accompanied by more rattling of chains. Then Kitto heard a faint sniffle and a whimper. Though no words were spoken, Kitto immediately recognized the sounds.

"Duck! My God, is it you! Where are you!" Kitto nearly shouted, joy leaping up inside him and catching at his throat.

"Kitto? Kitto? Kitto, is that you?" Duck's voice sounded far off, as if it echoed across an ocean of misery. Kitto strode forward into the darkness, promptly struck his forehead on a beam and stumbled—sending Julius flying—then pressed on, moving toward the sound.

"Kitto! Kitto!"

Duck crawled toward the sound, dragging metal behind him. He felt an outstretched hand take a fistful of his hair.

"Oh, Kitto!" Duck cried. Kitto covered his mouth with a hand and whispered something about silence. They fell into an embrace. Duck hugged him desperately.

Duck was not like Kitto. He did not do well alone—nor did he fancy the dark, either—and though it was only part of a day he spent in irons in the hold of that slave ship, those hours were the most harrowing he had ever known. His body shook with sobs.

"I've got you, Duck! I've got you!" Kitto whispered in his ear. Everything broke inside the little boy, and it was several minutes before his breath came back.

"But . . . but Mum!" Duck finally managed. "They took me away! They—"

"Hush now!" Kitto commanded. "Save that for later. We are not yet safe. We must get off this ship. Can you walk?"

"What in the . . . Kitto! There's some rat or something on me!" Duck felt clawlike hands moving up his shirt. He flailed at it and sent the creature tumbling. It squealed angrily.

"No, Duck! It's all right. That's Julius. He's a monkey. A pet. He's with me."

"Your pet?" Duck felt a furry bundle placed into his hands. He patted tentatively at the soft fur. Julius squirmed beneath the boy's touch and purred like a pussycat.

"Now tell me, Duck . . . can you walk?"

"They've chained me, Kitto. Here, around my foot," Duck told him, and guided his brother's hand to the

THE DAGGER QUICK

metal clasp around his ankle. Kitto could feel a narrow groove for where a key would fit.

Kitto's heart sank.

"You cannot slide out of it? You are sure?"

"I tried. I tried and tried! I got meself all cut up with trying. No use!" Duck broke into sobs and inadvertently began to squeeze the monkey. Julius squealed again and the boys nearly jumped.

"Julius, quiet!"

"Kitto, what will you do? Please don't leave me here, Kitto, please!" Duck begged. "They say I am to be a slave to some African king! Please, Kitto!"

"Stop it, Duck!" Kitto put a hand on Duck's wet cheek. "You be strong for me now. Strong, Duck! That's the only way. Can you do that?" Duck reached around Kitto's hand to wipe at his nose. He could walk on water or hot coals if it meant getting off that ship. He nodded.

"Now we need the key. Who would have that, Duck? Who put the lock on you?"

"I . . . I don't know, Kitto. Nobody told me any names. He's a big fat fellow, always singing. . . ."

Singing!

"In English or foreign? The songs."

"It ain't English, Kitto, and they ain't pretty, neither. Mum sings better than that even." Sarah Wheale had many fine qualities. True pitch was not one of them.

"I know the man and I will get the key. Stay here," Kitto added unnecessarily, "and make not a word."

"Kitto, don't leave me!" Duck pleaded again, clutching at his brother's wrists.

"Remember what I said now, Duck." Kitto's voice was stern. "Be strong and be quiet and I shall be back in a moment." The monkey leaped from Duck's lap to follow, but Kitto set him back and instructed Duck to hold fast. He did. Clutched him might be a better description. Poor Julius tolerated it this time, and tried to settle into Duck's lap.

Duck could just make out the outline of Kitto's body as he walked back in the direction he had come. The little boy tried his best not to whimper, but the darkness was so dark again once Kitto's hands had left his own. Julius curled into Duck's lap and proceeded to doze.

The faintest of glows appeared to Kitto once he reached the stairwell, and he made his way up quickly. He withdrew the dirk again and held it out in front of him with his left hand.

This time he did not slink down the hall. He walked, standing at his full height, the blade catching the candlelight. Kitto felt a great rage swelling up inside him from having seen Duck so misused, and he was ready to kill. He strode recklessly right into the mess, and suddenly became aware that the singing had stopped.

The reason for the silence was instantly obvious. The singer had pitched forward in his seat and joined his companion in dreamless slumber. The pewter cup lay on the floor in a dark puddle.

Kitto approached the man, carefully bending over

each side of him, scanning his body for a ring of keys. He peered around either side of the man's wide girth, but saw nothing around his belt line. He slipped the dirk into his belt again and rubbed his good hand on his trousers.

Sweet dreams, mate, he wished, and slowly extended his hand under the man's arm toward where a lanyard might hang around his neck. His fingertips disturbed something pressing against the man's tunic from the inside. There was the slight jingle of metal, and at that moment the man's head jerked up.

Kitto yanked back his hand, but it was impossible to conceal himself. He reached again for the hilt of the dagger, but then froze. The man's eyes half opened, he garbled a few words in Portuguese, then nestled his head back to the table again. When the first snores began anew, Kitto withdrew the dirk and squatted down on his knees.

Oh, for a pair of shears! he thought. Cutting through the man's shirt would be a delicate maneuver. The thought occurred to him to rap him on the head with something heavy just for good measure, but then there was the matter of the other man slumped just a few feet away.

Kitto possessed skilled hands, though—one of the benefits of the tedious hours he had spent with Father in the shop. Using Carroll's dirk, he cut a vertical slit a few inches long, and the black tip of a single key flopped out of the opening.

That's the stuff! Kitto set the dirk on the floor and reached into the opening. He felt the small metal ring upon which clung several keys of various sizes. He got down even lower, almost beneath the table, so that he had a better angle from which to work. He took the dirk again, by the blade now, and worked it against the leather strand that held the ring.

The lanyard gave and out the hole fell the metal ring. Instinctively Kitto reached for it with his wounded arm. His outstretched palm caught the key ring with only a small jingle sounding, but the sudden movement was enough to make him gasp in agony.

Oh God, oh God, oh God! Kitto clenched his teeth, and beads of sweat dimpled his forehead. He rested for a few breaths beneath the table until his head cleared. The men snored.

"Is it you, Kitto?" a small voice whimpered from the darkness once Kitto returned to the hold. Duck's chains dragged on the floor, and Julius sprang up to greet him.

"It's me, Duck. I have keys." Their hands found one another again, then Kitto squatted. "Show my hand to the lock," he said, and Duck guided him. There were a half dozen keys on the ring. Kitto fumbled with them.

"Oh, please hurry, Kitto! What if they catch you, too!" the little boy wailed.

"Hush, Duck! You must decide in your mind that we are going to make it out of here. Do you understand?"

"You sound like Mum," Duck told him. He was

quiet while Kitto's fingers worked the keys. Finally one slipped smoothly into the slot.

Come on now, Kitto pleaded, turning his wrist. There was an audible click. The clasp opened and slid to the floor with a clatter.

"That's it! I am free!" Duck threw his arms about his brother's shoulders, sending Julius sprawling and screeching for the third time. Duck felt so happy to have the chain off him he could have shouted, but Kitto slapped a hand over his mouth.

"Now let us go! But listen, Duck," Kitto whispered, the new challenge of getting the boy off the ship looming before him, "this will be very difficult. There is a man on deck. We must not let him see us, so you must be terribly quiet. Do you understand?"

Duck nodded fervently.

"No whispering even," Kitto said, remembering that Duck did not really know how to whisper.

"What about Julius?"

"Don't worry about him," Kitto answered, although he was plenty worried the monkey would foul things for them. "He'll come along on his own." As if in answer, Duck felt a strong pressure moving up his arm. Julius settled in on his shoulder.

"Hold on to my belt." Kitto stood and turned, guiding Duck's hand.

Together, the two of them made their way soundlessly up the stairs, past the glow of the mess from which a chorus of snores could now be heard—one baritone and one bass—and up the stairs toward the main deck. Kitto's nerves were steady now after his successes, and he had the throbbing pain in his shoulder to distract him from fear. Duck did not. His teeth chattered. Tears slipped silently from his eyes.

Reaching the upper deck, Kitto peeked his head out into the starlight. Through the rigging and masts he could see the man sitting on the barrel in the stern, his pipe smoke rising up. Kitto ducked back into the shadows.

"He's the bad one," Duck said, already forgetting his instructions about whispering.

"We must not let him see us."

"Why is your face all black?" Duck asked, seeing it for the first time.

"No questions, Duck! Just listen. I will take you to a rope. We climb down it and into the water."

"I must swim?" Duck asked anxiously. He was a better climber than swimmer.

"Only for a moment, if that. There is a boat hiding below, filled with friends." Kitto looked about the deck for a sign of them, but when he saw no one, the thought struck him that something had gone very wrong. "They will see you coming down the rope and bring the boat around to pick you up. But, Duck, you must beware of splashing, and no crying out no matter what!" he stressed.

"Not a word, I swear it!"

"Then take my belt again and off we go."

Crouching behind any mast or bulwark that provided cover from the man at the stern, Kitto led them to the port rail at the ship's waist where he had come up. Duck padded after him, utterly silent. In the shadows they came upon the grappling hook. Kitto was about to instruct his brother on shinnying down the rope when he saw that Duck had stood fully upright in the starry light.

He jerked at Duck's shirt, but the boy pulled away. He had seen something. Someone.

"Duck!" he whispered. "Get down! In the shadows, or he'll see you!" Duck lowered himself slowly and turned toward his big brother. It was the first time that Kitto had really seen Duck's face since he had found him. It was an awful sight. His cheeks were streaked with dirt and tears, and a dab of encrusted blood had dried around one nostril. Duck had huge blue eyes, but just then they showed something other than fear.

"Kitto, it's Abe! It's him over there!" he said breathlessly.

"The man, you mean?"

"No, the boy. They call him Abe, but that's not his name."

"Yes, him. He's a slave, I think, Duck."

"We can't leave him here, Kitto." The boy's face had gone hard and his eyes flashed.

Kitto shook his head. "No, Duck. No, no, no. Just put that out of your head. We'll be lucky enough ourselves to get off the ship without being seen. There's no

room for him in the boat. Now come on and stay close."
Kitto stood and turned to head farther toward the bow,
away from the guard, but he felt no hand on his belt.

Duck was standing again in the light, the monkey
still on his shoulder.

Kitto turned back and grabbed his brother by the
arm, but Duck wrenched himself free.

"Elias Wheale! You'll get us killed," Kitto hissed.

"He brought me a mango."

"A what?"

"A mango. That's what they call apples here. Abe
did. He brought me one when I was down there in the
dark."

Kitto scowled

"He's a slave, Ducky. They'd have told him to bring
it to you."

"No, Kitto. He did it on his own."

"And how do you know that?"

"Because they beat him for it. Right in front of me,
and worse than *anything* Father ever did! Two men, one
of them that same one over there—he whipped him with
this big rope that had knots all down it. . . ."

"Yes, but, Duck . . ."

"Mum wouldn't want us to leave him!"

Kitto closed his eyes in defeat. If there was one lesson that Sarah had instilled in the boys over the years, it
was to be strong for those who could not be so. She had
planted a thought in little Duck that no one could uproot.

"I'll not leave Abe here. I won't do it!"

Kitto shook his finger at him. "Then it's all your fault if we end up dead, or scrubbing some African king's backside," he said. He scanned the deck again. *Where is Peterson?* "I'll do it, but only if you do what I tell you, right?"

"And you promise you'll get him?"

"I promise, but first let's get you safe." This time Duck took his belt again and the two of them made their way toward the bow of the ship. Once a safer distance had been put between them and the stern, Kitto tucked Duck into the darkest shadows he could find behind the foremast and instructed him to keep tight hold of Julius.

"If I don't come back, you go down that rope without me," he instructed, pointing to the grappling hook in the rail.

"I swear it," Duck said.

In the relative safety of the shadows, Kitto made his way aft, walking half bent. Shortly he could make out the sounds of labored breathing, and a rubbing sound, which he figured must be the slave boy working at his task. He peeked out from behind the mizzenmast. Sure enough, the young slave boy was hard at work, bent over a long strip of brass that ran along the stern rail, and facing him, lying on his side across the lids of three barrels, lay the lone guard. He had propped his head up on an elbow and was enjoying his pipe.

Kitto hefted the dirk in his hand. Swickers's words came to him. "If you need to stick a man from behind . . ."

Kitto looked down at the butt end of the knife. It

was hard and blunt and heavy. He would not kill, just maim.

But what if I fail? What then? Kitto wiped his brow as if to wipe the thought away, and the back of his hand received a smear of tar. It was a thing that must be done and he must do it. That is all. He peeked around the mast again, seeing the man's soiled tunic and the curl of his dark hair. Kitto saw himself in his mind's eye stepping forward and bringing down the dirk with all his might on the man's skull.

It will be as I see it, he commanded, but his stomach churned.

CHAPTER 23:

Saved by a Slave

Kitto slipped out from behind the mizzenmast, the pale glow of the remaining stars casting a faint shadow on the deck behind him. Three steps away. Two.

Kitto raised the dirk in his hand so that the hilt would come down first. He had picked out the spot just behind the man's ear and was about to bring it down with everything he had when the boy working happened to catch a strange reflection in the brass. He turned.

"Ai!" he wailed.

Instantly the sailor whirled, knocking to the deck a pistol that had lain hidden on the barrel tops with him. Kitto lunged, but the man raised an arm in his defense. Their forearms and bodies crashed together.

The empty barrels tumbled, Kitto and the sailor with them. Kitto's grip on the dirk slipped and it spun off. The advantage of surprise gone, the sailor quickly gained the upper hand. He whipped his fist through the air as the two of them tried to find their feet, and caught Kitto across the jaw. Kitto's head snapped back, but he managed not to go down. He scanned the deck desperately for the dirk.

Duck, of course, had not waited in the shadows. Nor had he gone down the rope. In fact, he had followed Kitto just a moment after his brother had left, with Julius scouting the way from his shoulder. Duck watched in horror as the man struck at Kitto again. Kitto tumbled back but then launched himself again at the man, fueled by rage. The man threw three punches that Kitto ducked as he tried in his turn to land a fist into the man's groin. Kitto scooted between the man's legs to avoid his grip and scrambled onto his back. There he pulled at the man's hair and gouged at his eyes.

"Kitto!" Duck gaped in fear and shock until Julius leaped from his shoulder, let out a scream like a thousand fingernails dragged on a slate, backflipped on the deck, and jumped into the fray.

"I'm coming, Kitto!" Duck ran forward pell-mell and dived through the air over a barrel in his path, landing at the man's feet. The man had just managed to disentangle Kitto and hurled him over his head onto the deck. Kitto landed in a heap.

Duck wrapped his arms around the man's ankle, turned his head, and sank his baby teeth into the soft flesh just behind the man's knee. Just a few years earlier, Duck had been a monster of a toddler; neighborhood children were forbidden to play with him. Julius, who grappled with the same leg on the man's thigh, saw Duck and did what monkeys do. He clamped down on the man's thigh, his sharp teeth piercing through trousers and skin. The man wailed in agony.

In an instant, though, he had flung Julius aside by his tail and grabbed a fistful of Duck's hair. Duck whimpered as he was lifted above the sailor's head. He braced for the tremendous blow that would come. But the man did not throw him. Instead, Duck was held motionless in the air, staring up at the stars.

"Put that thing down, boy!" Duck heard the man say. Duck craned his neck around. He was not talking to Kitto. Kitto had barely managed to push himself to a sitting position. The man was speaking to the slave boy: the one Duck knew as Abe.

Abe wore a tattered pair of trousers that ended at the knee, and was naked from the waist up. He was all elbows and ribs. His skin was very dark, and from his efforts polishing the brass, it shone with perspiration. In one hand he held the pistol, and in the other the dirk.

"Shut your hole," the boy said quietly, trying out such words for the first time.

"Don't go being a fool now, Abe-boy. Put down that pistol."

"Put the little boy down!" Abe commanded. The man did as told. Duck landed on his bottom hard enough to rattle his teeth.

"Ow!"

"Give me that pistol." The sailor stepped forward. Abe was no stranger to a pistol's operation. His thumb reached up and cocked the hammer.

"You are good at watching," the boy said. "You watch while I work. Now you watch me kill you." He had a clear, high voice, full of fierce pride.

"Take it easy with that thing now, boy."

"Abe!" Duck cried, finding his feet. "That one there is my brother! He is here to rescue me! Rescue us!"

Abe looked at Duck, then over at Kitto. He shook his head.

"I will be a slave no more. Not for anyone."

"Not a slave," Kitto said thickly from where he sat. Julius had run over to him and was nuzzling the crown of his head against Kitto's hand. "You come as a free man."

"Liars!" barked the sailor. "They're just thieves! Slave stealers. They'll sell you off to worse than Mawbry."

"It's not true!" Duck shouted.

The sailor nodded emphatically. "That's right, Abe, all they'll do is sell you off. Not worth it. But you're smart not firing that pistol. I'll see to it Captain Mawbry hears of your loyalty. He might just grant your freedom too, if you just hand it over."

To this Abe laughed darkly. "Around you I act stupid, but I am not stupid."

"You will join us as a free man!" Kitto said again. "Free! But we must hurry before more men return to the ship."

Abe looked down the barrel of the pistol. Kitto could see that he struggled with indecision. Could he trust this painted boy sprawled out on the deck?

"Please, Abe! I made him come over here to help you. You have got to come!" Duck pleaded.

Just at that moment there was sound and movement over at the anchor cable. All turned and Abe's pistol swung in that direction. The sailor seized his chance. He leaped forward and struck Abe across the jaw, wresting the pistol free. Julius screamed and did another flip as Abe crumpled to the deck.

The sailor whirled the gun around, pointing it in Kitto's direction. Kitto was still there, but before him stood a wall of four men with blackened faces and bared pistols. A fifth, Peterson, was still pulling himself over the rail. Swickers stood out in front with a knife blade jammed between his teeth, reaching out with primed pistols.

"Came just in time, I see," Carroll said, stepping forward and snatching away the man's pistol. The sailor had a wide-eyed look of fear.

"We waited a bit, Kitto. Didn't want you to think we had no confidence in you," said Jenks, flashing his teeth.

"Thank you," Kitto muttered. He pointed to where the boy lay in a heap. "The boy might need some help." Isaac stepped forward and shook Abe gently. The boy recoiled from the touch when his senses returned, but seeing Isaac, he stopped struggling and was helped to his feet.

"He comes with us," Isaac announced to the group.

"That's what I been saying!" Duck threw in.

"Are there any more like him below?" Isaac asked the man. Whether from fright or resistance, the man did not answer. Isaac stepped forward and into Swickers's line of fire. The sailor was tall himself, but Isaac had to look down at him to see eye to eye. "Are there any more slaves?" he barked.

The man's confidence returned. He sneered. "Rot in Hades, you ape." Isaac grabbed the man by the front of his shirt. His massive bald head whipped down and caught the man across the bridge of his nose. Duck winced at the sound of a crunch.

"Isaac, there are none like you, man," Jenks said. Isaac lowered the sailor gently to the deck.

"There are no more," Abe said. "The rest were taken off today."

Swickers belted his pistols and withdrew the knife from his teeth. He kicked the unconscious man to his back and raised the blade.

"No!" Kitto nearly shouted. Swickers turned slit eyes to him. Kitto held up his hand resolutely. The sailor moaned.

"No," Kitto said again. "My brother has seen enough of the world already, Swickers. Just give him a good rap on the noggin and let's be gone." Swickers grunted his assent, then brought the butt end down on the top of the man's head.

"We should go," Kitto said. "There are others below deck." He turned to the boy who stood next to Isaac, looking wide-eyed at the blackened faces. "I thank you, Abe. You saved my life, and my brother's, too. Come with us, and we shall repay the debt."

The boy spread his feet in a wide stance and stood

up tall. "I will come. But my name is not Abe. I am Akintunde. In your tongue it means 'brave.' You call me Akin."

"Lovely," said Jenks. "Now that introductions is all proper? . . ."

"Aye," said Peterson. "We have been too long as it is. Swickers, get the boat and bring it port side where Kitto went up. It'll be easier going down by the rope than the anchor cable."

Within a few minutes the party had slid down the grappling hook's line and into the awaiting boat, where Swickers manned the oars.

Now that he had left that ship for good, the full weight of relief hit Duck. He nearly tackled Kitto when his brother was lowered into the boat and buried his face in Kitto's shirt. Kitto patted his brother's head and spoke soothing words while he wept. None of the men spoke, and the rowing began. Even Julius seemed to understand Duck's misery and petted at his wet cheeks with his tiny, coarse hands.

Kitto looked out from where he and Duck sat in the bow and saw all eyes but Swickers's, who manned the oars, upon him. He could not but see the pride—nay, the admiration—that shone on their faces through the tarred masks.

"I can't quite believe that arm of yours is still attached to your body," said Jenks, once Swickers had ferried them a safe distance away.

"It feels near yanked out."

"I will fix it when we get back," Isaac told him.

"That was a terrific fall, wasn't it? We all was holding our breath then, I tell you!" said Carroll.

"A fine time to play about like a monkey swinging on a vine when there was work to be done," Jenks added.

"I'll see to it the captain hears about this, Kitto," Peterson promised. "We'd not have done it without you."

Duck nuzzled into his brother's chest and hugged Kitto some more.

"I would have fought better, Kitto, if I still had that dagger you gave me."

"Has Mother got it, then?" Kitto said. Duck nodded, then shivered and burrowed into Kitto.

Swickers put his back into his work, and Akin turned to watch the *Crucible* fade into the night.

"This calls for celebration!" Peterson announced. "We shall raise up to Kitto Quick, who probably saved us all our lives this fine evening."

"Huzzah!" the men cheered.

"But his name is Kitto Wheale, not Kitto Quick!" Duck protested. The men chuckled, and Isaac tousled Duck's hair.

There was a great lot of bellowing and slapping of shoulders when finally they reached the *Blessed William*'s decks.

"Cheers for the Pirate Quick, may he be a William or a Christopher! And may the luck of neither ever run dry!" called Peterson.

"Bring on the music!" bellowed Jenks, capitalizing on the moment.

Peterson conceded and soon Whitney produced his fiddle and broke into a rousing jig, and in no time the three boys were being paraded atop the shoulders of the men: Kitto atop Carroll, Jenks hoisting Duck, and Akin on Isaac. The men danced themselves breathless during an endless jig that kept Whitney's arm sawing until sweat poured down his brow.

Joy is infectious, and upon Jenks's shoulders Duck found his smile again. Jenks spun him and tossed him until he grew dizzy. Swickers whacked at a stalk with a huge knife, then handed up to Duck a cut of sugarcane—the first ever Duck had tasted—delivered to the *Blessed William* earlier that day. The little boy chewed at the stringy stalk until sticky sugar water dripped down his chin.

Heavy feet stomped the deck to Whitney's beat, and the whole ship seemed to vibrate with joy. Kitto broke into giggling himself as Carroll spun him around and around and the men threw shavings of sugarcane up at him, his eyes dancing in the lantern light.

More of the crew returned from their evening ashore in a merry state, and soon a circle of dancing men surrounded Kitto, Akin, and Duck. Akin had lost all trace of wariness. He gamboled about with the rest of them, despite the fresh stripes on his back from his most recent whipping. Ferris the Irishman had quick little feet, despite his years, and stepped into the middle of the circle to show off his fancy footwork, his head bobbing to the beat. Duck tried to imitate him, and the men howled and clapped and called for more.

Julius leaped about from shoulder to shoulder. The sailors liked to watch the little monkey, because when excited, Julius would scream that distinctive wail and whirl in backflips on the deck. Jenks found this terribly funny and began taking wagers on how many such flips Julius would do, when Kitto saw what was happening and put a stop to it.

Finally Whitney's strength gave out, and as if on cue the men tumbled to the deck. The throbbing in Kitto's shoulder had begun to spread into a deep ache that gave him the chills.

Isaac pointed toward Kitto. "I must set the boy's shoulder."

"Aye. It's going to hurt like the devil, lad," Peterson warned.

Isaac stood and beckoned Kitto to follow him. Duck rose to go too, but Jenks pulled him down and distracted him with shadow shapes he made with his hands from the light of the lantern. Kitto and Isaac made their way to the side of the ship, near the rail.

"Let me feel it," Isaac said, and took Kitto's sagging arm in his hands. His skilled fingers pressed into the flesh. Kitto gasped.

"It is good. I feel it. The arm has come out. I shall put it back." The nostrils of Isaac's broad nose flared.

"Sounds easy enough."

Isaac shook his head. "It hurts more going back in," he said.

"Oh, God!" Kitto whimpered. "Best get it done then." The men believed him to be brave now. He hoped he would not disappoint them by wailing in pain.

Isaac walked Kitto toward the rail and leaned him back against it so that his shoulder blades rested on the rail itself. Then he raised Kitto's wounded arm, set the boy's palm against his own shoulder, and held Kitto's elbow straight with the other hand.

"Take a deep breath," Isaac told him.

Kitto did, between gritted teeth, and as soon as he inhaled, Isaac let out a guttural grunt and Kitto felt a terrific thrusting toward him. He was pinned against the rail, his own bone being driven into his body. The pain was so intense that he gave out a wail despite himself, and saw flashes of white light behind his eyes. But then it was gone, or at least much receded. Kitto looked up at Isaac through watery eyes.

"Is it over?" His hands shook and his mouth was dry. Isaac rested a hand on his head.

"It is over. You will be sore, but it is over."

"Thank you, Isaac," Kitto said, extending his left hand as best he could.

"It is I who thank you," Isaac said, taking it. "You honor us all this night."

"It was not so much," Kitto said.

Isaac shook his head. He lifted his face toward the moon, which had broken through the clouds. His eyes glittered with a dignified look. "It is very much. There is more to you than any of us know, Christopher Quick. More even than you know."

Kitto, too, stared up at the crescent moon. He did not feel particularly brave or worthy of Isaac's praise. He felt lucky, though, and he could not remember having felt that before.

"Men respect courage, young Kitto," Isaac said, nodding toward the group. "You will find they do not forget it."

CHAPTER 24:

A Captain Defied

"Ferry approaching!"

Whitney pointed with the fiddle bow toward the approaching boat. Peterson held William's brass spyglass to his eye and chewed at the inside of his cheek.

"Is it the captain?" asked Carroll. Every ear hung on the answer.

"Aye," Peterson affirmed. "And Van, I believe. Look lively, lads! Whitney, put that noisemaker away, and someone mop up the deck! Hop to, hop to!" he fussed, scrambling about and urging the sluggish sailors to action like a mother hen.

"Jenks, the ladder! Put her over!" he shouted, and Jenks did as he was bid. Kitto and Duck stood at the rail and watched the approaching boat. The captain sat at the stern alone, Van at the bow, and the ferryman pulled away at the oars.

"Is that Daddy?" Duck asked hopefully. He stood at Kitto's elbow and leaned over the rail, picking his feet off the deck and kicking them in the air. It was late and Kitto had not the heart to explain it all.

"It is not. That is William Quick. He is the captain."

"Yes, I remember! He looks like Da." Duck nodded. "Enough to be his brother."

Kitto said nothing. Akin walked up next to him and looked out at the approaching boat.

"That is the captain," Kitto said, pointing. Akin nodded. He could tell from the sudden change in mood among the crew that something important was happening.

"Is he . . . a good man?" Akin asked. Kitto turned to him. He saw the concern in Akin's eyes.

"You will not be made a slave again, Akin. I promise. But the captain . . . he might well be angry. I was not supposed to go onto the ship to get Duck, here. He ordered me to stay behind, and I disobeyed him."

"You will be whipped?"

"No. He is not that kind of captain."

"It is good you will not be whipped. I will not allow it." Akin had seen men with tempers. Most could be treated like children and the bad temper would go away. Only occasionally could they be dangerous.

"Ahoy, Captain!" Peterson hailed the boat. Van raised a hand from the bow, but William did not return the greeting. Whitney cast over the rope ladder, and Kitto and the rest waited while the captain paid the ferryman. Van waited too, as it was the custom for the captain to be the first to disembark.

"Good to see you, sir!" Peterson called out cheerfully, stepping forward to help his captain from the ladder to

217

the deck, holding a lantern high to light his way. William wore a stony expression. He did not so much as nod toward Peterson, but stepped forward into the center of the circle of men and boys. He surveyed their faces. His eyes came to rest a moment on Akin and Duck, then on Kitto, where they lingered and seemed to convey some hidden import.

Van ascended the ladder behind the captain, and after casting a furtive glance in Kitto's direction, he pushed through the gathering, snatched Julius from a barrel top where he had perched, and disappeared below deck without a word. Kitto watched him go, feeling a vague sense of foreboding.

"This is not the orderly ship I had expected to return to, Peterson," Willam said, his eyes running along the spent shreds of sugarcane littering the deck.

"Aye, sir. We celebrated a bit on account of our success. Looky . . . we brought back the lad without a hitch!" Peterson had a pale, drawn look. He knew his captain well enough to know when he was in a fix.

"And another prize, I see," William said, nodding toward Akin. "You have not been so daft as to bring a slave onto my ship, have you, Peterson?"

"Of course not, sir! I never . . ."

"He is no *slave*! He is my friend," Duck declared, taking a step forward into the circle of lantern light. "I told Kitto he had to come with us." William turned slowly to face the little boy, his eyebrows arching.

"*You* told *Kitto*?"

"Yes, sir!" Duck continued. "Kitto undid my chains

and we were going to climb down into the boat, but I told him we had to take Abe here with us. But his name is really Akin." Kitto put a hand on Duck's shoulder and squeezed. Duck stopped talking.

"Is it true, Kitto? You left this ship and went out after your brother?"

"You see, sir," Peterson began, but William raised a hand to silence him. Uneasy looks passed around the circle.

Duck nodded vigorously. He wanted to brag on his brother. "Oh, did he ever, Captain! The rest of the men stayed on the rowboat, and Kitto came up all alone! He saved me! And we would have been fine, too, but for that sailor who nearly killed us all. But then Akin here got his pistol. . . ."

"Hush, Duck."

The captain nodded. He had a strange look that Duck mistook for a smile. "No, please! This is very enlightening. It is good to know what happens when I leave orders for my men."

"Sir, if you'd let me . . . ," Peterson tried again.

"Shut your mouth, Peterson! You will hear from me in my quarters!" William snapped.

"Captain, it was no one's fault but my own!" Kitto said, stepping forward.

"I have not asked you to speak!" William barked, raising a threatening finger. "I am the captain of this ship and my orders are to be carried out! When they are not, there are consequences."

"Peterson had no choice, Captain! I held him at

gunpoint!" Kitto fumed, but William's fury had mounted and he did not hear.

"Get this ship ready to sail! Swickers, any more time is lost, and it will be your head. Mr. Peterson, my quarters. Now!" he thundered.

"Aye, aye, sir," Peterson whimpered, but the captain had already stormed off.

"Van . . . Van! Come now! Don't act like you're sleeping!" Kitto prodded at the motionless figure curled up in the hammock. Julius popped his head up from where he huddled into his master's side. Van did not move. Duck stood at Kitto's heel.

"I am tired. Long night," Van answered, but his voice did not sound sleepy.

"Did you not see? My brother is here! He is safe now. I got him out myself," Kitto boasted. "Do you not want to hear the tale?"

"Maybe later, Kitto."

"What is wrong, Van? Something is amiss. I know it. Did you see that Mawbry character?"

"Aye, we did. The captain outplayed him too, and came home with most of the man's money, from what I could tell."

"Ha! That's terrific!" Kitto cheered, giving Van's shoulder a slap. Van did not flinch. "It is terrific, is it not?"

"It is."

"Why ever are you so glum, then? And why is the

captain so foul? I thought he might rip one of our heads off up there!"

"I have my reasons, and the captain has his own. Ask him if you like. As for me, I am tired, and I would appreciate you leaving me be. Your brother is here now, Kitto, prattle on with him." With that Van rolled over farther in his hammock and said no more.

Kitto stepped away, stinging with rejection.

"All right, Van. I'll leave you be. For now." He turned and trudged off. Duck followed.

Van craned his neck around to watch them go, then settled back in, lowering his head to the rolled-up blanket he used as a pillow. The room was dark and quiet but for the creaks of the timbers. Van squeezed his eyes shut, but of course that did not work. Holding Julius tight, he felt it coming.

The tears spilled, rolling along the bridge of his nose to drop through the holes in his rope hammock.

"Disrated," Peterson said flatly.

"No!"

"Aye. It is true. Disrated." He shook his head. "After all these years, too. Somebody else will be first mate."

Kitto stuck out a hand to steady himself against the wall.

"Did you tell him, Peterson, about me holding the pistol on you?"

"I tried. I got most of it out, but he didn't seem to hear a thing. I knew he would be upset, but . . . well, I never thought I would be disrated, not after all we've been through." Kitto thought Peterson might actually cry. He knew Peterson looked up to the captain with great admiration, loved him even. Kitto felt as if he had been kicked in the stomach.

"I shall go and talk to him," Kitto said.

Peterson shoved off the wall. His look hardened. "Stay out of it, Kitto. You've done me enough good as it is. You and your stunts." Kitto watched him stalk off down the passageway and disappear.

Kitto strode down the hallway. Duck ran to keep up.

"What's disrated mean, Kitto?" Duck ran into his brother's back when he came to a sudden stop at the captain's door.

"It means Peterson's not the first mate anymore, thanks to me. And I'm not having it!" Kitto rapped his knuckles on the captain's door beneath the pewter dolphin.

"Be gone!" the voice inside thundered.

"You stay here," Kitto whispered to Duck. He tried the latch. It gave and Kitto shoved hard. The door sprang inward and clattered against the wall. He stepped into the small room and left Duck standing in the hall.

William was sitting up in his bed, his back against the wall. He glared at Kitto but said nothing.

"You have a difficulty with following orders. Anyone ever tell you that?"

Kitto closed the door behind him. "My father did, once or twice."

"Your father is dead!"

The captain said it loud enough for Duck to hear, though that was not his intention. In the hall, Duck took the news like a sharp slap across the face. His mouth dropped open and tears filled his eyes. Duck was struck by the words. It could not be. *Father is dead?* He slumped to the floor and buried his head in his arms. Kitto stepped back into the hall.

"I am so sorry, Duck." Kitto patted his brother on the head, then closed the door and left him alone with his grief.

"I did not know he was there," William said, scowling even more darkly.

"You didn't know!" Kitto snarled. "Of course you didn't! I am beginning to think there is nothing of use you do know!" Kitto threw himself down on the chest across from the table.

"Keep it up, lad, and the back of my hand will find a way to close that mouth of yours yet," William said slowly. "Don't think being a cripple gets you special consideration around here."

Kitto drew a sharp breath, then returned the man's glare.

"Yes, my foot is bent. But at least you don't see me cowering in a corner whenever things get rough!"

"The devil take you," William retorted.

Kitto let out a heavy sigh. "Uncle. I do not understand. Why are you not celebrating with the rest of us? My brother, Duck, he's right out there in the hall! Free!"

William considered his answer a long time.

"I seem to have a weak spot for betrayal," William finally said, and tugged at his mustache.

Kitto shook his head. "I did not betray you," he protested. "I just did not want one of those men risking his life. . . ."

"That's not what I meant, but shame on you anyway for not following my orders." One of William's characteristic smirks managed to curl itself upon his lips. "Actually, I had a feeling you would do just that."

"Then what betrayal?"

William Quick gave a long sigh and stared at the wall. "I wonder if you know what it is like to hate a man, Kitto. I do. And one man I hate is Phillip Mawbry. We know each other from years back, he and I. I mentioned Madagascar to you? Well, Mawbry was there then, along with every other cutthroat who took to sea. My nemesis, that man. He always seemed to get the better of me, have a laugh in a tavern at my expense, woo the woman I fancied, secure a deal with some merchant with whom I had spoken first, or pull out an ace of spades just when I had him against the wall over the gaming table." William reached out absently with a finger and picked at a splinter in the woodwork. Kitto remained quiet.

"It was a game of Swiss Tarot tonight. You play with a deck like the one I showed you earlier. It was just Mawbry and me and some other fat slaver who could barely string two words together. It's not my game, Swiss Tarot, but that's what the fat man wanted and Mawbry fancies it. And of course I started losing soon after we had begun.

"Mawbry watched my wilting stack of silver. He saw I was near out. A small crowd had gathered. I had a lady on each arm—though not the finest sort, of course. So Mawbry states loudly that he thought he had better just turn in, seeing as how I had barely enough to pay the ferryman, and he hated to leave a bloke busted.

"I managed not to choke on my olive nor come across the table and grab his chicken neck," William said, the muscles in his jaw flexing. "The ladies all twittered. Hee-hee-hee!" William mocked in a falsetto, then stared evenly at Kitto. "I have a sore spot, lad, for twittering, when it is aimed in my direction.

"I knew it wasn't time yet to let Mawbry go back to his ship. Night had come—but only just—and I knew the mission to get your brother would not yet have begun."

"Whatever did you do?"

"Not a thing. I could come up with nothing. Mawbry began to collect his winnings, to drop them coin by coin into his little leather satchel. I looked on helplessly, watching our little plan unravel before my eyes and without a clue as to what to do, and then there was Van tugging at my elbow. *Van!*" William sneered when he said the name.

"Yes, you brought him with you," Kitto said, not liking the snide tone.

"I did. And it was a good thing too, as it turned out, wasn't it? Very good. 'Have you forgotten, Captain

Quick!' he says. 'You had me bring a few extra pieces on my person for just the sort of moment as this,' he says, and out he pulls a ratty little sack from somewhere loaded with silver and drops it down on the table."

"He held your money for you?"

"I am no fool!" William sat up and rapped his knuckles on the wall next to him. "I do not hand a sailor—any sailor—a bag full of silver and set him loose on shore!"

"Well, where did he get the money then?"

"Yes. Where? How? From whom, and for conducting what services? Those are the questions worth asking, and only one answer satisfies them all."

"And what answer is that?" Kitto asked reluctantly. He could see that this was turning against Van, and he was ready to defend his friend.

"Is it not obvious?" William sat up and pointed at Kitto. "Your *friend*, Augustus Van Arkel, is the rat."

CHAPTER 25:

The Defense of Van

"Van? The rat? Are you meaning? . . ."

"Yes, the rat! No one, not any sailor anyway, has a pocket full of silver, Kitto. Not one. Do you know how many bar tabs I had to clear back in New York to gather the crew? The barkeeps there let the sailors drink without paying, and the custom is the captain who wants to hire one must clear his tab before a man may leave. None of this crew has a farthing to his name. Your precious Van was no different."

"He was indebted to the barkeep?"

"No. Not that. But a strong wind would have blown him over back in New York. He was pale as death when I first saw him. I have gone days with near nothing to eat, and I know the look in a man's eyes. Van had it. When I first saw him across the tavern, he was snitching chips off the barkeep's own plate. Only someone pressed to the wall with hunger would risk getting brained for a chip or two."

"He might have been saving his money," Kitto said, not believing it himself.

"Oh, yes, that's it," William said sarcastically. "He just had not found something worth buying yet, is that it?" William sneered. "Not a chance. I was there. I know the look of desperation, and Van had it. And I hired him *that* night, and since then he has been handed but a few shillings once we left New York. Yet here he is tonight with a bag of silver all tied up neat and hidden in his trousers!"

Kitto looked at the sweating man before him, with his stained shirt and his face covered in uneven stubble. As much affection he had felt in the weeks past for this man, now he felt equal disgust.

"What did you say to him?" Kitto said in a low and menacing voice, so low and so menacing, in fact, that William's head snapped up, and he eyed Kitto the way a man might look at a wild bear he had stumbled upon in the woods.

"What do you mean?"

"What did you say to Van?"

"I should have said to him he would never set foot on my ship again, and for the life of me I don't know why I did not! So shocked I was, I suppose. I liked that little urchin too, Kitto. I may be the captain, but I am not above affection for a good hand. I said nothing to him! Nothing needed to be said. Just handed back his satchel of silver once my pile of winnings grew. He knew and I knew. How I managed to win Mawbry's money with my head swimming like that I'll never know."

"Tell me this, then, uncle. Van is the rat. He collects

a pile of silver for telling this Morris fellow where and when we sail. His life now depends on no one aboard this ship knowing of his betrayal. So why would he pull out that silver in order to help us, when it could only reveal his treachery? Why?" Kitto demanded.

William stared out from beneath heavy eyebrows. "I don't know. Guilt, perhaps. Maybe he suffers guilt for what he has done."

"You do not know. You have an idea, is all. You condemn Van, but you do not know!"

William sat up. "I am alive because I listen to what I hear and I act! I don't have to know. Van Arkel is the rat. He got that money by treachery, and once I know it for sure I will spill his blood, I will."

The resentment in Kitto bubbled up and spilled over. He stood up too quickly and the chest on which he sat slid back.

"I don't care how he got it! I don't care!" Kitto cried, his voice shrill.

"Then you are a fool!" William told him. "And keep your voice down."

"My brother is safe!" Kitto said accusingly. "He is safe, and without Van's actions he would be on a slave ship heading to the African coast! I do not need any further proof of Van's good character!"

William stood unsteadily and returned the pointing finger at Kitto. "Your brother is here. But let me assure you—your brother is not safe!"

Kitto thrust out his open hand and knocked the

captain squarely in the chest. William fell back on the bed and struggled to right himself, his face screwed up with outrage. Kitto's voice trembled as he spoke. "Tomorrow morning, when you wake up feeling sorry for yourself, you will reinstate Peterson as first mate."

"Over my dead body," William said, his eyes glowing like two cinders.

"You'll do it, sir, or I'll sing to every man jack on this ship what's on that island, and I don't mean just the spice!" he whispered.

William's eyes snapped to focus, his unsteadiness suddenly vanishing.

"What in God's name did you just say?" He sat up. Kitto retreated a step.

Kitto did not quite know that of which he spoke, but there had been clues enough to know that nutmeg was not the only thing on the island. The bit about the shoulders. There was something else, something that neither Father nor William had been ready to share. "You heard me. I'll tell them all. So in the unlikely chance you ever find the treasure again, you won't be able to dupe these sailors into taking less than their full share!"

Kitto stepped out of the room and slammed the door shut.

The *Blessed William* weighed anchor and set sail before the faintest haze of morning had made glow the island's rocky hilltops. The orders were given by Captain Quick, although he did not emerge again that morning from his cabin, not even to haunt the deck with his spyglass to see if their departure had been shadowed by any of the ships huddled in the lee of the great island. There had been, thankfully, no sign of Morris.

Kitto busied himself with comforting Duck and locating a hammock for Akin. He and Duck would share his own hammock, as there was plenty of room for the two of them, and Kitto could tell that his young brother was much shaken and needed what little mothering he could offer. Duck had taken the news of Father hard. After much sobbing, he had calmed to an uneasy and exhausted stupor. Kitto lifted him into the hammock, petted him on the head, and told him stories about what Father would be doing now in Heaven. The boy fell into a dream of his father cutting staves in the Garden of Eden.

As for Akin, Kitto had lost track of him and wandered about in the dark searching, until he saw him curled up asleep in the shadows beneath the mizzen-mast. When Kitto stooped to rouse him, a hushed voice called down from above.

"Leave him, Kitto." Kitto looked up and saw Isaac coming down from the rigging. The large man dropped soundlessly to the deck in his bare feet.

"I have a hammock for him below," Kitto said. "I thought he would be more comfortable."

Isaac smiled and nodded at Akin. "There is the best sleep he has had in years. The sleep of a free man. I know that sleep, and I know what it feels like to awaken from it and know how big and beautiful is the world. He will awaken with the sun this morning."

Kitto nodded. Isaac had a wonderfully deep voice and such an accent that when he spoke it was as if he were speaking in music. "Yes, of course you are right."

"I am not sure he will remember where he is when he wakes. My face will ease his worry more than yours." Isaac placed a hand on Kitto's shoulder. "Your uncle. He did for me many years ago what you have done today for Akin. It is a great thing. I know you have fought tonight with the captain."

Kitto nodded and hung his head.

"William is not a great man, but he has done great things. We have a saying, my people: 'Only the view separates the mountain and the valley.' Men are not born great, not kings even. Men become great by luck and by choice. Your uncle has angry spirits that ride upon his shoulders and whisper evil into his ears. But he does not always listen to them, even when you think it is all he hears."

Kitto looked out at the dark, rolling sea. "I fear that his greed will swallow him up . . . and my family and all of us with him."

Isaac cast an eye about. "It is dangerous to speak too openly. But you are right. That is one of his devils, this greed. But remember, too, that we are here. Five of us aboard this ship would be dead were it not for William.

"Not one man in a hundred could have led us through what he has. And as for greed"—Isaac looked out with disdain at the members of the crew strolling the decks—"it has eaten his soul no more than any man of this crew. They are in as much danger from their own selfishness as from his."

Later Kitto replayed the conversation in his head as he settled himself into the hammock beside Duck, tucking an arm underneath his brother and pulling him close. Duck nestled in and moaned slightly, then slipped off again to a dreamless sleep. Kitto lay on his back and clenched his eyes shut.

Dear Lord, help me to see and make real a safe ending to this voyage. . . .

Kitto awoke in the early morning hours when Van dropped out of his hammock and to the deck. The friends acknowledged each other with a nod, but said nothing so as not to awaken Duck.

It was well after sunrise before Duck stirred and opened his eyes. He and Kitto lay entangled from the night before, and Duck pushed away Kitto's arm. Everything around him seemed suddenly strange.

"Where am I?" Duck wailed, his voice taking on the sound of panic.

Kitto shook him. "It's all right, Duck. You're on the *Blessed William*. We came and fetched you yesterday. Do you remember?" Duck did, all in a rush. He lay back into the warmth of his brother's shoulder.

"Mummy?" Duck asked. Kitto took a moment to answer. He looked around at the room they were in and saw that three or four of the hammocks were still occupied.

"Come on, let's go on deck. We can talk there." Kitto helped his brother down, and the two of them went above. Kitto found a private spot near the stern, far enough from Peterson, who worked the tiller arm.

"Are you good and awake?" Kitto asked. Duck nodded, then yawned and wiped the grit from the corners of his eyes.

"Mum is still aboard the ship you started out on."

"With the bad men? The one with the spider on his eye, and the one without no nose?" Duck shuddered.

"Yes. But tell me, Duck. How came it that you and she ended up on that ship?"

The little boy told the story as best he could, about how the tattooed man had overtaken him and Mum in their carriage on the road to Truro, how the man had paid the driver to swap horses, and had taken the reins of the carriage. Duck told Kitto about his bright red teeth in great detail. He had nightmares about them still, and about that terrifying spider tattoo over the man's eye that seemed to writhe when the man spoke.

"Mum was acting so strange. The spider man got up in the carriage with me and then Mum got down onto the lane."

"What for?"

"He told her to. He said she was being rude."

"Rude?"

Duck nodded. "She looked so scared, Kitto. I ain't never seen Mum scared."

"Of course she was scared." Kitto had never seen it either. "So then what happened?"

"He let her back in and he rode us to the edge of the wharf. We got into a rowboat and he rowed us out to the ship. They put us in a little room below and closed the door. We waited a long time and I had to pee, but Mum said I had to hold it."

"And?"

"Then the other man opened the door. The one with the nose bit. He was all pale, like he was hurt or something."

"That's the captain. What did he do?" Kitto asked.

"He told Mum to cover my ears and she did. Then he said something to her. It must have been awful bad, Kitto, because she kept pressing harder and harder on my head until I thought it would burst!"

"He is a bad man, Duck. The worst."

"You don't have to tell me, Kitto. Mum called him Black Heart. Said to stay away from him. But it wasn't like I had any choice. They kept us cooped up in that little room almost the entire trip!" Duck remembered the crawling feeling he got being shut up in that tiny room and shuddered. "But sometimes that captain did stop in, and then Mum . . . she would change."

"What do you mean?" Kitto wondered.

"That was the scariest part, really. When the Black Heart came in, she would speak rudely to him, the way she did when a man brought a pistol into Father's shop. Real high and mighty. He would ask all sorts of questions about Father, something about pepper or something. . . ."

"Nutmeg?"

"Yes, that's it! Nutmeg!"

"Keep your voice down, Duck," Kitto warned. Peterson glared at the two of them and gave a small shake of his head.

"But, aren't these men friends?" Duck was confused.

"Yes, but still we have secrets to keep. Even from Van."

"Black Heart and this Captain Quick had secrets?" Duck asked. Kitto nodded. "That's what *he* said! And every time after he had left, Mum would just come apart, Kitto. She would shake and shake. Sometimes she even cried! Oh, God, Kitto! That was worse than those men, seeing Mum like that!" Duck had to take several deep breaths into the wind to right himself. Kitto squeezed his shoulder.

"She was sick with worry over you. It will be easier for her to be strong now that you are not on that ship with her."

"I don't know," Duck said, shaking his head. "When they took me away from her, Kitto, I could hear her screaming, and begging, and—"

Kitto gave Duck a sudden jostle.

"Don't let's speak of that," he said, and Duck could see Kitto had to take his own breaths now.

"And, Kitto . . ." He swallowed heavily, trying to steel himself. "Daddy? What . . . what happened?"

"Morris shot him, Duck. Black Heart, with the bad nose."

Elias Wheale could be a tough little fellow when he wanted to be. It did not work so well for him just then. His blue eyes filled with tears. Kitto leaned over and put his forehead against his brother's.

"I want Mummy."

Kitto nodded. "Me too."

CHAPTER 26:

Painful History

FOURTEEN DAYS SINCE CAPE VERDE

The days passed and turned into weeks. Duck took a liking to Van, and whatever funk Van had been in after his trip ashore with the captain wore off after a few days. In no time he and Duck were playing games of blindman's bluff whenever Duck could pull him away from Kitto and the barrels. Van introduced Duck properly to Julius and instructed him about keeping the monkey out of trouble. Van made it Duck's official duty to mind Julius when he and Kitto worked, and it made Duck feel quite the man to be given such a task.

Akin played with Duck some as well, but mostly he was off proving what a good sailor he could be. On hot days he would dash about with a bucket of water and a ladle for the men on duty, or he would holystone the decks without being asked. Captain Quick appreciated industry, and in no time he had taken in a tunic and trousers with needle and thread himself for Akin to wear. Soon Akin fell into Van's old job as cabin boy.

The excitement of Cape Verde seemed impossibly distant now that endless sea stretched out in all directions from the *Blessed William*. Routine settled in aboard the ship. Kitto and Van worked like dogs. They had completed just two thirds of the barrels despite their efforts. The winds had been to William's liking, and he told Kitto they would need the barrels for their task in perhaps not much more than a week. At this rate the job would not be finished, but another ten days or so beyond that and Kitto was confident he would be ready. He had never so fully occupied himself with a cooper's labors before. He had skilled hands, but they were not so powerful as Father's were, nor as tireless. In the mornings they ached something terrible, and he could barely hold a mallet.

"Oh, fiddle!" Kitto ran a finger down the stave he had just trimmed with the adze, holding it up at an angle.

"Such language, cooper," Van chided, nodding to the wall where Julius and Duck sat. "What's got you so vexed?" The tropical sun shone down into their little alcove through the grated opening. Van was shirtless and his tan body glowed in the light, his muscles flexing. Duck nibbled on a mango seed and tried to tease Julius with it.

Kitto sat down and leaned against the wall, pushing his own damp, curly locks from his forehead. "The devil occupies my thoughts today, I suppose."

"To blazes with him!"

"Very funny. And watch your mouth, will you," Kitto scolded, nodding toward Duck. "Van," Kitto began after a pause, "let me ask you. . . . Have you ever been on a ship during a battle?" Van took a few more passes with the saw, then let it rest in the groove.

"I have, Kitto. Thrice."

"Was it awful?"

"Once, yes. The other two times, just a few men got hurt before we managed to damage the other ship enough to make off."

"And the one time, then. What was it like?"

"Awful. Bloody. I cannot say as I remember it so well. I had only eight years at the time."

"Eight years old! What were you doing at sea? Was your father the captain?" Kitto asked before he realized how ridiculous a question it was. Van laughed a little too heartily.

"He was not."

"How did you come to be a sailor, then? You've told me so little about yourself," Kitto remarked.

"Ah, that." Van pulled over a finished barrel and took a seat. He had hoped Kitto had not noticed his silences. "My parents got sick and died when I was but a lad."

"Oh," was all Kitto said, but now Duck's curiosity was piqued.

"Did you have any brothers or sisters?" Duck piped up from the corner of the room.

Van stared at Duck a long moment before he

answered. It almost looked to Kitto as if he resented the question. "I had a sister."

"Is she still alive?"

"Duck!"

"What a thing to ask!" Van snapped. Duck looked up at him with wide eyes, too young to have known his impertinence. "Of course she is!"

Duck had grown up with an older brother who barked at him now and then, so he recovered quickly.

"She older or younger?"

"Younger."

"Like me?"

"Give it a rest, Duck," Kitto cautioned. He could sense what his brother could not in Van's reserve.

"More like Kitto. Little younger maybe."

"So where is she now?"

"Shut it, Duck!" Kitto protested.

Van glared at the little boy between strands of blond. "I do not quite know. She is with a family, or so I assume. Probably in Newport, Rhode Island, working as a scullery maid or some such. Mercy and I—"

"Mercy?" Kitto blurted. Hearing that name again caught him up.

"Not nice to interrupt, Kitto," Duck scolded. He knew that much about manners.

"Yes, what of it?"

Kitto's face flushed. "Nothing. Sorry, go on."

"Mercy and I got sent to a home for orphans after our parents died. She was very young then. About your age, Duck. And she was cute as a button. One day I woke up just as she was being taken off by some family. They had a carriage out front of the building. I ran out half naked to catch that carriage, but it was too fast for me." The muscles in Van's jaw flexed.

"They didn't even let you say good-bye?"

Van shook his head.

"And she is there still, with that family?" Duck pressed.

Van hung his head and dug his toe through the sawdust on the floor. "I know not."

Duck wanted to know more, but even he could see that to speak of it saddened Van. Duck tugged at Julius's ear. The monkey slapped at his hand. An awkward silence filled the workroom.

"Did they treat you well, at least, at the orphanage?" Kitto asked.

The older boy snorted as if humored but did not answer and was not amused.

Father Smythe. Van remembered him like it was yesterday. He had a big round nose that always glowed red, and a heavy cane he carried everywhere. Van remembered the skinny little boys in their bunks on either side of him, shivering beneath their blankets—but not from the cold. Father Smythe would walk up and down the dark dormitory, tapping his cane against the metal bed frames, leaving no one any peace.

Tap. Tap. Tap.

There are things a person can never forget.

"They did not treat us well," Van said finally.

"Oh. I am sorry."

"So what did you do about it?" Duck asked, warming up again. Kitto glared at him and shook his head. But Van seemed to like that question.

"What did I do?" Van smiled, and saw in his mind's eye Father Smythe's loose limbs splayed out at the bottom of the stairs, his cane arm pinned beneath his body. Kitto felt gooseflesh rise up his back and along his arms as he saw the sickening leer on Van's face.

"I got my revenge, that's what I did!" Van whispered.

He stood up abruptly from the barrel and returned to the saw. Kitto and Duck exchanged wide-eyed looks. Back and forth went Van's arm. Back and forth, back and forth.

The moment of tension passed. Duck flicked his wet mango seed across the sawdust, leaving a trail, to see if Julius would go after it. He did not. Kitto turned back to his own work. He tossed aside the rough stave he had just ruined. He found one that would work well from the stack when there was a thump of wood hitting the floor as Van made it through his bundle of staves.

Van spoke cheerily, as if they had just been speaking of eating pasties or skipping stones. "I ran away after that. Ended up at the docks in Newport, where I hid. Fell in the water once and nearly drowned, but a fisherman pulled me out."

"You did not know how to swim?"

"Nor do I still, same as most seamen," Van answered,

shaking his head and grinning. "The common wisdom is that it's better to go down quick with the ship and be done with it."

Kitto shook his head slowly. "What an absurd notion."

"Yes. But then it comes from the Royal Navy. Someday I will learn, perhaps. I ended up stowing away on a coal barque heading along the coast. Hid beneath a pile of sand ballast down in the hold."

"What did you eat?" Duck asked. He had grown hungry again and wondered whether Julius and he could filch another slice of bacon.

"Eat? At first I didn't. I managed to catch and kill a rat, which is no small triumph, but couldn't stomach the thought of biting into it. I got good at figuring who had a soft spot for a skinny stowaway. Found the cook to be such a man, so in the wee mornings I'd sneak up to the kitchen and he would load me up with biscuit, then I'd go back to my sand pile. Once we reached Boston, I jumped ship and ended up a powder monkey on a British frigate. We trolled up and down the American coast, from Boston to Jamaica, always on the lookout for pirates."

"And how did you end up with the captain here?"

"The Pirate Quick? I was in a tavern in New York. The captain of the frigate I was on had dumped me when some merchant's son wanted the job of cabin boy. There was no work to be had then in New York and it was hard going. I got word one day there was a notorious captain who had appeared out of thin air and was cobbling together a crew."

"William Quick is well known?"

"In some circles, though not well thought of. I had not heard of him, but the men in the tavern had. They said he had stolen some loot from the great Henry Morgan and his buccaneer band of cutthroats during the raid of Panama some years ago. All the tavern dogs had thought Quick was dead, but there he was, buying drinks for thirsty sailors."

Kitto tried not to betray his interest, but he nearly jumped when Van said the buccaneer's name.

"If that were true," Kitto mused, "why join Quick's crew? He being a thief and all."

Van shrugged. "I needed work. And money. And any man who can cheat a scoundrel as big as Henry Morgan and all his mates, too, and live to tell about it must have some luck running on his side."

"Luck!" Kitto laughed. "You should tell him that. He thinks himself the most unlucky person to have lived."

"Then maybe I chose captains poorly. But from the way he spoke to those huddled around him, he made it sound like we were to be retrieving some unknown and valuable cargo. He did not say much else. We all figured we knew what that cargo must be."

Kitto whispered, "The treasure from Panama?"

"Kitto! We're not supposed to talk about that!" Duck protested. Kitto had made as clear as he could to Duck the tangled web of their involvement in this whole adventure. "You said not even to Van!" Of course his brother had not fully understood the conversation.

"Oh, he did, did he? Keeping secrets from me, are you?" Van poked a finger at Kitto. Deep down he was glad. Secrets were a burden.

Kitto pushed his hand away. "Just trying not to let Duck here spill all the beans," he managed, and turned away. "But what was the cargo everyone thought it must be?"

"You would know better than I would, eh? He's your uncle," Van said, and squatted down next to Kitto. "All I know is I have hardly seen a shilling out of him yet."

Kitto eyed his friend for a moment, remembering the conversation he had had two weeks before with William.

"In Cape Verde," Kitto ventured, "where did you get that bag of money you gave to the captain?"

Van frowned. "He told you?" Kitto nodded. "He thinks the worst of me, doesn't he?"

"He wondered how you came by such a pile," Kitto admitted. Van was quiet a moment.

"I stole it," he said quickly.

"Stole it! From whom?"

"Back in Falmouth. I wandered around a ship-wright's yard. And when he was off talking with some rich merchant, I slipped in and stole his bag of tools, then found someone down at the docks who was will-ing to pay a pretty price for it." It was a lie, of course. Van had been to the yard, and had wandered about with the idea of making off with something of value, but his conscience, after already having taken such a beating during his meeting with Morris and Spider, would not allow him to go through with it.

"A shipwright!" Kitto exclaimed. "I know that man! He's a good fellow, too!" Kitto dropped his adze on the deck and pointed an accusing finger at Van. "I would not have expected such thievery of you, Van! I thought you were a better man than that." Kitto turned his back on his friend and made to return to his work. Van caught him by the arm and spun him around in his strong grip.

"Not so fast do you judge me, son of a cooper!" Van dropped his saw on the deck and stood. Kitto stood too, to his fullest height, toe-to-toe with the much larger boy. Julius and Duck stared up at them. Duck held the monkey tight to ward off a bout of backflips.

Van poked Kitto's chest with a finger.

"Not all of us have had the privileges you enjoy," he said, but there was a flustered look to Van that did not fit him well.

"Gives you no right to steal!" Kitto poked right back.

Even Duck knew enough of Van by now to know he was not the type to take a smaller boy poking him in the chest. Duck shot to his feet, catapulting Julius across the room. Julius somersaulted over a pile of staves and protested vigorously. Duck balled up his fists and held them before him like primed pistols.

"Maybe not," Van admitted, ignoring Duck. "But it

ain't for me I earn my money, and what I do with it matters more than some rich merchant's precious bags!"

"Merchant? You said you stole a shipwright's tools,"
Kitto said, his eyes narrowing.

Van turned his back to Kitto and picked a few scraps
from the floor. "Shipwright is what I meant," he said,
trying to cover his slip, but there was something unlikely
in his tone.

"A bag of silver for a bag of tools? Sounds like a *fine*
trade to me." Doubt filled Kitto's voice.

"It was a big bag. They were fine tools!" Van threw
back with a snarl.

Even Duck could see through Van's blunder. "He's
lying, Kitto," Duck said. Van stepped toward him menacingly, but Duck raised his little fists high.

"And what would be so valuable to obtain that it
would be worth casting aside your honor, Van?" Kitto
pursued. Van looked away and made as if he would not
reply. Kitto leaned in even closer. "Are you my friend or
not, Van? Tell me the truth."

A silence grew between them. Kitto felt himself
hanging on to it like a line thrown out to a drowning
man. "*Are* you my friend?" he whispered.

"I wish I were, Kitto." Van took a deep breath. "I
would like to be." He would indeed.

"Then explain yourself as a friend would."

Van grimaced and shook his head. "It is ridiculous,
my explanation. But it's true."

"Bet I know," Duck said. He reached down and

picked up Julius by the scruff and tossed him toward his master. Van cradled the monkey in his arms with as much tenderness as a new mother. "'Tis that sister of his."

"Shut it, Duck," Kitto said, but Van cast Duck a begrudging smile. Julius offered his chin, and Van scratched the tender flesh beneath with his finger.

"No, he's right. Go on, Duck-head."

"You need money to go get your sister back, and make a home with her," Duck explained. Van blinked and his mouth dropped open. Duck could tell he had hit the mark, and he smiled triumphantly. "You're going to go save her the way Kitto saved me!"

"Ha!" Van chuckled. "The brightest lad on this ship you are, Duck! You're right." His smile vanished. "I never even got to say good-bye to Mercy. After the carriage made off and I went back to the orphanage, Father Smythe gave me a whipping and told me she was off to live out her sorry life and I was to think of her as my sister no more."

"Bloody!" Duck spit, saying the worst word he knew. The older boys snickered.

"Duck, watch your tongue."

Van nodded. "Aye, you're right, though. Heartless that man was who took her from me. But he got his. Anyway, I got this mad notion then, that I would go off and make my fortune, then return for her and take her away. We could be a family again. So I've been scraping together every piece of silver I can get my hands on for years now but never seem able to earn more than just what keeps me alive. I ain't stopped trying, though."

Kitto did not know what to say, so he just stood quietly.

"Ridiculous, I know. She probably has long forgotten me. I was little more than Duck's age when the thought came to me, after all. But in all this time there's not been a better thought in my head."

"Sounds valiant to me," Kitto offered.

"Me too," Duck echoed.

"Thanks, mates. But every year it seems more unlikely. Yet now I've been working toward it so long I can't bear to let it go."

"But then what, Van? You can't take her on a ship, can you?" Duck asked.

Van smiled down at him. "Then no more ships for me. I'd take up a trade in Rhode Island. Coopering maybe." He gave Kitto a poke. Kitto prodded him back.

"You could be a cooper, Van. A good one even."

"If I had a better master to learn from." Van pushed again, and in a moment the two boys were play wrestling. They danced about the room a bit, until Kitto's foot turned beneath him and he fell against the wall. Van pulled him up and the two boys shared a warm smile. Duck felt a pang of jealousy at their friendship.

"What's her name again?" Duck asked.

"Mercy," Kitto answered.

"Ah. Well, don't you worry, Van. Mercy won't forget you. I am six and I'd never forget my Kitto." He meant it too. Kitto stepped over and tousled Duck's head roughly.

"I'm not sure I was such a good big brother when I had the chance," Van lamented.

"I doubt that," said Kitto. "But tell me. That money from Falmouth. If it had such value for you, why offer it to the captain over a game of cards he was already losing?"

Van looked over at Duck, then down at his feet. "I couldn't very well stand there with silver lining my pocket and watch the same thing happen to you, Kitto, as happened to me all those years ago."

Kitto's eyes misted over and his Adam's apple bobbed.

"You're a good man, Van." He held out his hand to shake. "I am in your debt."

Van suddenly startled and stepped away from Kitto's hand like it was a hot poker.

"No!" he shook his head. "Nobody owes anybody anything. Certainly not me." Van turned and fled the room before Kitto could see tears welling up in his eyes.

CHAPTER 27:

Prepare to Engage

EIGHTEEN DAYS SINCE CAPE VERDE

Kitto and Duck swung in their hammock fast asleep, Duck tucked in the crook of his brother's arm. The curl of the hammock had a way of wrapping the boys up in each other's limbs as the evening wore on, but the closeness suited Duck just fine. The embrace filled the loneliness Duck might have felt being separated from his mum. Kitto liked it too, though he would not admit it aloud.

This very morning, though, was to be the last hammock the brothers would share for some time.

On the deck above them, high atop the mainmast, Akin perched with a fistful of biscuit hoping to attract a morning seabird, but the *Blessed William* was too far at sea by now for that. There was just enough sunlight from the approaching dawn for a survey of the horizon line to the north.

"Sail ho!" Akin called in his loudest voice. "Sail

ho!" He fumbled for William's spyglass, which he carried with him, and held it up. The vessel he beheld outclassed the *Blessed William* in every criterion: size, speed, crew, guns. Every one of her square sails spread wide in the morning wind.

"Sail ho!" he shouted again. The voice might have been weak, but far below, the call set off a frenzy of activity. A bell rang. Peterson sprinted toward the stern, shouting orders, nearly flying down the stairs toward William's berth.

Without so much as a knock, Peterson charged in. To his surprise he found William strapping on a belt of pistols.

"Sail, Mr. Peterson. I heard the call. Bring up all hands, if you will. Run out the guns and prepare to engage."

"Aye, aye, Captain! I am afraid they've got the wind on us, sir." Peterson did not bother to describe the ship.

"Of course they have the wind! And they shall keep it. But we have the heart. And the first broadside will be ours. Spread the word the first man to cripple that ship gets steak with the captain from here to Barbados." William threw Peterson a smile and slapped his brass buckle.

"You are a fine first mate, Peterson. That foolishness of mine back in Cape Verde . . ."

"I appreciate you reinstating me, Captain."

"I would not want to sail any other way, man, than with you by my side."

Peterson beamed. "I will not disappoint you, Captain." And with that, Peterson charged out, hailing for all hands, never more eager to prove himself in battle.

Kitto sat up so fast in the hammock when he heard the call that Julius and Duck were flipped out of it. Fortunately for Duck, he fell upon Van, who was already pulling on his shirt. Julius was not so lucky and landed on his head.

"Stop your fooling, Duck!" Van said, pushing him away. "The moment has come! Come on, Kitto. Stay close to me and all will be well." He meant it more ways than one.

"But wait!" Kitto looked down into Duck's wide and unblinking eyes. "What do we do with Duck? If it is *the* ship, it's the very one who just sold him off into slavery!"

Duck's jaw set. "They won't take me alive!" he shouted, raising his tiny fists in the air.

Van absently gave Duck's head a shove, and Duck sat heavily on the deck, scowling.

"Just let me fight!" Duck said. Van scowled in furious thought.

"Wait!" Kitto's face brightened. "They don't know!"

"What don't they know?" asked Van.

"Captain Morris does not know we have Duck. Probably they don't, anyway. We could hide him. Yes! We could put him in a barrel!" Kitto shouted. Van nodded enthusiastically.

"Brilliant!"

"I ain't getting in any barrel," Duck said, shaking his

head. "I don't even like barrels." Duck had been confined enough to small spaces aboard the first ship; he was not going to choose even smaller quarters now.

"It just might work," Van continued. "Down in the hold. Near the back so he's not discovered when they take the ship."

"Take the ship!" Kitto protested angrily. "How about a little confidence, Van Arkel?"

"Whatever outcome then."

"I said I ain't getting in no barrel!" Duck did not like the dark. Not one bit.

Akin ran in, breathless. "I saw a ship and I am ready to fight!" His eyes were wild and determined, his mouth set in a snarl. He had high cheekbones and a narrow chin he held up proudly. Even after the comparatively rich meals aboard the *Blessed William*, a strong wind could knock him down.

"We heard. Come on, Akin," Van said. "You and I'll fetch food for Duck. We're going to stow him. Kitto, get him to the hold and pick out a barrel. We've got to hurry!"

Kitto snatched Duck by the hand and ran. Duck grabbed Julius in time and tucked the monkey beneath his arm. He had little trouble keeping up with his older brother's awkward gait, but still Duck dragged his heels. He had seen enough of a ship's hold.

"Kitto! *Kitto!*" Duck protested as he ran. "It will be dark down there! I am afraid of the dark!" Kitto ignored him as he charged into the carpentry workshop and pulled down a barrel they had just finished. He pried up the round lid, then flipped it over. He began to hammer a scrap to its underside that Duck could use to hold the lid down from the inside.

"It's a tight fit, the lid, but something to keep it down might help," Kitto said as his hands worked feverishly.

"I am scared!" Above them they could hear the strident shouts of the sailors making ready. The decks above thundered with the footfalls.

Kitto stopped working and leaned down to Duck. "Do you remember? The story of the rabbit, the one where he hides beneath the farmer's shed?" It was a story that Sarah used to tell; the cornered creature is forced to hide in the dark with the spiders and is terribly afraid until he discovers that if he is quiet enough and speaks softly, the dark talks back to him, and he learns it is not so frightening after all.

Duck nodded. "'Tis a *stupid* story, Kitto."

"Hush. You make friends with the dark. And remember like Rabbit to whisper." Kitto finished hammering. He grabbed a stick of charcoal he used to make tally marks on the wall for each completed barrel, and he drew an arch with two spots above it on the barrel's side.

"A drawing of a smiley face!"

"That's so I can tell which one you're in."

Kitto drew another arch with two dots above on the lid. "He doesn't look too happy, does he? Someone might have a look inside. Now in you go, Duck. Just to try it!"

Duck felt slightly better now with the story in his head—even if it was a daft little morality tale—so he sprang into the barrel and hunkered down, keeping Julius tucked in his arm. There was plenty of room for the two of them, but poor Julius gave out a shriek. Moments later the monkey retreated to the barrel lip, looking down on Duck accusingly.

"Come on, Julius!" Duck pleaded.

"I doubt he'll go in for that, Duck. But don't worry," Van said, returning. "I'll have him check in on you. Bring you bacon if you're still in there tomorrow morn."

Akin stepped forward and lowered a bag of biscuit and a few strips of salt pork.

"You be a good boy. We'll take care of you," he said.

"But I don't like biscuit!"

"Shut up, Ducky!"

"And I need to relieve myself!" Duck wailed, though he didn't really.

"Hop out now and we'll get you to the hold," Kitto said. Duck climbed out, then Van and Akin each grabbed an end of the barrel and hustled down the corridor. Kitto followed behind with Duck, a chisel in one hand. Going down another dark, narrow stairwell was like being swallowed up by a mighty sea serpent to poor Duck.

"Couldn't I just hide on deck, wrapped in a sail, maybe?" he suggested meekly, but Kitto did not heed. *"Please!"*

They trod carefully now through the darkness. Van and Kitto had been in the hold countless times and knew its many nooks and crannies. They found an out-of-the-way corner and set the barrel on its end along with some others. Using some spare cordage, Van lashed it to the other barrels so that it would not roll with the ship.

"Take my hand and walk this way," Kitto instructed, and he led Duck back down the narrow lane between the ship's hull and the stacked barrels. "Feel this barrel here? It's got more salt pork. I'll put a notch in the top so you'll know which it is."

"I don't like salt pork."

"Soon you will like it even less," Van called to him.

Kitto made the notch and pried up the lid carefully so that it could still be set firmly in the top. He showed this to Duck, and warned him to keep the lid down or the rats would get to it before he did.

"Rats?"

"Of course. They are friends with the rabbits," Kitto said, referring to the story.

"Oh."

Kitto led Duck farther along the passage. "These barrels here? These big ones? There is water in them. You can get at it down here." He guided Duck's hands and showed his brother how to work the tap.

"Now you could last for weeks."

"Weeks!" Duck nearly swooned at the thought.

"It won't be that long," Kitto assured him. "Just saying you could." Kitto led the way back to Akin and Van.

"We need to get up there, Kitto," Van said gravely.

"In you go, Duck!" Kitto gave him a quick hug. Duck clung to him.

"When do I come out?"

"I'll get you," Kitto said. "Otherwise you stay in here and come out only for food or to make your water."

"And where do I do that?" Kitto and Van conferred. Van gave him instructions to another remote corner of the hold, where the sloshing bilge water was a few inches deep.

"But I'll go batty if I stay in there all day!"

"Better to be batty than booty," Van said sternly. Duck looked ill as he clambered into the barrel. Akin dropped the dry goods down on Duck. The reek of salt pork made his eyes water.

"You too, Julius!" Van dropped the protesting monkey down into Duck's lap. "Keep tight hold of him!" Van instructed. Duck clutched Julius. "Let him out afterward or he'll scream his bloody head off."

"Don't get shot! Not any of you!" Duck called up as Kitto set the lid down and Duck's world went utterly black. "And don't forget us down here!" he shouted, his voice cracking.

"Come on!" Duck heard Van say, and the boys were gone.

Kitto trundled after Van and Akin, a sickening taste in his mouth that he knew to be fear.

It'll be all right, he told himself. *It will be all right.* The words did little to quell his fears as he hustled to keep up.

Up on the main deck, men shouted and hurried in all directions. Sunlight streamed through the open hatches, and the deep rustle of heavy chains and squeaky iron wheels filled the air. Timbers shuddered as the guns were run forward on their trucks so that their ends protruded out from the side of the ship.

Kitto struggled to keep up with Van and Akin as they charged past the teams of three men at each cannon. They bounded up more stairs and to the stern quarterdeck, where they found Carroll standing at attention, awaiting word from his captain, who stood at the very stern of the ship, spyglass in hand. Whatever ill look William had awoken with had left him now. He stood proud and captainlike, a pair of polished black pistols hanging from his bandolier. The boys turned to look astern. The dark ship was drawing nearer. Kitto could see the throng of men crowded at the oncoming ship's rail. Each wore red on his head.

"Is that some kind of uniform, the red?" he whispered to Van. Van gulped.

"It's so they don't hack each other to pieces once the fighting starts and we're all mixed together." Van's hand automatically reached down to pat a bundle concealed in the pocket of his pants. He would not put on his head scarf until the last possible moment.

"They plan to board us, Captain!" Carroll announced.

William snapped down the spyglass. "Peterson!" he called. Amidships the first mate turned. "You and the quartermaster get cutlasses to every man jack. Port-side gunners, take up small arms and come to the upper deck. Starboard side, prepare for broadside!"

"Aye, aye, Captain!" Peterson returned. He ran up and handed a ring of keys to Carroll.

"You boys come with me!" Carroll barked at them.

"Hit the deck! Get down!" William suddenly screamed, and then everyone was screaming it at once. Kitto and Akin were so startled by the cry that each went rigid. Van tackled Kitto and hooked Akin about the neck, bringing them both down.

In the next instant there was a harrowing roar as the air around them ruptured in explosion: splintering wood, the ringing and pinging of brass being struck by lead shot, the ripping of sails, the whistling past of shot thrown too high.

An anguished scream cut through the air. It was Baker, a balding Scottish fellow who had just begun climbing the mizzenmast to act as a sharpshooter when William made his call. His body struck the deck just a few feet away from the boys, landing heavily in a tangle of arms and legs and blood. The man landed in such a way that his head was turned directly toward Kitto, his blue eyes open, and it seemed to Kitto that for a moment they gazed at each other in shocked surprise. No one rushed to Baker's aid; it was obvious he needed none. Kitto squeezed his eyes shut and gritted his teeth and felt a fear so elemental, so tangible, it was like the walls of his chest were closing in on his heart.

His eyes popped back open to see William looking

at him, his face too just an inch from the deck. Some shipmasters—usually those with a history in the Royal Navy—resist taking cover when their decks are raked with grapeshot. William Quick had no such qualms.

An absurd, beaming smile lit his face. "A bit slow following my orders, nephew!" the captain shouted. "Bad habits will be the death of you!"

"Get off me, will you, Van?" Kitto managed to say, realizing it was Van's weight that made it difficult to take a breath.

Van stood and dragged Kitto to his feet.

"Akin, stay here to be my messenger," William instructed, the spyglass again raised. "You boys be off, and, Kitto, do learn how to duck a bit faster." A broad grin spread across William's face. Life made sense to him when he was in a fight.

"Come on, then! Follow Carroll!" Van shouted. He pushed Kitto toward the waist of the ship. Kitto's foot caught and he nearly stumbled down the stairs after the quartermaster, who was several steps ahead, his booming voice ringing loudly.

"Starboard gunners, prepare for broadside! All other hands, it's cutlasses and fists! They've a will to board us, the swine!" the stocky man bellowed.

"Huzzah!" A bellicose, throaty cheer rose up from the gun decks below. They ran down the stairs, and Kitto found himself staring into the contorted faces of the port-side gunners, rushing forward to get their cutlasses. Their eyes were alight with bloodthirst. To Kitto it seemed as if not a one felt the raw fear that clung to his own heart. Van pulled him aft, toward a small cabinet door barred with a lock. Carroll fumbled with Peterson's keys.

The quartermaster ejected an oath when the keys dropped to the deck, but he found the right one soon enough and swung the doors wide. Van stepped forward and grabbed two cutlasses in each hand from where they stood in a stack and, turning, pushed them past Kitto toward the grasping hands of the men.

Another explosion rang out above them, and another scream. The ship shuddered slightly.

"Full to starboard. Prepare to fire!" the cry resounded throughout the gun deck.

Van yelled to Kitto above the din. "You grab hold the pistols, the muskets! Give them to the men!" The quartermaster had opened the next cabinet down, and in it were a few dozen pistols with the classic stubby shaft that curved to a stout handle, and about half as many muskets. All were loaded with powder and shot. Kitto stepped toward the cabinet, grabbed two pistols, and turned. These were snatched from his hands instantly by the press of bodies. He turned and grabbed two more.

In a few moments the men had dispersed, making for the deck above. Van stood before Kitto with an armload of cutlasses. They felt the ship list beneath them as Peterson heaved the rudder and the ship turned.

"Our broadside's about to give 'em a real fight!" Van said. "We got the best gunners—" His words were drowned out in a high whistle and then a crash as the enemy ship's guns struck again.

"Blazes, they are fast!" Van said worriedly. *Too fast*, he thought. There was no one who dreaded this confrontation any more than did Van, and now that it had come to a head, he could not help hoping that some lucky shot might turn the battle for the *Blessed William*.

On deck, William pushed up from the deck for the second time. Beneath him his ship turned so that the length of its starboard side slowly opened up toward the enemy. He waited, patiently, like a man who had waited a thousand years and saw no need for hurry, his nostrils flared, his eyes unblinking. There were just six guns of any size on the starboard side. The *Blessed William* had not a shot to waste.

One shot in Hell, William prayed. *By God, I deserve that. Sweet Jesus and Desmond Jenks, the finest shot, if you please!*

It is not impossible for a smaller vessel to cripple a larger one, at least enough to escape. It had been done before, though the odds? William refused to calculate them.

Something at the approaching bow caught his eye. Disbelieving, he held up the spyglass and peered through it. He pulled it down again; the world-be-lost look on his face vanished.

"Fetch the cooper!" he croaked. "Fetch me Kitto, now!" Akin ran off.

"Captain!" Simmons popped his head up through

a hatch from the deck below. "The gunners await your command, sir!" The ship's quick pivot had been completed. So fast had it been that now the sails sloughed off and went into irons. There was no backup plan, no secondary strategy William would put into effect should his gunners fail at their task.

"Hold your fire until my call, Simmons!" the captain returned, his voice slightly shrill. William felt an eerie sense of unreality, like a nightmare, taking shape before him.

Below deck, Van helped himself to a pistol. Kitto held a cutlass, turning it in his hands. How would he help repel a boarding party?

"Kitto! Kitto!" Akin ran headlong into him and knocked him against the cabinet door. "The captain! He says come! You come now!" Van and Kitto exchanged worried looks.

"Good luck, mate," Van said, and held out his hand. Kitto was still beyond words at that moment, so he just took Van's hand and they shook. Akin pulled at his shirt, and he followed him up the stairs. Van watched him go.

Good luck, mate. His own words stung in his ears.

Akin led Kitto by the hand to where William stood, like a statue now, the spyglass pinned to his eye though the distance had narrowed enough to make it unnecessary. Kitto looked outward toward the ship approaching, and what he thought he saw brought his heart to his throat.

He reached up and snatched the spyglass away from William and lifted the glass to his eye.

It was not the brigantine's trim lines, nor the crimson scarves of the throng that arrested him. At the bow of the ship just this side of the boom, there stood a man in an oversize hat, a sickly smile of red teeth like a wound across his face, and a black mark over one eye. He worked a coil of rope in his hands around the rail and through the tied arms of his captive, then tied it off tightly. He waved toward the *Blessed William*, his hat in his hand, like a man might greet his family at the docks as he arrives home from a pleasant voyage.

The deck swayed beneath Kitto's feet as the ship rolled on the crest of a wave, and he tried desperately to keep the spyglass trained on the figure being tied to the rail. An eerie silence prevailed.

"The broadside is ready, sir!" Simmons insisted, his head peeking up again. "Do I have permission to commence firing? Sir!"

Silence answered the gunner's mate. "Captain, sir, shall I commence firing?" he called again.

"I bloody well heard you, Simmons!" William barked at him, then turned again to Kitto.

It was of course Sarah Wheale at the bow. The only mother Kitto had ever known.

CHAPTER 28:

Ringing of Steel

Sarah stood tall, bless her heart. She neither quailed nor struggled at the rope that bound her. There was a set look of defiance on her face, but through the glass Kitto saw too the same tinge of something Duck had witnessed that day a few weeks earlier on the road to Truro. The dress she wore—the same she had left home in—was soiled, and her hair was mussed as if she had slept in a barn. At the angle the *Port Royal* approached, Sarah stood directly in the path of the broadside. On the gun deck below, the shot was loaded; the men had already lit the strands of slow match to be plunged into the hole at the base of the cannon, setting off the chain reaction that would send deadly orbs of iron hurtling.

"I must fire upon her," William said quietly, though without conviction.

"You cannot fire!" Kitto protested, but he did not have to say it. He saw the look of uncertainty and confusion in William's face, an expression he would not have thought possible on the man.

"I must fire, and with Sarah there, I cannot fire.

I have lost the wind. We have no chance. It is over," William said. The voice was flat, without emotion. William stared blankly at the oncoming ship, unbelieving. All those years rotting in a Spanish prison, telling the rats stories of how one day he would break free and make himself a fantastically rich man. Had he really ever believed those stories? Had he not always known it would come to an end like this?

The men on deck stood at the rail, cutlasses and pistols raised, all eyes on their captain.

The weight of Kitto's fear lifted at the sight of Sarah. An elemental anger began to brew now inside of him. Kitto squeezed the cutlass in his hand so hard it quivered with the beat of his pulse. He reared back with it and slapped the flat of the blade against William's chest. William's trance was broken and he flashed bewildered eyes down at Kitto.

"We must fight. We *can* still fight!" Kitto shouted, holding the tip of his sword at William's chest. "*She* would fight!" He pointed across the water. Kitto's eyes blazed and his face had turned so crimson it was nearly purple. All eyes on deck were on the captain now and this odd but compelling boy. Truth be told, even the hardiest fighters aboard the *Blessed William* had begun to lose courage at the sight of the overwhelming force rapidly approaching. But to see a mere boy slap his sword against the captain's chest and challenge his courage—it gave heart to every man aboard.

"Huzzah!" called out Swickers in his hoarse voice,

and the decks erupted in a chorus of cheers. William looked evenly at Kitto and nodded slowly. Jenks, who had rushed up from below, turned his backside to the oncoming vessel, dropped his pants, and propped his pasty hindquarters onto the starboard rail.

"Come and get a piece of England's finest!" he crowed, and the cheers rose up all the louder.

William Quick snapped back to form. He pointed to the gunner's mate whose head floated in the hatchway.

"Mr. Simmons, hold fire! Summon all hands to the deck. Prepare to repel boarders!"

Within seconds nearly thirty men stood on deck, cutlasses glinting in the afternoon sun. Kitto searched for Van but could see him nowhere.

"Sharpshooters, have at them!" William called upward. Instantly, from both ships, the crackle of musket fire broke out. Above their heads four seamen perched in the lines; thin columns of smoke spit out from the yards and were quickly carried off by the wind. The men of the other ship did the same, firing steadily and dropping spent weapons down to men below who reloaded and handed them back up. Kitto's eyes were trained on Sarah. Musket shot whistled past her on every side. Spider cowered behind her for cover.

"Don't hit the woman!" Kitto shouted, but his voice was drowned out in the explosions.

A man with a musket fell screaming from high up in the rigging of the approaching ship, his wail audible to those on the *Blessed William*. William bellowed out enthusiastically. More shots were heard, and two men from his own ship, standing at the rails, were knocked backward into the men behind them, who picked them up and dragged the bodies out of the way.

Kitto surveyed the crowds poised at the rail of each ship, the Jamaican vessel approaching fast. Two dozen on the one side, easily twice as many on the other. The closer the other ship drew, the more time there was for the renewed zeal to diminish among the *Blessed William*'s crew, yet it did not. Some men were nearly bursting at the rail with enthusiasm, so eager to take up arms against an unknown and overwhelming enemy. Ferris clenched a dirk in his teeth, a notched cutlass in one hand and a pistol in the other, nodding furiously. Every seaman carried a weapon in each hand, a blade of some type, and then either a pistol or an ax, or grappling hook, a gaff used for bringing in large fish, anything they could get their hands on that could be used to deadly effect.

Kitto looked again but could not find Van in the crowd; Akin had left William's side to stand at the back of the group with a cutlass and a determined but terrified look.

Where is Van?

Still the ship came. Kitto could make out the worn and dirty faces of the men on the other ship, and at the stern, near the helmsman, his eyes met with those of the noseless man, John Morris, where he stood unmoving at the tiller. The man looked right at Kitto with a malevolent stare of satisfaction. He called out an order, and two men at the rail upturned the buckets they carried. A stream of chopped up fish innards, bones, and bloody chunks cascaded down into the water.

"For the sharks," William said. "John Morris always liked the sharks. . . ."

Kitto looked forward again and found his eyes meeting Sarah's, who had now caught sight of him on deck. Her stolid features melted into a mask of agony and terror.

"Kitto! Kitto! Save yourself, Kitto! They'll only kill you!" Sarah wailed, her shrill voice cutting across the gap between the ships. Kitto's heart leaped. Spider, who had taken cover behind her from the sharpshooters, cuffed her hard on the back of the head with the butt of his pistol. Sarah fell sidelong into the rail, exposing Spider. A musket ball whistled by him and he hit the deck. Kitto felt a terrific surge of rage; he stole a look up at William and saw the captain with pistol raised, his jaw clenched so tight his cheeks shook.

"Do not fire, sir!" Kitto squeaked. "You might hit her!"

A call sounded from the approaching ship. The sails were quickly reefed, momentum carrying the ship the last several lengths. A half dozen men on the other ship dangled black grappling hooks from each hand, awaiting the moment to throw them at the *William* and lock the two ships together until the battle had been completed.

"Mr. Simmons!" William barked over the snap of gunfire.

"Sir!" the man replied. William motioned for him to come closer.

"Once their bow passes our stern, send a round of grape to clear their decks. Nothing forward of the mainmast, mind you. That woman is not to be touched!"

Simmons smiled and bounded off, the bow of the approaching ship coming on now. More shots rang out. One musket ball whistled as it passed between Kitto and William, then walloped into the mizzenmast behind them.

"Isaac! You and the cooper get that woman to safety! Fitzpatrick, Peterson, Williams, you'll stay by my side. We'll get below their ship and light their magazine."

"Their magazine! But, Captain, even if we could do it, it'd blow both our ships!" Peterson answered shrilly. The magazine was a small room usually in the lower deck of a ship that housed the lion's share of gunpowder to be found aboard. A ship like the *Port Royal* carried enough gunpowder to destroy the entire ship and everything in its immediate vicinity.

"Then get your crew to cut us free of that ship when they tie us together! They will take no prisoners!" William barked. "None but me."

The bow of the other ship crossed their own stern. Though the rails of the approaching vessel were still several feet off, a handful of berserk fighting men leaped across and onto the *Blessed William*, throwing themselves into the men awaiting them. Barbaric howls and the ringing of steel against steel immediately filled the air. The awaiting round of grapeshot burst forth, but the other ship, riding slightly higher on the crest of the wave, took most of the round to her side. The lazy arcs of a dozen grappling hooks curved through the air, hitting the *Blessed William*'s deck and dragging along until they found purchase. Several hooks fell beyond the mass of men at the *Blessed William's* rail. One sharpened tine hooked Whitney by the ankle as it was swept along the deck. He fell backward, and he screamed as the hook snagged his heel and dragged him toward the rail. Impaled and screaming, Whitney flailed. Above him, Ferris stood with his cutlass raised, but could not swing at the rope for fear of cutting off his mate's leg.

With a sickening crunch the two ships crashed together. Timbers splintered. Gunfire burst from all directions, and a cloud of smoke drifted before Kitto's unblinking eyes. William bellowed orders, but Kitto could not hear a word. The chaos set his untrained mind reeling. Men hacked wildly at each other. William dashed away into the fray, then leaped over the rail and onto the enemy ship, three or four men following him. Kitto saw a hatch open on the other ship. Men began streaming out of it, though the first four or five were cut down by the staccato fire of the sharpshooters in the ratlines.

Kitto felt a strange heaving inside him. He turned his head and gagged, vomit splashing against the decks and his own boots. He spit and turned again toward the melee.

Kitto ran. He ran toward the fighting crowd of men, toward where the rails stood close enough that he could jump. A movement to his side made him turn. There, a wild-eyed bearded man came running at him waving a freshly reddened cutlass.

"Ahhhh!" The man ran screaming at Kitto, raising his curved sword over his head. Kitto rushed straight at him, then ducked to his knees at the last moment, swinging his own cutlass for all he was worth. He heard a whiffling in the air where the man's blow overshot its mark and arched over his head. His own blade caught the man in the right leg, just above the knee. The man's momentum carried him over Kitto. Kitto scrambled to his feet and ran again toward the rail.

He leaped. The dark blue-gray of the water beneath him passed by in slow motion, and for a moment Kitto feared that he would not clear the opposing rail. But then he was at it, his feet striking the top of the rail, his body pitching forward into the back of one of the other ship's men. He fell to the deck hard, as did the other man. The wind knocked out of him, Kitto pulled himself unsteadily to his feet and swept his hand about for the cutlass he had dropped. He looked up to see a snarling Isaac hack down at the man Kitto had just knocked over. Kitto fought down another wave of sickness as the blood rushed out over the bleached deck boards. Isaac pointed to Kitto's cutlass a few feet away. The giant man turned and engaged with two men who rushed at him.

Kitto lunged for the weapon and began running for

the bow, dodging small groups of entangled fighters. There he found Sarah hunched over the rail alone.

"Mother! It's me! I am here!" He pulled her arm, but she did not turn. Kitto could see the hair matted with blood at the back of her head. For an awful moment he thought her dead, but then Sarah lifted her head. Kitto hacked twice with his cutlass, severing the cords that bound her.

"Can you walk, Mum? We must hurry!"

"Kitto!" she moaned in a weak voice. "Oh, Kitto. Sweet boy, you're alive! But Elias! They have taken my baby." She fell into Kitto. Kitto kneeled with her and lifted Sarah's face by the chin.

"No, Mum! I have rescued him! He is hidden aboard our ship. But we must hurry!" Sarah's head jerked free.

"Yes! It is true! But if we're not off this ship in a moment, all will be lost!" he said, remembering William's intention to blow the ship and how Peterson had paled at the notion. Kitto put Sarah's arm over his shoulder, supporting her with one hand and leaving his sword hand free to swing. They stumbled their way slowly across the heaving deck, the two ships caught in a series of rolling waves. Only at the center of the ships did the two vessels ride close enough that he could lead Sarah over to the *William*, but the action was too frenzied there to consider it. Kitto scanned the deck for some clue, his eyes traveling over the tangle of men. Then he saw it. At the port-side stern of the ship hung a small rowboat. It hung in the air several feet above the deck, made fast by ropes. Kitto rushed toward it, dragging Sarah with him.

It was a small boat that was made ready to be used in the fight but now stood ignored. Kitto leaned Sarah against the rail and began hacking blindly with the cutlass at the ropes securing the boat to the mizzen yard.

"No, Kitto!" Sarah shouted, her head clearing. "Lower it!" Kitto saw where she pointed; a line securing the boat passed through a block and tackle at a lower spar and was tied off near the deck. He dropped his cutlass and rushed to work the knot, cursing his clumsy fingers. Behind him men yelled out in frenzy and in pain. The knot gave and without warning the rope zipped through the block and the boat plummeted. It banged into the rail as it fell but cleared it and continued to fall. One of the boat's oars hooked the rail as it passed and ripped clean out of its oarlock, spinning silently out of sight. The rope continued to whiz, then went slack when the boat hit the water with a hollow wallop. Kitto tied off the line in a dash.

Sarah stepped up to the rope and looked at the boat far down in the water. It might not seem so far from the deck of a ship to the surface, but when one faced the prospect of reaching it by sliding down a frayed length of hemp, it seemed a great distance indeed.

"Can you manage it?" Kitto began to ask her, but before the words were out of his mouth, the stalwart woman stepped onto the rail, wrapped her limbs about the rope, and shot out of sight.

CHAPTER 29:

Shark!

Kitto leaned over the edge. Sarah had landed awkwardly, but righted herself quickly in the boat and waved for Kitto to follow. He retrieved his cutlass, stepped up onto the rail, and took hold of the rope with both hands. The ship reared up suddenly on a rising wave and his stomach went to his throat, but he jumped and wrapped his feet about the line. He looped his sword arm around it so that the rope rested against his sleeve, then let gravity take its course.

The heaving boat caught him hard and he fell into it next to Sarah, who struggled to orient the single oar. Kitto found his feet and managed to remove the oar from its oarlock. The little vessel rose again on a wave, and Sarah fell to the bottom of the boat, her hand going to the wound on her head.

"Stay down, Mum! I shall take us about."

With quick work of the cutlass, Kitto cut the rowboat free, then took the oar in hand and leaned over the bow to attempt to paddle. The enemy ship's hull loomed over them, massive like a towering black wall.

As Kitto reached forward into the water, the bow of the boat kept rising on the swells and knocking him in the chin. He leaned out farther still, and felt Sarah take hold of him by the ankles. Kitto pulled at the water for all he was worth with the single oar, and slowly the boat edged toward the stern.

With great effort, they rounded the stern, the sounds of the fighting returning in full volume. Several more strokes carried them out into the open space between the ships. Kitto did not turn towards the chaos of violence boiling above him but kept reaching forward, frantically pulling the water.

Swift motion attracted his eye and he turned. Men with swords raised high jumped from one vessel to the next. A shot was fired and a man aboard the *William* who had been engaged in a death struggle at the rail with another seaman was propelled backward over the rail, spinning crazily in the air as he fell, then crashing into the water between the two ships, a dozen yards from where Kitto labored. The man did not resurface. Kitto's oar struck against a large chunk of wood, and a few feet away the body of a man facedown in the water rose and fell in the swells. Farther off, another man in the water thrashed his arms uselessly. He could not swim. His flailing arms sent up a flurry of white water, but his voice was quickly lost in the water that came up over his head on a swell.

The two entangled ships rubbed their hulls together with the waves, creating an awful grinding sound, and causing the splintering of timbers.

"Pull, Kitto! Pull!" Sarah encouraged, and Kitto gathered strength from her words.

The boat crept forward. Just as they neared the stern of the *William* and were about to pass around it to relative safety, another movement brought Kitto up short. Toward the open sea, a smooth, fluid motion jarred with the scene. He and Sarah both turned to look; a single gray triangle pierced through the surface of the water, cutting a graceful arc. It disappeared beneath the swell of a wave, but two others took its place in the trough of the wave behind it. Then another appeared. And another and another. The fins moved past the rowboat's stern and into the channel between the two ships.

"Oh, Sweet Mary in Heaven!" Sarah exclaimed. A man who'd been thrown overboard had managed to stay afloat between the ships by way of a large splinter from the rail. The triangles moved in his direction. He saw them coming, wailed pitiably, and frothed the water with his kicking legs. The sharks circled him for a few seconds, then darted inward as if of one mind. There was an awful wail, and then the man went under. Fins swarmed and tails thrashed. One of the sharks floated fully into view, rolling onto its back lazily like a dog and exposing a gleaming white underbelly to the sunlight.

Kitto had just turned back to the task before him, when from the deck of the *Port Royal* he saw a body being lifted into the air. Kitto saw a flash of bright red on the sailor's head. This man was held up by another, and as this second man stepped to the *Royal's* rail and heaved, both faces turned and Kitto could see them: the man who did the throwing was William, his face contorted and red as a beet; the man being thrown overboard was no man at all. It was Van, the red scarf slipping off his head as he went.

"Van!" Kitto shouted. Van cried out and flew through the air. He kicked and twisted as he fell, his blond locks matted. Headfirst he went, his terrified face staring down at the approaching water.

"Van!" Kitto screamed again. He half stood up and the sudden change in the boat's balance nearly upset it. Van crashed into the water with a huge splash.

"Kitto!" Sarah shouted in dismay, clutching at the gunwales. "What, Kitto! What is it?"

"There! It is Van! And he can't swim." Kitto pointed to the bubbling circle of water where the young man had gone in. To Kitto's surprise, his friend's head broke the surface, and Van now flailed about at the water, his mouth wide and gasping for air. He struck at the water ineffectually, barely keeping himself afloat.

Kitto froze in a crouched position for a full second. He could hardly row the boat closer to where the ships grinded up against one another just beyond Van. Nor could he paddle away and leave his friend to die.

Sarah's face filled with anguish as she understood the thought passing through Kitto's mind. She wanted to tell him he mustn't. To forbid him to do it. But she was already sickened by the sight of the dying men around her, and she had not the strength left to stop Kitto from doing what was right.

Instead of protesting, Sarah wrenched up one leg of her soaked skirt, grabbed beneath her petticoats, and withdrew something, which she held out to Kitto.

"Take it!"

Kitto took the dagger. It was the very blade Father had given him the night they went to see William, the one Kitto had given to Duck to pass on to Sarah.

Kitto flipped the knife so that the handle lay across his palm. He hurriedly untied his boots, the crooked foot catching like it always did. Precious seconds passed. Sarah watched the shoes that she had stitched with her own hands fall in a heap on the floor of the boat.

Kitto stood again, and when the boat found a steady spot in the trough of two waves, he dived.

Well beyond Van, the sharks were still hungry. The reek of fresh blood had excited them into a frenzy.

Sarah watched the fins and the sinewy gray bodies thrash beyond, then saw Kitto's head break the surface as he headed straight toward them. Van flailed about on the surface, gasping for breath, about halfway between the boat and where the sharks finished their meal.

"Dear Lord, who art in Heaven . . ." she began. "Please, Sweet Mother Mary, do not take my boy. . . ."

Kitto's arms revolved expertly, reaching forward and pulling the water toward him, kicking strong and confident strokes. In the boat his efforts had been so awkward and clumsy. Here they were sure. Here his foot did not slow him. He kept his head above water now as he swam, keeping an eye on Van, whose movements had begun to slow.

See it in your mind's eye, Kitto! Make it happen!

Within a few seconds Van would begin to sink. Kitto knew that. He had never pulled a drowning man from the water. He knew it could be as dangerous for the rescuer as the rescued. A drowning man could easily, in his panic, grab hold and force the rescuer under, drowning them both. Kitto had witnessed drowning men saved on more than one occasion down at Falmouth Wharf, where there are many men about and many who do not know how to swim. Each time, the skilled swimmer had grasped the drowning person across the chest and held him tight, performing a sidestroke to swim back to shore with one arm.

I can do it! he told himself.

Beyond Van's thrashing arms, Kitto could just make out the gray tips of the fins sparkling in the sunlight, still clustered around the remaining shreds of the last victim. Kitto did not think about them. He did not fear them. In fact, he had no fear at all in that moment. He must reach Van, or Van would die. Every particle of his being focused on that one point. That is all there was in the whole world. Whether or not Van saw him coming he could not tell, since his friend thrashed about so clumsily and his head came up and went down beneath the water with each wave.

Three strokes before he reached Van, his friend's

movement abruptly ceased and Van slipped beneath the surface.

Kitto took one more stroke, then dived. His head slipped beneath the waves and silence engulfed him. He kicked downward and reached out. Van's body had gone slack. Down he went. A large bubble floated upward from his open mouth. As he slipped deeper into the water, Van's arms lifted over his head, and his eyes—still open—seemed to look up at Kitto. Kitto kicked and stretched out; his fingertips brushed against Van's, but still his friend sank deeper and had not the wherewithal to reach out himself. Knowing that this would have to be his last attempt, Kitto kicked and kicked with everything he had. Three more feet he descended, five . . . six! Van's body seemed to gather speed in its descent. Kitto propelled himself downward, reaching out.

His hand struck something and he grabbed at it. He had squeezed his eyes shut at the last moment, and opened them now to see that he held Van by the wrist. Immediately Kitto heaved up, righted himself in the proper direction, and began to kick and pull at the water, the surface far above him glowing with a gentle light. His left hand still clung to the knife, and he nearly dropped it as he swept his arms along. His lungs burned. Still he kicked. Through the clear waters off to his left he saw that two of the sharks had broken away from the frenzy, and had taken up slow, widening arcs just below the surface of the water.

Kitto's lungs felt like they would rip from his chest

THE DAGGER QUICK

when he broke the surface and gasped. He yanked Van up, but when his friend's face lifted from the water, his eyes were closed and he took no air.

"Come on, Van! Stay with me!" Kitto shouted.

He slipped his arm around Van's shoulder and chest and grabbed on beneath his left armpit, just as he had seen done in Falmouth. The sea was not particularly rough, but it rolled steadily, and Kitto struggled to keep Van's head above the swells. He took two strokes . . . three . . . four, and halved the distance between himself and the rowboat. There Sarah clung to the gunwale, a look of frantic abandon contorting her features. She held the oar out in her hands.

"Hurry, Kitto, hurry! The sharks!" she called to him, seeing the main body of killer fish break apart from their tight clump at the meal they had finished and join the others in ever-widening arcs. Two more strokes. One more.

On this last stroke, the terror of the battle, the panic, the frenzy, finally got to Kitto. He gasped for breath, and his left arm slapped down into the water with a splash, carrying down a hundred air bubbles with it. Something in the vibration that last stroke emitted stirred the prehistoric brain of one blue shark. It interrupted the course of its arc and veered toward Kitto and Van. The shark sensed instinctively that another meal awaited. It quickened its pace.

"Grab on, Kitto! Hurry!"

Kitto grasped the oar and Sarah pulled with every bit of strength she possessed, recklessly standing up in the rowboat. Kitto lifted half out of the water and shot toward the side of the boat. He reached the gunwale and hooked an arm over, dropping his knife into the boat.

"Van first!" Kitto cried, lifting his friend's body toward the gunwale. Van's head lolled loosely on his neck. Sarah took Van beneath the arms and heaved. The boat rocked dangerously but Van rose up. Sarah fell backward into the bottom of the boat, dragging Van with her. She scrambled out from beneath the body and tried to regain her footing.

There was the fin, slicing through the water, making directly for Kitto. Sarah saw it. She struggled to rise again, but slipped. Kitto was trying to pull himself up on the gunwale, but the heaving rowboat drifted from him. Closer the fin came. Closer. Sarah's eyes widened. The gray triangle lowered slowly into the water as it closed the last few yards, and then breaking the surface was a huge black gash of jagged teeth and a streaming, shining white belly.

"Shark!" Sarah screamed. "Kitto, SHARK!" Finally Sarah got her footing. She leaped toward Kitto and grabbed hold of him by the arms, their faces just an inch apart.

"Kitto! Kitto!"

The shark struck. Sarah held tight. Kitto's eyes flashed.

"Mum!"

Then he was torn from the gunwale. The waters closed over him.

CHAPTER 30:

Adrift

Van came to his senses in the boat as sunlight dazzled his eyes. It glinted off the blade of the magnificent dagger Sarah held—blade down, her arm reared back, her whole body poised, one foot up on the gunwale of the boat.

Van tried to speak but sputtered seawater. Sarah leaped through the air and the boat lurched.

"Madam!" Van shouted, or tried to. He heard the splash of water as her body hit. He gagged again, vomiting seawater, his eyes blurring. He did not see that Sarah's dive had been true; he did not see that she had plunged through the water and ripped a vicious wound along the dorsal side of the shark bearing Kitto away. All he saw was the boiling white and red water several yards out when he came to his wits moments later.

Van snatched up the oar and found his feet. He could make no sense of the furious splashing whatsoever, but the red in the water gave him the strong urge to vomit again. Then Sarah's head emerged, her hair streaming behind her, the tresses covering a darker form. It was Kitto!

"The oar!" Van screamed. "Take it! Take it!" He held it out over the water. Sarah flailed once, then grabbed the blade. Van hauled it in quickly until they were alongside the boat.

"Get him! Get him up!" Sarah was breathless. Van heaved Kitto's unmoving frame out of the water and into the boat, setting him down roughly. Then he wrestled to pull up Sarah, her soaked dress streaming. She dropped the dagger she still clutched at Van's feet.

"He's hurt! Kitto is hurt! Quickly, we must help him."

Kitto's body lay sprawled in the bottom of the boat, and there a pool of blood was already staining the bleached boards. Van gasped.

"His . . . his foot!" He pointed.

Where the clubfoot had once been, only a jagged shred of purpled flesh and gleaming white bone remained.

"Kitto!" Sarah rushed to him, taking the boy's face in her hands. "Kitto, can you hear me?" Kitto made no answer, his face going ever paler.

Van tugged at his belt. "I can help him!" he said. "I seen it before! Several times." Van stripped the leather belt from his waist.

"Oh, hurry! Please hurry!"

As he whisked off the belt, Van felt the hidden satchel of silver slip down his trouser leg and fall to the bottom of the boat with a muffled jingle. Van gave it a quick kick.

"Hold up his leg, madam." Sarah did as told. Van

threaded the leather end of the belt back through the buckle to make a loop. "A bit below the knee we put this." Together their fingers worked hurriedly to slide the loop of leather over the wound. The blood spilled from it in a steady stream of drops and spurts. Kitto moaned, but his eyes were closed. Van saw that the wound occurred about midway between the knee and ankle. The bone looked bitten clean through.

"Tighten it now, yes?" Sarah said, and Van wrenched back on the leather. The loop tightened and Kitto's leg jerked beneath the pull. He stirred, but Van held him tight.

"See it, Kitto. See your strength in your mind, my son. You shall be all right."

Van pulled back with his left hand as he braced his right against Kitto's shinbone and the belt buckle. He grunted with effort to get it to go tight. Instantly the flow of blood lessened. Van took the leather end into his mouth to hold it, then worked the buckle with both hands.

There was no hole in the leather to insert the prong of the buckle and hold it fast against the leg. Van jammed his thumb on the back of the prong and pushed with all his might. Sure enough, he could see the leather whiten on the far side as the prong began to push through. He pushed some more, gingerly now, until the very end of the yellow brass poked through. The prong slipped through the makeshift hole.

Inspecting the gory wound, Van held up Kitto's leg beneath the knee and released the belt. The wound dripped a few drops of blood, but the flow had obviously slowed.

"Have you done it?" Sarah whispered.

"I think so," Van said. "I'd like a bit more to tie it off." Both their eyes searched the empty vessel. Van crawled to the stern and reached over the side at each corner, hoping to find a strand of sturdy rope dangling from one of the hardware loops there. From one dangled a chain. He pulled it up from the water. The slack end came up after several feet, but a chain was no good to him. He swung the unattached end into the boat, swearing coarsely and without remembering to apologize. Then he jerked his shirt over his head, his bronzed muscles going taut as he rent the article at the neck and the shirt split in two. He reached over and dipped each one in seawater.

"The salt is good for the wound," he said.

"Yes? Yes. You can save him then. You can, can't you? Tell me you can!"

Van nodded. Maybe he could. He had seen it done. He had seen men in battle stumble about without a hand or a foot, cleaned off by grapeshot the way a hot knife whisks through summer butter.

Each wet strip of shirt he tied around the gnarled end of Kitto's wound, just below the belt tourniquet. He finished tying and settled against the boat's side, resting Kitto's leg on his lap. A wave of exhaustion splashed over him, and he allowed himself the pleasure of closing his eyes for a moment.

The wind had picked up considerably now, but the waves were not yet more than easy rollers. The sky had gone gray as he knew it would, but for a moment he forgot about the storm he could feel coming like a squeezing pressure behind his eyeballs. The distant popping of pistol fire speckled the air.

"The ships." Van opened his eyes reluctantly to look where Sarah pointed, her face creased with apprehension. "We must try to get back to them!"

The *Blessed William* and the *Port Royal*, still locked in combat but both still with just enough sail unfurled to catch the rising wind, had already moved off several hundred yards. It was almost as if the rowboat had waded into a different current, determined to put distance between them and the embattled ships.

"Not even with both oars could we, I shouldn't think," Van answered. "And we've got but the one."

"But my Elias! My sweet boy, he's on that ship. Kitto told me. . . ."

Van nodded. "Aye, he's there, and hidden. He's safe."

Sarah looked at him incredulously. "Safe? For how long will he be safe? Or hidden?" She turned back to the ship and furiously wiped a tear from her cheek.

"Do you think they'll come back for us?" she said after a moment. "Surely they'll turn around when the fighting is over. . . ."

Van did not answer. He did not imagine that he knew all that stirred in the dark mind of John Morris, but he found it a strange notion to think such a captain would have qualms about leaving two boys and a woman behind, especially when to one of those boys he now owed a pile of silver. He did not share his thoughts, but instead looked down at Kitto's stump.

Kitto stirred and gave out a moan.

"That's it, love!" Sarah said. "I am right here and you are safe. Can you hear me?"

Kitto opened his eyes wearily. They rolled without focusing, shut, then opened again, and this time found their bearings.

"Van," Kitto whispered. Van felt his whole body go cold.

"Yes, Van is right here! You saved him, sweetheart. He's right here." Sarah gestured toward Van. "Come closer. Let him see you."

Van could not refuse. He propped Kitto's leg onto the rower's seat, where it would remain elevated, then slowly inched his way toward the bow. Kitto's cheeks were pale, but his dark eyes were clear and piercing.

"Are you in pain, Kitto? Is there something I could do?" Van asked, swallowing against the lump in his throat. Kitto stared at him unblinking for several seconds.

"It was you," he said finally.

Van felt his breath catch.

"What is that, sweetheart? What is that you say?" Sarah said.

"It was you, wasn't it?" Kitto whispered again. Van turned away, his face flushing.

"You were the rat." Van said nothing, but he felt his insides coil.

Sarah looked from one boy to the next, baffled. "Rat?

Kitto, no. He was fighting on your side, remember? You dived into the water to save him."

Kitto drew a jagged breath. "Tell her," he said.

Van's eyes flooded. He closed his eyes and sat back in the bottom of the boat. There it was. All in the open now. And time to admit his crime. Van opened his mouth to speak, to finally unburden himself of the guilt and trade it instead for shame. Only a croak came out.

"I . . . I do not understand," Sarah said, mystified still.

Van buried his face in his hands and wept. The wind whistled and the boat rolled. When Sarah reached out and squeezed his shoulder and muttered something comforting, something mothering, a gesture now so faintly familiar to Van it was like something he had once dreamed and forgotten, it only made the pain harder to bear.

Finally he composed himself. He took a deep breath and looked Kitto in the eyes, surprised to see trails of tears leading from the corners.

"I *was* the rat," he began. "Your uncle hired me in New York, but then Captain Morris found me before even I first set foot on the ship. He offered plenty. It was for my sister, you know. It was always for her."

Sarah withdrew her hand slowly from Van's shoulder. "Captain Morris offered you payment? For what?"

Van reached down to the bottom of the boat and grabbed the leather satchel that had fallen out when he removed his belt. He handed the bag to Sarah. She turned it in her hands and knew what it contained.

"When we docked in Falmouth, Spider found me and told me what Morris wanted. So I followed William when he left the ship and visited your husband's shop." He looked down at Kitto. "Kitto's father. I told Morris where it could be found. And he paid me that bag of silver."

Sarah's face had drained. Now the hand holding the bag began to shake. She lowered it to her lap.

"My husband is dead," she said. "Black-hearted Morris told me so."

"I didn't know they would . . . ," Van began.

"My young son is lost out to sea in a ship full of men shooting guns, men who would sell him as a slave."

"I swear I . . . ," Van tried again.

"And my Kitto, here, nearly killed by a shark and might possibly still . . ." That was a thought she could not complete. Van saw the fury in her eyes now. They bore into him like hot brands.

"And you tell me you did not know! Do not you *lie* to me, young man! Had you not met that black captain before? Or his vile henchman, Spider? You *did* know!" Sarah flung her arm savagely. The satchel flew out over the crest of the nearest wave, then disappeared behind it. She turned back to Van.

Van nodded. "Yes," he said. "I did know."

The admission took the heat out of Sarah. She hung her head, her wet tresses hiding her face. Her shoulders shook.

Kitto spoke. "You owe me your life," he said weakly. "You owe us." He reached out weakly and found Sarah's hand.

"I have lost two parents now," he whispered. "You have too, Van. But I am lucky and have a third . . . maybe the finest of them all." Kitto's eyes filled with tears and he could not continue.

"Kitto, I love you with all my heart," Sarah said. "You are every bit my son."

"And you my mother."

The soughing wind rolled over the lonely boat and across the gray water.

Van cleared his throat. "I owe you both my life," he echoed. "My oath is nothing, and my life is sorry, but what it is, I give to you. I will see your family united, madam, Kitto, and safe. There is nothing I won't do for that."

And for the first time in some weeks, Van thought he might just be able to live with himself.

CHAPTER 31:

Storm

ONE DAY LOST AT SEA

Van scanned the gray and menacing sky. He was surprised it had not overtaken them yet. Kitto and Sarah lay huddled in the bow. The sea waters were dark for the Caribbean, as dark as Van had ever seen them. A particularly large wave suddenly heaved the little boat high and nearly upended the craft.

"Heavens!" Sarah flailed about. Van took hold of a gunwale.

"Yes, madam. I am afraid those heavens are about to show us their might."

"A bad storm, then?" she asked, trying to shelter Kitto from the rising wind. Van did not answer. His mind spun the problem of such a tiny craft afloat in a hurricane. Maybe there was a little they could do.

"We'll need those shoes of yours, madam, if you don't mind," he said. "And Kitto's boots, too. For bailing when the rains get heavy. If the water gets too high in the boat, we won't be able to ride up the sides of the waves." Sarah immediately began to work at the buckle of her shoe.

"And we need some drag, too," Van muttered, then remembered the chain at the stern. He fetched it and the oar and fed the chain through the hole in the oar's handle, then paused again to consider how to keep the chain and the oar connected. The temperature had dropped ten degrees in the past hour. Shirtless, Van shivered.

"I am sorry, madam, but . . ."

"What is it?"

"I need you to give me as much of that dress as your dignity can spare, madam."

"My dignity can spare plenty." In a few moments Van was tearing a strip from the hem of the dress and using it as a cord to secure the chain to the oar. The rest of the material he tied tightly to the blade of the oar, then threw the oar out over the stern. The chain caught and the oddly adorned oar floated in the water behind them.

"Why did you do that?" Sarah sat in her shift now, inspecting Kitto's stump and sprinkling it with seawater.

"The oar shall drag behind us. Keeps us aimed in the right direction, so these waves don't catch us crosswise and flip us." As if on cue, a massive riser lifted them so rapidly it made Sarah's heart flip, then dropped them just as quickly. Sure enough, the boat stayed aimed in a perpendicular path to the waves.

"You've seen storms as bad as this at sea, then?" Sarah asked nervously.

"Many times," Van lied.

Kitto opened his eyes to a bloated and angry sky, gray almost to black. A bolt of brilliant yellow shot out from a cloud, followed by a muted rumble. The wind whipped and sang.

It had been the sloshing water at the bottom of the boat that woke him. It was several inches deep now and cool. He put his hands into the water and tried to push himself up a bit. Van and Sarah were hunkered down on either side of the seat, frantically bailing out the water with Kitto's and Sarah's shoes. He could feel the heat in his clubfoot, and he knew there was something wrong there, but he knew not to look.

"Is there water?" Kitto asked weakly. His throat was afire.

Sarah and Van froze. Sarah stole a look at Van.

"What's that, sweetheart?" she said, smiling wide with relief to hear his voice. Both Van and Sarah craned forward to hear him.

"Is there water?" Van's look of wonder melted into a huge grin. His eyes filled with tears.

"Is there water? Is there water!" He gestured about with Kitto's gnarled boot in his hand. "Did the shark take your eyes?" Van laughed. Sarah was laughing too, and for a few blissful seconds the two of them could laugh at the ridiculousness of it all. Even Kitto came close to a smile.

Another clap of thunder ripped the skies. A huge rising wave lifted the boat heavenward. Van and Sarah fell into each other and nearly atop Kitto. Kitto watched an enormous wall of water rise up above the boat. Still the boat climbed higher and higher and higher, racing up the huge wave.

"Hang on, hang on!" Van cheered, and the boat did. The crest of the wave rolled beneath them and immediately they were sliding down its backside, thrown to the other side of the boat.

"I think I shall be sick," Sarah said weakly, clutching at the gunwale.

"Is this a storm?" Kitto said.

"It's a hurricane," Van answered, and pushed himself back to start bailing some more.

Another boom of lightning opened up the skies, and it began to rain. Huge raindrops fell in sheets, instantly blinding them.

"Here's your water!" Van screamed, and now he was bailing like a dervish, the little rowboat seeming to catch every drop. Sarah tore a section of material from her shift and held it toward the rains. This she held to Kitto's mouth, and he sucked at it ravenously.

Another huge wave raised their boat. The boat crawled up, more sluggish this time, and the very crest of the wave curled several gallons of seawater into the boat before dropping them off its backside.

"Oi!" Van shouted, his face a stunned look toward something in the distance.

"We're sinking!" Sarah said frantically, scooping the water out as fast as she could. Van had stopped bailing. "Hurry!" she commanded, but Van did not move, and another gray monster rose up behind them. Again the boat climbed up its side, and from where Kitto sat it seemed the boat ascended a nearly vertical wall.

Still Van did not bail, and at the crest the boat took on several gallons more. Van grinned like a well-fed cat.

"Huzzah!" Van cheered. "Huzzah, huzzah, huzzah!" He fell on his back in the boat and kicked his legs in the air.

"The water, you madman!" Sarah screamed. "Bail this water now!"

Van sat up and scooped out a shoeful, still grinning.

"It's land, madam! Land! Clear as day, not more than a mile. We're heading straight for it!"

Sarah paused enough to smile.

"Thank God," Kitto breathed. Land. He would make it to land again.

Sarah returned to bailing. "Then bail for your life, Van, or we'll never make it."

Van lowered the shoe into the water and set about scooping out with Sarah. Even Kitto did what he could, cupping his hand and tossing out tiny handfuls of sea-water, but the level never seemed to diminish.

They kept at it for ten minutes. Fifteen. Sure

enough it was land, and in little time they could all see it with every wave that lifted them high.

"What will we? . . ." Sarah began, looking worriedly toward the looming dark shape of the island over the point of the bow.

"What's that?"

"Will we crash?"

Van paused long enough to take a look himself. The island was less than a half mile off now, and Van could see quite clearly the crashing of white surf well off the line of the shore.

"Looks like reefs!" he said above the wind.

"Reefs?"

"Reefs." Van felt his insides quiver. Only hours before he had flailed about in the open water, too frightened of his inability to get air to realize that sharks were circling. Now he would be in it again, and the water much angrier this time.

"What does that mean?"

"If we're lucky, the boat will make it over them." He scooped out two more bootfuls of water. "Then maybe we can keep the boat upright and just wash up on the beach."

"And if we strike the reef?"

"Then you help Kitto swim to shore."

"And what about you?"

"I don't swim."

"There's the oar! You could get the oar, could you not?"

Van looked astern toward the oar following behind like a dutiful mutt. It wasn't a half-bad idea. He wondered if it had the buoyancy to keep him afloat.

For a moment the howl of the wind ebbed slightly, and a new sound made the three occupants crane their necks to see. A few hundred yards ahead now the water boiled white. Wild mare's tails of spray leaped up, lashing against the rocky outgrowths just below the surface of the water.

"It's soon upon us!" Van announced. "Madam, you ought to get ready with Kitto. Get a good hold of him and all. If we hit, it will knock us over for sure!" Sarah abandoned her shoe and crawled to Kitto, embracing him.

"It's all right, Mum," Kitto whispered in her ear. "I can see it in my mind's eye. We'll be all right." Sarah kissed him fiercely on the cheek.

"Hold tight to me, Kitto. Hold tight."

"The dagger?" Kitto asked. "Do you have it?" He lifted his head.

"Leave it, sweetheart. It is nothing."

"Let me hold it," he said. "I want to hold it." Sarah splashed about in the boat's bottom until she found it. She wrapped Kitto's hand about it.

"Make sure you hold to me and not that dagger," Sarah said.

"I will."

Van was at the stern of the rowboat, hauling in the chain and working the knot that held the oar. Another large wave lifted them up. It curled at the top and dumped a huge load of water into the vessel before passing beneath them.

"Any moment now!" Van shouted. He freed the oar from its binding. "You take Kitto when we go over," he told Sarah. Sarah nodded, a mixture of terror and determination written large on her features. She wrestled her way underneath Kitto so that she could put an arm about his chest.

When it happened, though they had been watching the reefs come for what seemed like an eternity, it came swift. A wave lifted them. It seemed to roar from a foaming mouth, and below them the water boiled white. The dark island loomed, but was probably still nearly a quarter mile off.

"This is it!"

"God be with you!"

And then the roaring filled Kitto's ears. It was as if he were inside all the rage of the whole ocean. He felt Sarah's grip tighten. The boat below them was suddenly above them. The world spun. Something hard struck him on the bridge of his nose, but he had not even the time to reach out to fend it off because he was whirling through and under the water. He kicked with all he had and pulled with his arms, though which direction he paddled he could not tell.

But then there was air. He gasped and heard Sarah do the same.

"Kitto!" she called in his ear.

"I'm fine, Mum!" he answered. "I can swim, I think," he managed, but then another wall of wash covered them and they were blinded and submerged again, tumbling in a sea of bubbles. Again they pulled for what felt like the surface, and again they broke clear of the water.

"Van!" he shouted, his voice weak and pitiful against the howl of the wind and the angry sea.

"I saw him make clear the boat!" Sarah shouted. Another wall of wash took them.

How many times it happened, Kitto could not count. Each time they were knocked under, and each time they fought their way for the surface. Sometimes Sarah held him, sometimes they parted for a moment. Kitto thrashed at the water with his dagger hand as if battling a wild beast. Always there was hardly time to take a breath before they were covered over again, and in that instant, too, they paddled fiercely for what they thought was the shore. After a few minutes Kitto could feel lethargy taking him. He had just begun to wonder if they would make it when he felt his foot strike something below water. Then he heard shouting.

"Over here! Here!" It was Van, galloping from the beach toward them in the surf, a huge grin spread across his face. He tossed Kitto over his shoulder and pulled Sarah by an arm.

"I cannot believe it. It's a miracle! I could kiss a priest!"

Sarah was pushed to the point of exhaustion. As Van brought them to shallower water, she stumbled on the sand.

"Put me down and get *her*," Kitto said. He crawled on all fours out of the last of the wash as Van helped Sarah. Kitto was surprised to see the dagger still clutched in his right hand. He dug its fine blade into the sand to help pull himself forward. Ahead, a dark wood of palm trees rose in front of him.

The rain had slackened to a steady drizzle. Kitto crawled up the lip of land where the trees grew to the edge of the beach, and rolled himself into the welcoming arms of the green undergrowth. Van dragged Sarah up and, panting, pointed to a palm tree a few feet farther in.

Kitto followed, as best he could, nearly crawling. A flash of lightning lit the air around them, and the thunder boomed. Kitto saw that they were in some sort of forest of palm trees and strange plants he did not recognize.

Sarah caressed his cheek and gave a weak smile.

"We made it, sweet darling," she said.

"Aye, we did!" Van answered, still exultant. "That oar saved my neck. Rode it like a dolphin the whole way in." Kitto lay on the leafy ground. Adrenaline was ebbing now, and with it the pain in his leg returned. He lowered his cheek to a smooth leaf and allowed his eyes to close. Sarah unwrapped his fingers from the bone handle of the dagger and tucked it into the hem of her shift.

"Tell me, Van. What is to be done for him?" Sarah said, trying to whisper above the patter of the rain on the leaves above.

"We need fire. Once the storm is passed." He looked

around, wondering where he would ever find dry wood. It would have to be done. His eyes and Sarah's met, silently communicating the urgency. Another flash of lightning illuminated the world. Van saw Sarah's eyes dart away to some spot behind him, widening with surprise. He whirled around to find they were not alone on the island.

CHAPTER 32:

Ontoquas

What Van saw gave him a start. There stood a girl—so far as he could tell—with jet-black hair streaming wet, and skin the color of baked sand. She was clothed only in a tattered pair of seaman's pants that came just below her knee.

Another bolt of lightning lit the air, and Van saw one thing more—she was holding a pistol, aimed right at him. He stared at it in fear and stepped back.

"Good God! It's one of them man-eaters!" Van choked, his eyes on the pistol. "Give me the dagger!" He had heard the stories, gruesome ones, about the Carib Indians that still lived on some of the islands. The girl's stern expression cracked for a moment to a smile.

"I eat turtle," she said. She spoke in a clean, though accented, English. She looked down at Kitto, who gaped at her from the ground. Her eyes moved to Kitto's wound.

"Can you . . . would you help us?" Kitto said. His face was pale. The girl lowered the pistol.

She nodded once. "Come. Come!" She beckoned.

She turned and disappeared into the dark forest behind her.

Van turned to Kitto and Sarah. "I don't know," he hissed. "I don't like it. She could be taking us to their braves. Maybe we run off now while we have a chance."

"No," Kitto said. "We trust her, Van. Come help me up." Begrudgingly Van relented, and in a moment the three of them were forging through the broad-leaved forest, following the girl as best they could. She certainly knew the way well, and they had a hard time following her, but whenever Van would stop and scan the darkness for some sign of where she had gone, she would reappear and they would set off. In a short time they reached a small clearing in the woods on a slight rise, and in its center was a shelter, a lean-to construction made of branches in the shape of a cave. Van hunched low to step through, carrying Kitto now piggyback style. Inside, it was dry and spacious, the air still.

"Here's a spot for you to lie, Kitto," he said, and Sarah helped him to set Kitto gently on the floor of matted leaves. Kitto immediately closed his eyes and fell into a dreamless sleep. Sarah bit her lip and combed her fingers through his wet hair. The girl knelt at her side and looked at her, reading the care and worry in Sarah's eyes.

"Mother?" the girl said. Sarah turned to her and their eyes met. Sarah nodded.

Van spoke. "Tomorrow, in the morning, if the storm is passed, we need to find dry wood to make a fire. I need . . ." His eyes drifted to the ragged stump at the end of Kitto's leg. "I need to seal the wound. Do you understand?"

The girl nodded. "I have wood." She had a high voice, but clear, and other than that first moment when she had smirked at Van's suggestion of making a meal of them, she had maintained an impassive, though not unfriendly, expression. Van looked about the shelter. There was a stack of upturned turtle shells and in the corner what looked to be a weathered chest, the kind found on ships. He wondered how it had gotten there. And how had the girl gotten on the island? How long had she been there?

"Are you alone?" he said to her. The girl nodded.

Sarah moved from Kitto. "Thank you for helping us," she said. "What . . . what is your name?"

The girl looked at each of them a moment as if considering how to answer.

"Ontoquas."

Sarah had her repeat it, then tried it herself.

"Ontoquas, then. Thank you, Ontoquas."

Kitto slept the fitful night of a tortured soul. Sarah slept not at all. She held Kitto tight when the pain would wake him and his body seized rigid. She sang softly to him, songs she had sung to him years ago when he had woken with nightmares. It seemed to bring Kitto some measure of peace.

In the middle of the night, Sarah looked down to see

Kitto's eyes wide open. It gave her a terrible start until he blinked and turned his head to her.

"I'm sorry, Mum," he said.

Sarah shook her head and ran a hand across Kitto's cheek. She felt a tear moisten her fingers.

"You have nothing to be—"

"I could have saved him." Kitto could see it all so clearly. There in the shop. His heart pounding. "I had a pistol. I could have shot sooner. . . ." Sarah placed her fingers over his lips.

"He was my da!" More tears.

Sarah smiled sadly. "Oh, Kitto. Someday you will be a father, a fine man, and you will understand. Being a parent means there is another life that is more precious than your own. Your father would gladly give his life for you, Kitto. And I would do the same." Sarah bent to kiss him on the forehead.

"I am so scared, Mum," Kitto said.

"Yes," Sarah said. "Of course you are. But look what you have done! Such pride you should have! Look how you have carried yourself. . . ."

Kitto closed his eyes and remembered his proposal to William to be the ship's cooper in his father's stead. He remembered his arguments with William over Van. He remembered the harrowing venture onto the slave ship to rescue Duck, and the moment when he jumped over the embattled ships' rails to do all he could to save Sarah.

He remembered the look of fierce determination on

his father's face in the workshop as he turned the pistol he and Morris wrestled with toward his own body and away from Kitto.

Father would have done anything to save me. Anything.

Kitto's body stiffened again, though not with physical pain this time. Sarah held him as the grief flowed through him, and when it subsided again, gradually, like a lowering tide, exhaustion won out.

The sound of wood crackling woke him. He drew a delicious breath and felt oddly calm. Kitto lay alone now on the leaf-covered floor. The stillness of the earth felt new to him, and he found himself rocking his head slightly, side to side, as if he were still at sea. The motion was like an old friend. Kitto opened his eyes slowly and found himself staring at the sea chest just a few feet away in the corner of the lean-to. His mind still slack with sleep, Kitto did not truly comprehend what he saw at first.

But then he did see. He saw the hardware of the chest, particularly the front latch mechanism—pewter, unremarkable but for the small casting of a dolphin. A dolphin arched, as if leaping through the air.

Kitto smiled. He sniggered slightly. How funny it was. How perfect.

"Kitto," Van said, kneeling behind him. "I'm going to have to burn you. There's an ax head, what was in that chest over there. I'm heating it now. Once it's red-hot . . ." Van stopped when he saw Kitto's smile. He stepped lightly to Sarah, who sat by the edge of the fire

Ontoquas had made in the stone ring near the opening of the lean-to.

"Madam. I think he's gone a bit batty," Van said. "He's smiling like he's happy when I'm telling him I'm going to burn him. That ain't right."

Sarah stepped around the fire ring to Kitto. She put her hand to his forehead.

"No fever." She leaned to him. "What is it, son?"

Kitto whispered. Sarah leaned closer. "Say it again." Pause. "What is here?"

Van joined Sarah, leaning close too. Kitto whispered again.

"*That* chest? No!" Van turned and rushed over to the chest in the corner.

Sarah spoke again. "Van is going to have to burn you, Kitto."

"I know, Mum," Kitto whispered. "I'll be all right."

"You can see it?" Sarah asked. She caressed his cheek.

Kitto smiled. Yes, he could see it. In his mind's eye he could see that it was true. He knew what that meant now. He could see that he would live. Kitto believed it with all his heart. He would live out what he saw. He knew it like he knew his name, like he knew the grotesque curling joints of the clubfoot that was no longer connected to his body. He could see it, and he would make it true.

"Then I will see it too," Sarah said. Van whooped behind them.

"By God, he's right!" Van shouted. "He's right! Captain Quick had a chest just like this one! I seen it a thousand times in his cabin! I can't believe I hadn't noticed. This belongs to Quick!"

"I do not understand," Sarah interrupted. "What does this mean?"

Van held his arms above his head, his face alight with triumph.

"It means this is Quick's island!" He hooted loudly, then danced about the lean-to as Ontoquas stared. Kitto smiled wide and closed his eyes.

"We're rich as kings, by God! Rich as kings!"

A PIRATE GLOSSARY

Brethren of the Coast: A loosely organized group of privateers and pirates who roamed the waters of the Caribbean
Sea in the seventeenth and eighteenth centuries. Some of
them were **privateers**, sailors who would get permission
first from their government to attack ships and colonies of
their enemies, and some were **pirates**, those who attacked
and robbed whomever they could and still get away with
it. Mostly these sailors were of English, Dutch, or French
descent, and mostly they attacked Spanish ships, because
Spain was the main power in the New World and it often
refused to do business with other European peoples there.

buccaneer: Nowadays we use this term to mean "pirate," but
back in Kitto's day, it just meant someone who knew his way
around a ship and was willing to attack the Spanish settle-
ments in the New World. Spain was an ultra-superpower at
the time, mostly because it got to modern-day Mexico and
South America before the rest of Europe, killed or enslaved
the native peoples, then stole and mined the silver and gold
deposits found in those places and took them back home.
Don't think the Spanish were hated because of the atrocities
they committed, though. They were hated by other European
sailors because they got rich easily and were not interested in
sharing.

dirk: An old word for a short dagger. Sword fighting takes a good bit of room for swinging. Wielding a smaller weapon was a good choice when jumping onto another ship to engage in battle.

Henry Morgan: The most famous of the Brethren. Historians still argue whether or not he was a pirate. Even his contemporaries were not sure what to make of him. He spent a short time in prison in England after his attack on Panama, but ended up returning to Jamaica as an appointed lieutenant governor. Was Morgan a villain? You will find out in *The Dagger Quick*'s sequel what a man named Exquemelin thought of him.

jolie rouge: A French phrase that means, roughly, "pretty red." It referred to the original pirate flag, which had neither skulls nor crossed bones. In Kitto's day, when a pirate wanted a merchant ship to stop so that it could be robbed more easily, he shot a cannonball over the merchant ship's bow. If the ship did not stop, the pirate flew a bright red flag, which translated into, "Now, we're going to kill all of you first, *then* rob you." It was not until about 1700 that some creative pirate devised the idea of a black flag with a scary picture on it to do the job of the *jolie rouge*. The pirate's term for these nifty black flags became Jolly Roger, a clear mispronunciation of the old French term.

lubber: Short for landlubber, an awkward, stupid person who was utterly clueless when it came to the basic operations of a sailing ship. You did not want to be called a lubber.

Panama: One of the richest Spanish cities in the New World. Henry Morgan led a band of more than a thousand buccaneers across a mosquito-infested jungle to attack Panama in late 1670 and early 1671. While the attack was a success, the buccaneers did not come away with nearly the plunder they had expected.

press-gangs: At different points in English history, naval ships needed more hands before they could set sail. To get more people, gangs of sailors would roam city streets at night and round up anyone who looked able bodied. These poor kidnapped souls would be "pressed" or forced into service.

ACKNOWLEDGMENTS

I owe a huge debt of gratitude to my agent, Carolyn Jenks. She took a risk on a total unknown entity (me), and did so with plucky determination and good cheer. Her efforts landed me with a top-notch publisher in Simon & Schuster, and a skilled and supportive editor in Paula Wiseman and her team. The character of Jenks in the story is named for Carolyn. Carolyn's staff was also crucial in delivering this project to such a fabulous publisher. Jeff Saraceno put huge energy into the marketing of the manuscript. Andy Fuller brought his exceeding talents and energies to bear in similar fashion. And Raleigh Dugal's exceptional skill as an editor helped me make the book in your hands much better than it otherwise might have been. I deeply appreciate the hard work of all these folks.

I am fortunate to teach at such a dynamic and inspiring institution as the Paideia School. If only more schools in this country were more like it. Some wonderful people at Paideia sustained me throughout this process. Teacher/writer Greg Changnon not only got me to Carolyn through his friend and writer Anne Echols, he inadvertently gave birth (birth?) to the turd Simon wrestled with by encouraging me to rework the beginning. Natalie Bernstein, librarian extraordinaire and creator of the best children's literature blog out there (The Pithy Python), was my most vocal fan and also helped me with revisions, as did Martha Alexander, who called me up in bed one night to berate me for a cliff-hanger ending. Thanks, too, to Mary Lynn Cullen for her contacts and support.

Many kids helped me, and each one is going to kill me for not mentioning them specifically. I promise you all Blow Pop peace offerings. Reading the manuscript aloud to classes was the single-most-helpful step in my revision process. I do want to specifically thank Bridget J., Will F., Sarah B., Eli P., Sarah D., Moey R., Morgan T., for some extra marketing blitz.

And lastly thanks to my family, who put up with me when I was bleary-eyed and near comatose from waking up at four a.m. on too many consecutive mornings to chase this dream. I hope you'll think it was worth it.

Turn the page for an
exciting sneak peek into
the next Dagger Chronicles
adventure, *The Dagger X*

SEPTEMBER, 1678

"Please. Please."

The words woke Sarah with a start, her heart in her throat. The Indian girl knelt at her side.

"Is it Kitto? Has something happened?" Sarah bolted upright in the lean-to and looked over to where Kitto lay awash in pale moonlight. He lay on his back, the rise and fall of his chest smooth and steady. Sarah breathed again. She berated herself silently for having fallen asleep. She told him she would watch over him!

That morning Van had held the red-hot head of an ax to Kitto's leg, where the shark had torn away his bent foot. Sarah had held Kitto down by sitting on his chest and pinning his arms to his sides. Van had set a stick in Kitto's mouth to bear down upon to keep from biting his tongue when the pain hit. And had it ever hit. Sarah shivered at the memory.

"*Quog quosh*," Ontoquas said and then translated. "We hurry."

"Is there something wrong? What is it?"

Ontoquas shook her head. "I did not know you *wawmauseu*." Ontoquas frowned, wishing her English allowed her to say it the way she could in the language of her own people. "I see you with him today. You are a good mother. *Nitka*."

"I do not understand, Ontoquas."

The Wampanoag girl's brow knitted. She reached out for Sarah's forearm and gave her a gentle tug. "You must come."

"Where?" Sarah bit her lip. She looked over at Kitto. "I do not want to leave."

"Please. He is not far."

He?

"Is there someone else on this island? Is there a ship?"

Ontoquas shook her head. "Please come." Sarah pushed herself slowly to her feet. This native girl was such a puzzle to her. Who was she? How had she come to live alone on this forsaken island? And was she truly alone? Sarah swore that she could sense some other presence, some other life, lurking in the dense jungle. All that day the girl had disappeared for stretches of time, sometimes returning with a freshly killed turtle or a split coconut or a bucket of fresh water, but other times with nothing at all save for a worried look.

From habit Sarah ran her hands along the front of her shift as if to smooth it, but the tattered and sun-bleached material was long past such ministrations. The dress that once covered it had been lost to the sea during the hurricane that nearly killed them all.

"For a moment, then," Sarah said, and followed the girl out of the lean-to.

It was a primitive domed structure, made by Ontoquas's own hands from woven tree limbs skillfully tied together with reeds, and broad palm leaves covering the frame and providing protection from the rains. Van slept on a pallet of palm leaves at one end of the dwelling, snoring lightly. Sarah stole one last look at Kitto. Were his cheeks truly that pale, or was it the moonlight? He looked peaceful enough. She turned back to the native girl.

Ontoquas led her along a narrow path that carved its way through thick foliage, heading deeper into the island. The way was slow going, with fallen tree trunks and patches where the thick undergrowth forced the path into wide sweeps. After a few hundred yards the ground rose up beneath them in a gentle hill.

How much farther? Sarah wondered. She stopped and looked back in the direction they had come. As she had since they first set foot on the island, Sarah felt now the eerie sense that somewhere in the dark wood there were eyes watching her. She turned back and chided herself. The girl had disappeared around a bend in the rising trail. Sarah was just about to call to her to say she could not go farther on, when Ontoquas came back around the bend. She beckoned to Sarah with urgency. Sarah pursed her lips, but made her way up the last several yards, surprised to see a flash of teeth on the Indian girl when she reached her.

She is smiling! Sarah drew closer. The look on Ontoquas's face was more than just a smile. The girl's face beamed with love and joy and pride so radiantly that it brought Sarah to a shocked standstill. The girl pointed toward the ground just a few feet ahead. There lay a tiny clearing in the wood, a circle bordered with stones, fallen logs, and brush shrouded in dark shadow.

Sarah peered toward the circle. In the middle of it, bathed in pale moonlight, slept a baby, a tiny African infant. The baby slept on his back, his arms up by his head. His stomach gently rising and falling with his breath. Sarah gasped when she understood what she was seeing.

"A baby! What is an infant . . . where did . . . is the baby yours?" Ontoquas held a finger to her lips. She knew the baby would be very angry if awoken in the middle of the night.

Now Sarah was even more confused. How did this baby come to be here? The girl was too young to be a mother, and even in the dim light Sarah could see that the two could not be directly related. The girl's lighter skin, her straight hair—she had to have been a native of the Americas. But the baby was much darker, with a thin layer of curly black hair and a wide nose that flared with each breath.

He was beautiful.

Ontoquas watched the *wompey* woman step over the barrier she had built to make sure the baby could not escape—not yet necessary since he did not crawl, but she could not bear to leave him in the open woods, even if this island had no animals that would show an interest. Sarah squatted down and scooped the child up expertly. The baby gave a startled jerk and his eyes shot open, but Sarah immediately rose and began to bob him up and down and run the tips of her fingers over his tiny black curls. The child's eyes drooped, then shut again.

"He is beautiful," Sarah whispered.

Ontoquas nodded. *"Weneikinne."* Sarah stepped about the enclosure with the child in her arms, bouncing gently with each rhythmic step. Ontoquas felt a pang in her stomach as she watched and knew it to be jealousy. Whether the jealousy was aimed at the baby or the woman she did not know. She felt pride, too. Without her, the tiny one would be at the bottom of the sea.

When she looked up again at the woman, she could see her cheeks were wet with tears. Ontoquas said nothing, but let the woman walk her little one around the circle, bobbing as she went. She knew the *wompey nitka* was thinking of the other child, the son of hers who they had said was somewhere lost out on the sea.

Finally the woman wiped the tears away and stepped close so as not to wake the baby. "He is so young. How have you fed him?"

Ontoquas shrugged. "I chew turtle in teeth," she said, pantomiming the words. "Then I . . . I kiss it to Bucket."

"Bucket? That is his name?" Sarah smiled.

"A bucket saved his life. And me."

Sarah looked back at the shining baby in her arms. "You have done so well, Ontoquas. He looks quite healthy. I would never have thought a girl of your age . . ."

Again silence won out.

"I helped my mother with my *netchaw*, my . . . brother. Before."

Before. Sarah nodded, wondering what horrors this child had faced. "Your mother taught you well. But I must know, Ontoquas, how did it come about that you and this baby are here together on this tiny island with no other soul in sight?"

Ontoquas sighed and lowered herself to a fallen log that formed one barrier of the pen. She puzzled, staring hard at the floor of matted palm fronds.

"It is long, our story. And my English . . ."

"Your English is excellent, young lady. Astonishing. You should be proud of it." Sarah looked back down the rise in the direction they had come. "Kitto is asleep and will stay that way long enough."

"You do not need to go back?"

"Tell me your story, Ontoquas."

JULY 1678, TWO MONTHS EARLIER

"The skin is cold on this one, captain."

The first mate pinched the woman about the forearm and relayed his message through the kerchief he pressed to his face. The woman in question, dark-skinned yet somehow frighteningly pale about the face still, clutched at a naked baby in her arms with the little strength she had left. The man examining her could scarcely believe she could stand.

"And the eyes, Mr. Preston. Note how sunken they are. Blast!" Captain Lowe grimaced as he made a mark in his precious ledger. He carried the book with him on deck each day, using it to calculate what little profit might be made from this journey gone awry.

"Make your way down the queue, if you please," Captain Lowe said, "while I decide what is to be done . with this one."

"Aye, aye, Captain." Mr. Preston moved to the next

slave, inspecting a wispy dark man for signs of disease.

At the head of the line stood a girl not older than twelve. She stood out by virtue of her skin color and the texture of her hair. Her skin was the color of wet sand, her hair black as India ink and falling straight over her ears and forehead. It had been longer, but the slave trader in Jamaica had taken sheep shears to her locks to ward off the lice.

Unlike her fellow captives, Ontoquas had not hailed from Africa. Her people—the Wampanoag—had lived for thousands of years in lands that would one day be named "Massachusetts" after the people it had been taken from and the language they spoke. But she, too, was a slave.

The line of slaves formed a ragged arch along the outer rail of the ship's quarterdeck, so Ontoquas could clearly see the diseased woman and the tiny naked boy she cradled in her arms. Ontoquas remembered her little brother, Askooke. He was not much older than this baby when the *wompey* men came to take them away. She used to help Mother bathe Askooke down at the river. Whatever happened to him?

The woman with the baby sagged, and the baby nearly spilled from her arms. Ontoquas almost leaped from the line to save the infant from being dropped to the deck, but checked herself at the last moment.

They will beat me. They will stop my food as they did to the others.

Ontoquas turned away, a defense she had learned to save herself from witnessing the horrors that this life had shown her.

"This one looks well enough," Mr. Preston said, moving farther down the line. Ontoquas looked out over the rail and tried to conjure up Askooke's face in her memory. Somehow her brother's image had begun to fade.

From behind her came the sound of a heavy burden hitting the deck, followed by startled cries. Ontoquas turned despite herself.

The woman with the baby had fallen, pitching forward onto the quarterdeck's planks. Her last effort had been to protect the baby, turning so that her body cushioned the infant's impact. The baby, curled tight, rolled several rotations outward to the middle of the quarterdeck and came to rest on his back. He let out a tiny wail, and Ontoquas felt her heart might break, but none of the white sailors seemed to pay the child any heed.

"Mr. Preston!" Captain Lowe said. "See to that one." He flicked his pointed chin toward the collapsed woman.

The first mate returned to the sick woman, his kerchief again pressed to his face. The captain watched as the officer pressed his fingers to the woman's neck, then her wrists. Mr. Preston looked up with arched eyebows.

"She's dead, Captain!" he said.

"Dead? Are you quite certain?" Captain Lowe ran a finger down a column of numbers in his ledger.

"Aye, Captain. Keeled over right where she stood." The captain scowled and added another mark to his page.

"Very well, Mr. Preston. Toss the body overboard, if you please."

"Bowler! Simpson!" Mr. Preston barked toward two sailors nearby at attention. He pointed at the woman.

"You heard the captain. Put her overboard."

Ontoquas knew enough of the white man's language to know what they had said. Again she tried to turn away, but somehow she could not take her eyes from the pitiable baby lying on deck, kicking his legs out now and crying out for someone to pick him up.

The two sailors stepped forward and took hold of the woman, one by the wrists, the other by the ankles. They moved toward the rail and the line of slaves parted to make room for them. One woman in the line held her hands over her face; a man with wide eyes withdrew in fear, as if he might be the next to go overboard.

The sailors positioned themselves by the rail, one of them pausing to get a better grip. Then they swung the woman's slack body back and forth several times, as they would a sack of grain. In a moment she was tossed into the air and out of sight.

The men turned around and paused. They were looking at the wriggling baby lying on the quarterdeck, its empty howls being carried off by the wind. Mr. Preston followed their gaze. He, too, seemed puzzled.

"The wee one, Captain?" the first mate said. "What is to be done with that?" He pointed to the child. Captain Lowe, busy with the calculations of reduced profit this latest inconvenience had caused, did not want to be interrupted.

"Just toss it overboard as well," he said with a wave of his hand, his eyes never leaving the page.

"The baby too, captain? It appears fit enough."

Captain Lowe jerked his head up in frustration.

"I said overboard! Are you daft, Mr. Preston!" Captain Lowe pointed at the infant with the feathered end of his quill. "The miserable whelp should not have been allowed on this ship in the first place. It must nurse from its mother to stay alive, and now she's dead."

"So we throw it overboard?"

"Can you nurse a baby, man? There is nothing more that can be done!" the captain said. "And it probably carries the sickness as well. Get it over before the others fall sick."

"Aye, aye, Captain."

Again Ontoquas tried to look elsewhere, and this time she succeeded. In the two years since her enslavement in the Caribbean—so far from her home—she had seen horrors that haunted her dreams: men whipped until they fell and then whipped more, children succumbing to the smoke in burning fields of harvested sugarcane, human beings bought and sold at market in chains, families and loved ones torn apart.

Ontoquas did not want to watch them throw a baby overboard—this baby with the tiny feet it kicked in the air.

Several feet away knelt a boy no older than Ontoquas: a white boy in a plain sailor's shirt and pants cut at the knee. Captain Lowe had ordered the deck holystoned, and the ship's boy had been assigned the task. The stone lay in front of him as he sat back on his haunches, breathless, having stopped to watch the unfolding drama. Ontoquas wondered what he thought of it. *How could he look on so easily?* The stone was large, two hands wide. Beside it a large bucket made from the bottom third of a cut barrel held fresh water.

Ontoquas's eyes locked on the stone, but she turned when she heard the first mate speak.

"Bowler, Simpson, damn your eyes!" Mr. Preston said. "Do as you're ordered, men!"

The two sailors who had cast the dead woman over the rail without a care now stood eyeing the infant. They each stole a glance at the other.

"You quite certain, sir?" one of them said, risking a flogging himself.

"Oh, for the love of God!" said Captain Lowe. He tucked beneath one arm his treasured ledger and strode to the middle of the deck where the baby lay. He snatched the boy up by one leg so that the infant dangled upside down.

"Truly, Mr. Preston! You should be embarrassed, sir. Never have I known Englishmen to be so squeamish." The baby rocked back and forth as the captain strode toward the rail. Its cries grew louder.

Ontoquas spun away, pressing her palms against her ears. The baby's cries were too terrible! Her eyes fell again on the holystone. She remembered the words of her father, Chief Anawan, the last time she spoke with him.

"We will lose our lives in our fight. It has been foreseen. But if we do not fight, Little Wolf, then we are no longer a people. If we do not fight, then we are already ghosts."

Ontoquas lowered her hands.

If we do not fight, then we are already ghosts.

Ontoquas stepped from the line of slaves, and with that first step she was a slave no more and never would be again. She took three strides toward the boy who stared at the captain, and kicked him savagely across the cheek with the sole of her foot. He sprawled back in a heap, then turned an incredulous look upon the girl as she hefted the stone.

All eyes were still glued on the captain and the infant dangling from his hand. His back was to Ontoquas.

"Captain! Captain Lowe, sir!" the boy called out.

The captain did not turn as he approached the rail. "Silence, boy, or I shall have you flogged. This is the work of men." Ontoquas raised the stone high and charged.

"Captain!"

The wind was out of the west that morning. It swept steadily across the quarterdeck. Captain Lowe had handed his hat to the first mate before grabbing the infant, and the pressing breeze revealed a pale spot of scalp on his head. He had reached the rail now and drew back his arm to heave the baby to the sea.

"Captain, sir, look out!"

Ontoquas took a last step and drove the holystone for the spot on the captain's skull with everything she had.

I will fight!

The stone struck without sound. The captain's head snapped forward. The ledger he held fell, bounced once against the rail, and whirled off in a flutter. The captain slumped into the rail and slid along it until he dropped to the deck in a tangle of loose limbs. Ontoquas plucked the crying baby from the deck and tucked him beneath her arm.

There was an instant of shocked silence, and then

the line of slaves broke apart, everyone running.

"All hands!"

The ship exploded into chaos. Voices yelled out in all languages. The captives ran in every direction, some in terror, others in rage. One man hurled himself upon a crouched sailor who had just jumped from the ratlines, and the two struggled for a knife the sailor held. Others charged out blindly and struck at any sailor they could find.

"Get them tied! Get them below!"

Ontoquas ran across the quarterdeck away from the sailors, but Mr. Preston cut her off. She stared at the dark circle of the pistol's barrel the first mate leveled at her.

Then she dove and tumbled, holding the baby close and trying not to hurt him as she rolled. There was a terrific explosion, and a woman nearby crumpled against the rail with a cry. Ontoquas found her feet again and dashed across the deck.

"You little devil!" shouted the sailor. He raised a whip. Ontoquas dodged and the crack sang out just behind her ear. She clutched the little baby tighter.

I must save this baby!

The man's face contorted in fury. He reared back again. Behind him she could see a surge of dark bodies emerging from the main hatch, men howling tribal war cries.

Again the man lashed out with the whip. Ontoquas lurched to avoid it and lost her footing on the wet deck planks, falling onto her back and nearly dropping the wailing infant. The deafening crack resounded against the rail behind her. A hand clamped down on her arm.

Ontoquas bore down on it. The man howled as the girl's teeth crunched against bone, and then she reeled as the butt of the whip came down on the top of her head.

Somehow she still held the baby. He was part of her now, her own brother. She would do anything for him. Again Ontoquas rose, the first mate separated from her by a wrestling crowd of sailors and slaves.

The whip crackled the air. Many months before, Ontoquas had come to understand that she would die, and die young, but with the infant in her arms, living was an imperative. If she did not live, the baby, too, would die. Ontoquas charged at the first mate, who had made his way clear to her, and scooted under his arm. Across the deck she scampered, the snap of the whip chasing her. She ran directly at the ship's boy—crouched in terror—the infant still cradled tight in the crook of her arm. Next to the boy rocked the overturned bucket.

"Leave me be!" the boy wailed.

"Get that one!" Ontoquas heard a sailor shout. "Grab her!"

Ontoquas lifted the boy's bucket by its handle. She turned toward the rail, and she ran like she had never run. She leaped as she had never leaped. One bare foot lighted upon the rail. She thrust against it and was over.

Through the air they flew, Ontoquas and her new brother, the bucket held above her head by its handle. The endless arms of the Great Mother Sea rushed up to greet them.